Honor Bound

R. C. Butler

Bulldog Press
Red Deer, AB

Copyright © 2016 by R. C. Butler

www.bulldog-press.com

First Printing, 2017

Warning: This book contains graphic sexual material and is not intended for anyone present at the author's birth.

Published by:

Bulldog Press

Red Deer, AB

ISBN-13: 978-0-9879958-9-6

ISBN-10: 0-9879958-9-8

Honor:: (n) /ˈänər/: adherence to what is right or to a conventional standard of conduct.

"Without integrity and honor, having everything means nothing."

Prologue

*H*er mind was spinning. She could blame the champagne, the warm night, or the adrenaline rushing through her from five hours of dancing. She could blame any of it, but she knew it would be a lie. Her mind was spinning and the handsome, uniformed man on her left was responsible. Corporal Jon Strand had her heart beating and pulse racing in a way it hadn't in years. He'd been the consummate gentleman, offering to walk her back to her downtown apartment, taking her arm along the way. His smile disarmed her. His soft yet powerful voice enchanted her. His presence caused an unknown sense of urgency and want. With every step closer to home her mind spun quicker. Unsure yet sure at the same time. Wanting him yet frightened. With every block her time grew shorter. Approaching the three storey modern complex, she needed to clear her mind. Make a decision. Did she trust her upbringing, say goodnight and wonder what could have been, or should she jump in and hope for the best?

"Vista Bueno Apartments, I believe this is you." His voice was calming and sincere as he eyed the front doors.

"Thanks Jon, it was kind of you to walk me home. I think I may have had a little too much champagne." She smiled, trying to act calm and confident while her mind reeled through the possibilities.

"I'm at your service ma'am. Of the troops, for the troops."

She laughed, the formality of his core motto breaking the tension as he had hoped. She gazed into his eyes, shook away her fear and took the leap.

"Why don't you come up for a bit?"

He smiled, leaned in gently and kissed her cheek. "Perhaps we should wait. It's been a fun evening, Liz, and I'd love to spend more of it with you but..."

"But Claire's upstairs... I get it, it's okay." She tried to hide her disappointment but the look she couldn't shake gave her away.

"Liz..."

"No, it's fine. Thanks for the walk home." She turned and bolted into the building before he could see the tears forming in the corner of her eyes.

He stood there, staring at the empty doorway feeling like a complete fool. She deserved better. He wished he could move on, open his heart once again but no matter how hard he tried he could not get passed it. He could not get passed Claire. Jon stared at his reflection in the glass doors and shook his head. Turning to leave, unsure where he was going, a high pitch scream pierced out through the night air, tearing into him.

His only thought, 'Liz.'

Chapter One

She didn't hear the first ring. In fact, she barely caught the second, but that wasn't surprising. Between the intensity of the orgasm and the deafening decibel level of her own screams as it hit, it was amazing she hadn't passed out.

"Jamie."

She heard her name but her mind was still elsewhere.

"Jamie, I'm pretty sure that's yours."

"Shit," she muttered reaching for the night table in search of her phone.

Ell couldn't help but laugh. It was an ego boost knowing that she had been able to take the beautiful redhead to such heights of arousal with only her tongue. She kneeled at the foot of the bed, watching Jamie transform back into the role of Detective Baker, scrambling to regain her senses.

Ell glanced at the clock, 1:12 a.m., and knew the evening was over. She withdrew herself from between Jamie's legs and flopped down on the bed slightly frustrated as Baker finally connected the incoming call.

"Baker. Yeah… shit… ok, I'm about twenty minutes out. I'll meet you on scene."

"Jones?" asked Ell watching Jamie pull herself from the bed and begin the search for her scattered clothing.

"Yeah, dead body downtown. Patrol's on scene but we're on rotation." She slid on her jeans, flipped her hair to the side and looked down at Ell, pausing at the site of her beautiful form laid out on the silk sheets. "Shit, Ell, I'm sorry."

Ell waved off her concerns, "You don't need to explain it to me. I know the job."

"Thanks." She leaned in, their lips brushing softly, Ell's hand snaked through the luxurious red locks and held her for just a moment.

"Do you want to tag along?" asked Baker, pulling back from the kiss while she still could.

"Nah, you and Jones can handle it, I'm gonna catch a few hours before the sun breaks."

"Ok, I'll text if anything comes up. Otherwise we'll get you a full report in the morning. Thanks for…"

Ell smiled, Jamie was always unsure what to say or do post orgasm. It was cute. "Anytime."

Baker snapped on her holster and shield, smiled awkwardly and let out a nervous laugh. "See you in the morning Lieutenant."

Ell's mind wandered, watching the detective's ass as she strolled out the door. Normally, she'd have reached for her nightstand drawer and a little relief from the sexual frustration but she knew that wasn't an option tonight. Her instructions were clear. No self-stimulation was allowed while her 'boy-friend?' 'dom?', shit she didn't know what Rob was, but she knew she'd follow his instructions while he was out of town. Of course he hadn't forbidden her from finding other forms of sat-isfaction and Detective Baker could be very satisfying. Granted, that had backfired this evening, leaving her far more frustrated and wound up than she could have imagined. She could picture the smirk on his face as she closed her eyes in hopes of sleep.

"Point Fayee," she muttered as she drifted off.

She couldn't have been out for more than forty minutes when the chime of her cell broke through her slumber. Ell, brushed the hair away from her face, cursed softly and reached out blindly for the phone.

"Shit's hit the fan. Need some brass stat. 218 3588 W Mandrin Ave. Vista Bueno Apartments. Dead Body - David Samuel Jellic – B"

"Had to tell her to text," she muttered, pulling herself out of bed and tossing on her jeans and a fresh white blouse.

"Ten minutes – E"

Baker responded almost immediately. "Took me eighteen with no traffic - B"

"Yeah, I figured I'd stop for coffee on the way – E"

Baker didn't respond. No witty banter, no smiley face, no 'fuck you' and Ell immediately knew something was seriously wrong at the scene. She'd skip the coffee.

Eight minutes and twenty-four seconds later Ell's silver Mercedes S550 came to a screeching halt outside the Vista Bueno Apartments. The car may have been overkill but Ell loved it and, when time was tight, it definitely got the job done. She took a quick look in the mirror, confirmed that she looked like she'd just crawled out of bed, shrugged and headed for the building.

Baker and Jones were positioned just inside the main doorway face to face with two military officers in full dress uniforms. The men were built, as was expected with military officers. Each stood nearly six feet tall and, from her estimate, a finely-toned hundred and ninety pounds. It was a nice view and, given different circumstances, she may have enjoyed it. As she approached Ell could hear Jones laying into one of the officers.

"... civilian and if you don't get the fuck out of our way and pull your team off scene I'm going to run you, and them, in for obstruction."

"Ma'am, I have my orders, no one goes on scene. If the Police Department has an issue with that they will need to take it up with Colonel Craig."

Ell didn't need the back story. She'd done a quick scan on David Samuel Jellic on the way there and knew this was going to be a jurisdictional nightmare. She looked over at Baker as she stormed through the doors. "Dead civilian?"

"Yes, sir," Baker knew there was no reason to elaborate.

Ell took two quick steps closing the gap between her and the uniformed officers. She eyed them up quickly. They were military police, private first class if she remembered the insignia correctly. She flipped them her badge, stepping in close to the talkative of the two guards.

"Lieutenant Ell Frost, Metro PD. Unless you prefer to spend the evening in lockup, you and your team will get the hell out of our way and clear my crime scene."

The private stood his ground. "As I was just telling the detectives..."

"Did I ask for a bedtime story? Stand down or we'll put you down, private."

The officer to his right let out an audible laugh, looking at the three ladies, shaking his head.

"Last chance, private."

"Listen, ma'am..."

Ell didn't wait for him to finish the sentence. She quickly grabbed his left wrist, spun it behind his back, used her right leg to sweep his out from underneath him and shifted her body weight and momentum to drive him face first towards the floor. The direct assault was unexpected and before his mind recoiled from the fall, Ell had his wrists cuffed and her knee between his shoulder blades. The other soldier reacted quickly and without thought as instilled by years of training. Instinct and adrenaline had him drawing his weapon as he stepped to close the gap. As the detectives were accustomed to, he underestimated Jones and Baker and focused his attention on the threat to his fellow officer. Baker had his wrist and firearm restrained before he could begin to level his weapon. Jones lunged low taking out his knees and the gun skittered across the floor as his two hundred pound form collided with the tiled ground. Jones struggled to fight off his attempt to roll to his back and Baker quickly applied her own cuffs, pressing a four inch stiletto heel against his throat.

"If I was you I'd settle the fuck down before my partner decides to take a step," snapped Jones as the soldier continued to twist against the restraint of the cuffs.

Baker removed her heel from his throat and leaned down grabbing him by the secured wrists and pushing upwards just enough to make him feel it.

"Do you like that?" she whispered softly. "The sting of the metal, the slight pain of the restraint? Keep struggling, big boy, it only gets better."

Overhearing the comment, Ell could not help but laugh. She pulled herself to her feet, allowing Detective Jones to disarm and take control of the officer she had pinned to the floor.

"Drag their ass's downtown and let them cool off in a cell while I get this shit sorted. If their friends are just as cordial I'm sure they'll have some company before the night is over."

Ell left them to deal with the two men and headed up to the second floor. An additional officer was stationed in the hallway outside of apartment 218 and she immediately knew this was not going to be a fun night.

"Lieutenant Ell Frost," she said, flipping him her badge and attempting to walk past. The man placed a well muscled arm across the doorway blocking her path.

"Sorry, ma'am. No civilians allowed on scene."

"Unless you plan on joining your two buddies from the lobby in lockup for the evening, you'll want to move that tree trunk you've placed across the doorway and drop the 'ma'am' shit."

This one appeared a tad more thoughtful. Turning his head, he called through the door, "Colonel Craig? I have a police lieutenant out here that would like to speak with you."

Ell recognized the Colonel before he made it to the hall. Colonel Anthony Craig had become somewhat of a celebrity lately. Thanks to a series of successful peacekeeping missions and a hostage rescue in the recesses of Columbia, his star was on the rise and he'd been getting a lot of press. Ell was not looking forward to the fight she was about to pick. She hoped the press was right about his calm under pressure demeanor and that it wasn't just a byproduct of his disarming smile and rugged good looks.

"Lieutenant?" he asked as he approached.

"Frost, Lieutenant Ell Frost."

"Of course, I should have recognized you. I believe we've shared a few front page spreads lately. What can I do for you?"

The photos hadn't done him justice. The man was young for his rank and had a ruggedly beautiful look. Coupled with the pure confidence, military body and tight fitting uniform, he was bound to make women swoon. Ell was not immune but, thankfully, the adrenaline from the episode in the lobby was still racing through her, helping to keep her mind off his chiseled jaw and on the issue at hand.

"You can pack up your men and get the fuck out of my crime scene to start."

"Pardon?"

"Colonel, you and your men are currently interfering with an active police investigation. Given your reputation, I am willing to give you the benefit of the doubt and not detain the lot of you on charges of obstruction, but I do have to insist that you clear my scene immediately."

"Lieutenant, I'm afraid we won't be doing that. First and foremost, this is MY scene. This is a military investigation and I have been asked to oversee it. I appreciate that you are attempting to do your job but your services are not required."

Ell decided that his 'confidence' bordered on cocky, a trait she disliked on its merit but loved to go up against.

"Listen, I'm in no mood to stand out here measuring... egos. I have confirmation that the victim is a civilian which means PD has jurisdiction here. If you have information in regards to the situation, I'll be more than happy to incorporate it into my investigation but we both know that a dead civilian means this is my scene. Clear your men, Colonel and stay out of my way."

"I'm not sure where you're getting your information, Lieutenant but the victim's status is... questionable."

"Nothing questionable about it, Colonel. David Jellic may have been one of yours yesterday, but as of thirteen hundred hours he's a civilian and that makes him mine. I have crime techs on the way and I suggest you and your team clear out before my scene is further contaminated and I have no choice but to level charges and haul your collective asses in."

To his credit, Craig maintained his calm composure, continuing to block her entrance. "Unfortunately, time of death has not yet been determined so, as I mentioned, the victim's status is unclear. Based on our findings, it is also irrelevant. The Department of Defense has registered this scene military jurisdiction. Based on Jellic's background, the suspects, witnesses and involved parties are likely to be military officers. That gives me the ball, Lieutenant."

Ell set her jaw and took a deep, calming breath. "It's time to take your ball and go home. 'Likely to be' gives you a courtesy call at most, if and when I make that determination, Colonel. Until then, this is a PD Homicide. Feel free to complain to the D.O.D, Mayor, or whoever else is on your speed dial, but, in the meantime, clear out and pray to god nothing's missing."

Ell set her stance, letting her fingers tap against the metal cuffs hanging loosely from her belt. She could see the stonewall glare in Craig's eyes shift, soften and turn, for a moment, to hesitation.

"In the interest of moving this along, let's say we agree to work together, in good faith, until we know what we're dealing with?"

"I don't play well with others, Colonel."

"Now that is not at all what I've heard," replied Craig, a sly smile crossing his lips, making Ell wonder who he'd been talking to.

"Fine, you can tag along, but keep the hell out of my way and get your techs off the premises. I work with my team and, for now, I'll keep you in the loop on results."

The Colonel nodded in resignation and asked the officer at the door to inform the team inside that the PD crime techs would be taking over until further notice. Ell tried not to look too sanctimonious as he did so.

Chapter Two

She had expected the scene to be messy, murder always is, but she was not prepared for what met her inside the apartment. The two-bedroom flat was simple, not overtly expensive, but clean and well organized. It was lived in but cared for. The living-room, however, was destroyed. The furniture was broken, flipped and covered in blood. The contents of every drawer and cupboard were strewn throughout the room and, as if set as a centerpiece for viewing upon entry, the victim was naked, bound, gagged and hung, inverted, from the ceiling on the far end of the room.

David Jellic had been a fit young man in his mid thirties yet it was hard to tell that from the state of the body. His hands and forearms were wrapped and tied across the small of his back with black leather strapping. A makeshift ballgag fashioned from a black belt and something she could not yet make out, covered his jaw. The body was suspended, upside down, from an extension cord that had been tied around his ankles and tethered to a large hook in the ceiling. The bleeding had stopped but his torso, arms and legs had been sliced repeatedly with a sharp thin blade. The cause of death was not immediately apparent. However, from the amount of blood staining the room, the victim had lived through some significant pain before it was over.

The Colonel watched her as she entered the room, waiting for a reaction that never came. Ell merely stood in the doorway, taking in the scene, her mind looking for subtle clues that could help reconstruct the hours leading up to her arrival.

"Have your techs been in here?"

"No, I had just done my on-scene analysis and was about to give them the go ahead. They've been confined to the rest of the apartment and interviewing the woman that found the body."

"Girlfriend? Records didn't indicate a spouse."

"No, we haven't found a direct connection. She's a civilian, Elizabeth Plante. She's not sure how or why Jellic was in the apartment but her roommate is military personnel and may have let him in."

"And the roommate is?"

"Missing. Claire Fenn, thirty-two year old female," he referenced his notes. "Plante had expected her to be home but we haven't been able to locate her. Her cell phone goes straight to voicemail."

"The killer came prepared but didn't shop for it. The extension cord, the belt, they speak to opportunity items."

"Could have found them on-site." Rique's voice rung out from behind them.

"About time, don't you live four blocks south of here?"

"Had to give your mom a lift home," he replied and Ell could tell from the sly grin that it wasn't his own bed she'd drug him out of. Her good friend, escort madam and sexual deviant, Angel Demarco, had been playing with her partner again.

"Colonel Craig, this is my partner, Enrique Shaw. Excuse his humor, it's an acquired taste. The Colonel will be assisting until we can determine jurisdiction."

Rique took his first hard look at the crime scene and winced visually. "As I was saying, the extension cord, the leather straps, the belt, these could have been found on-site. What makes you think the killer came prepared?"

Ell waved at the ceiling, pointing to the location of the body along the back wall, "You don't hang a plant in the center of a wall and I don't know of a plant hook capable of suspending a full grown man. That's a four inch stainless swivel hook with two inch lag bolts. It comes standard with most swings and suspension kits. Whoever hung it took the time to find a joist or insert pull bars in the ceiling to distribute the weight."

Rique nodded and stepped carefully towards the body, "L.T., take a look at the arm wraps." They were a series of flat wraps, evenly spaced, circling the thumb and looping between the arms. It was a professional threading technique used to tighten the restraint and resistance. "This is no amateur wrap. The perp had some experience with bondage."

"Hold on," cut in the Colonel, "Bondage? Suspension? Swings? Are you trying to say THIS was sexual?" He waved his hand at the blood soaked, overturned room.

"God no," replied Ell, "this was anger, rage and aggression. But the perp had knowledge of bondage and suspension. Perhaps in a sexual sense, perhaps in a professional one. Rique, get some photos before tech gets in to rip this place apart and let Sanders know I need a full work up on the body as soon as possible. I'm going to want a few minutes with Dr. Grayson in the next twenty-four hours, send her an email and give her a heads up. The profile's odd. Too many mixed signals. She may be able to tighten it down."

Dr. Anne Grayson was a good resource to have even if she did insist on poking at Ell's psyche along the way. She was one of the top profilers in the business and when she wasn't on loan to the FBI or some other acronym based organization, Ell valued her input.

Turning to the Colonel she left her partner to continue examining the crime scene. "Where's Ms. Plante?"

"In the second bedroom, she's pretty shaken up."

'No shit,' thought Ell.

They passed Detective Lund, head of Crime Scene, and his team of techs, just arriving and watched them scatter and begin dissecting the apartment. "The body is in the living room. You're clear to sweep as soon as Sanders finalizes the preliminary report on the victim. It's not pretty."

"They never are." grunted Lund on his way past. The late night calls left little room for witty repartee.

Ell rounded the corner into the second bedroom and found Elisabeth Plante curled up in a ball on the bed. Her eyes were red and her face ghost white. A young man in a full dress military uniform sat beside her, his hand resting gently on her leg. Ell eyed him up slowly. His tight body filled out the uniform well and coupled nicely with a disarming smile and soft eyes. Her mind wandered, briefly, and her skin flushed as she imagined his strong arms pinning her down. Cursing Rob and his torturous rules against self-satisfaction, she shook her head and struggled to focus.

"I thought you cleared your men out?"

"I did, Corporal Strand is a friend of the witness. He's not on duty this evening, but was first on scene, aside from Ms.

Plante. I figured you'd want to talk with him and he didn't seem very eager to leave."

"Sorry sir, Liz is pretty shook up. I just wanted to be here for her."

"Were you with her when she arrived home?"

"I was outside. We spent the evening together at the Collin's Red Ribbon Gala. It was a fundraiser to help support the families of fallen soldiers. I walked Liz home after the event. We parted out front, but when I heard her screaming, I high-tailed it up here. I found her in the hall just outside the living room curled up and in tears. I wasn't sure what to make of it at first but by the time I reached her it was pretty clear what happened. I'm not afraid to say your techs are going to find my DNA along with some mighty tender sirloin in the hallway carpet. Anyway, I carried Liz in here, called nine-one-one and immediately contacted my Sergeant, Sergeant John Jeffrey, as per protocol."

'That explains the Colonel's quick response', thought Ell.

"What time did you arrive, Corporal?"

"Approximately Zero-One-Hundred, Lieutenant."

"One a.m.," whispered the Colonel and Ell tossed him a snide glance indicating that his help was not necessary.

"Did either of you enter the living-room?"

"God no. Sorry, no, not after I arrived and I found Liz on the floor in the hall, I don't think she had been in there."

"I... I... I was going to go in," said Liz in a trembling haze. "but, the blood and... and... the man... I just screamed and I think I fell. Where's Claire? Is she... is she..."

"Ms. Fenn's location has yet to be determined. Her cell phone appears to be off. Do either of you know if she had plans this evening?"

"No, she was here when I left, she said she was staying in," replied Liz. "She'd had a long week at work. She works for the Judge Advocate and things have been hectic lately. It's why she was skipping the Gala, well that and... Jon..." Liz trailed off, looking at Corporal Strand.

Ell gave Liz a questioning glance and the Corporal answered for her. "Claire and I were engaged. We broke it off two months ago but it's been awkward for both of us since. We still work in related divisions and share similar social circles. We do our best to be cordial but often it's easier to simply avoid one another."

"And what was her relationship with David Jellic?"

"Jellic?" asked Strand. "None that I'm aware of." He glanced at Liz for confirmation.

"God no, we all knew about his court martial, it was pretty recent gossip in military circles, but we didn't know him or anything like that. Wait. Are you saying? The man I saw, the body? Was that Jellic?"

"Formal identification has not been made but early indications suggest so. What time did you leave here today?"

"About nine this morning, I work at a small café over on thirty-second. My shift ended at seven and Jon met me there to head for the Gala. I wanted to come home first but the timeline was tight so I took my dress with me and changed at work."

You mentioned that Claire works for the Judge Advocate, is there any chance she was involved with Jellic's case?"

"Claire's a paralegal. She deals with a lot of research but she's not really involved with clients. She may have done something for the case, peripherally, but she didn't mention anything. With all the gossip I'm sure she'd have said something."

"Thank you both for your time, I'm going to have an officer take down some contact information in case we have any follow-up questions. Ms. Plante, we're going to be in the apartment for a while yet, do you have somewhere you can go?"

"I have family in town," she replied, beginning to calm.

"Good, if either of you think of anything else please feel free to contact us, and if you hear from Ms. Fenn have her call me immediately."

Ell and the Colonel headed back down the hall, meeting Rique at the entryway, preparing to head out.

"Sanders is on scene, Lund's waiting for him to finish his on-site before the techs start on the living room."

Ell took one last look at the apartment from the edge of the doorway. Something was off. There was something she was missing but she couldn't place it.

"Shaw, hold up."

Rique stopped, turning back into the doorway.

"What's up, L.T.?"

"There's something off. Tell me what you see, what stands out as odd?"

"Not much. It's a pretty standard front hall. This whole neighborhood is built in a similar style. Aside from the purses and heels, this isn't much different from my own flat."

"Purses?" asked Ell.

"Yeah, to your left on the wood bench. It's pretty normal for ladies to leave them up here isn't it?"

"Sure, but why are there two?"

Chapter Three

R ique issued an APB on Private First Class Claire Fenn but Colonel Craig insisted on taking point on the missing persons case. Being a missing military officer with no indication of civilian involvement, there was nothing Ell could do to prevent it. The situation was becoming a cross-jurisdictional nightmare and she feared it was only a matter of time before someone attempted to strong-arm her off of the case.

The trip back to the eleventh precinct was quick but agitating. The pent up sexual frustration wasn't helping but there was something else about this one that wasn't sitting right. Something about the scene had pulled her in. This was her case now, her victim, and she did not intend to walk away and let the military take over.

The precinct was quiet, though she had not expected much activity at three-thirty in the morning. There bound to be a few drunk and disorderlies down in the tank, perhaps a couple working girls that were rousted overnight, but unless there was something high profile in the works, robbery/homicide would be a ghost town at this hour. Baker and Jones had settled into the bullpen and were filing the paperwork on the two military officers they had escorted in. Ell knew the charges wouldn't hold, D.A. Stranik would drop them in the interest of 'playing nice', but the work still needed to be done.

"Thanks for taking care of the grunt work, ladies. Did they give you any problems on the way in?"

"I think their egos were bruised more than their bodies," responded Jones. "They rode in like a couple of well scolded toddlers. How'd it go at the scene?"

"Grizzly. It wasn't pretty, but I'll let you review the photos and notes as soon as Rique gets the file and board going. This one's gonna turn into a fight for control and I have no intention of letting it go. It's still your case," she nodded at Detective Jones, "but I want to be kept in the loop."

Baker shook her head, the flowing red locks framing her sweet, innocent smile. A smile Ell knew held much more than it appeared.

"We've already transferred the case off in the system, L.T. You and Rique are the active investigators. We figured, you examined the scene, started the process, you'd be invested."

They knew her, knew she'd never be able to step aside once she'd done the initial on-scene. "Thanks, but I want both of you on this with us, if your case-load can handle it. I have a feeling I'm going to be spending too much of my time fighting to keep us involved. Colonel Craig is playing nice for now but he's not the type to sit in the background and watch."

Jones' eyes snapped up from her desk. "Craig? As in the Columbian Cutie, Craig? He can watch me anytime. What the hell is he doing looking into a simple homicide? Did we run out of needy hostages in remote jungles?"

"I'm not sure, but does hoping one comes to light in the next couple hours make me a bad person?"

"Maybe just a little," laughed Baker. Her soft giggle sending chills through Ell's body. Taking a deep breath she focused her mind and headed across the hall to her office.

Opening the door and settling into the desk chair, Ell took a moment to focus and take in the room. It was more a converted broom closet than an office, but she liked her private space. It was quiet and non-distracting. It also had one of the best computers in the precinct thanks to her personal I.T. slave Rob. Looking at the dual LCD monitors she felt a ping of longing. It had only been a week since he left for his 'let's build a robot overlord' conference but she was definitely beginning to miss him. It was an odd feeling. She'd never felt connected to someone before. Not like this. Not to the point of affecting her. Her body tingled at the thought of his touch, his soft hands caressing her skin, setting her at ease for just a moment before the hard sting of flesh on flesh coursed through her. Her mind fluttered, her skin flushed and she nearly let out an audible moan before coming to her senses.

'Fuck, I'm going to seriously hurt that boy for doing this to me,' she cursed, trying to regain her composure. Taking a couple deep breaths, she turned and wiggled her mouse, bringing the computer to life. The desktop popped up and she pulled up the case files Jones and Baker had begun compiling on David Jellic. She added her own on-site notes, knowing the other detectives on scene would do the same, and then turned her attention to a search on jurisdictional requirements. It was a conversation that was going to come up sooner or later and she intended to be prepared.

Having lost herself in the search she barely noticed when Rique knocked on her open door forty minutes later.

"L.T., I've added my site notes and started to put together a timeline and case board in the bullpen. Not much to go on yet but it's early. Baker and Jones went to grab a couple hours down time before their shift starts. Sanders should have a preliminary report by mid-morning and said he would contact you as soon as it's ready. The cause of death wasn't obvious at the scene although he said the significant blood loss may factor in. He estimated time of death as one to six p.m. but is hoping to tighten that up once he can do a thorough examination."

The timeframe was promising yet it still left the victim's status as a civilian arguable. Hopefully they could tighten it down before she had to speak with the Commader.

"Any word from the tech monkies?"

"Still on-sight. With the state of the room it's going to take them a while to catalog and process everything. I sent Grayson an email about a consult but wouldn't expect a response until the sun's back on this side of the planet. Still no hit on the APB for Fenn so I have uniforms canvassing any known haunts that may be open at this hour. I know we are not supposed to be running point on the missing person case so they've been instructed to be discreet."

"Good, we should also dig into the roommate and their relationship. It's not likely to play but dating your roommates ex-fiancé seems like something that doesn't go over well in most circles. There's not much else we can do until the sun comes up. You should get a couple hours in a bunk while you have a chance. I'm just finishing up some research that may help us hold on to the case. Odds are Colonel Craig is going to want to tie in his missing private as an excuse to claim jurisdiction. I don't plan on releasing the reins, nor do I need the military breathing down my back every step of the way."

Rique rubbed his eyes and smiled.

"I don't envy your job, L.T., but I'll leave you to it."

The seven a.m. shift change came quickly. Ell was still reviewing her jurisdictional argument when the traffic in the precinct halls began to pick up. Exhaustion was on the edge of her mind but the adrenaline of a new case had managed to keep the fog from flowing over her. It was going to be a long day.

She set aside her research for a moment and headed across the hall to the bullpen. The Jellic case may be hers but as the Lieutenant for robbery/homicide she had to make sure nothing else was falling through the cracks while she ran with it. As expected, her team were already hard at it. The bullpen was bustling with cop speak, the distinct aroma of stale pastry and tar-like coffee filling the air. If she didn't have a throbbing head ache and a hard ass reputation to protect she may have smiled. There was nothing as beautiful as the bullpen at full throttle. Beautiful and frightening. A symphony of organized chaos.

Her mind, focussed on the scene unfolding before her, cleared just in time to sidestep an elbow to the temple. Jenkins swung around, blindly, a half eaten bagel hanging from his lips and arms full of files.

"Christ! A little warning before you bust into pirouettes, Jenkins."

"Shit, sorry L.T.," he said, wrestling the remaining bagel from his mouth, "I didn't see you come in."

"That's the high level of observation I love to see in my detectives." She waved him off before he could apologize again. "So what's hot this morning?" Ell gestured at the stack of files he was struggling to keep balanced on his left arm.

"Oh, Brituski and I are on deck for testimony in the Donne's case this afternoon. I figured I'd better brush up on the official reports and make sure everything is in order."

"Donne's? Was that the idiot that tried to rob the Brinks' truck on fifth?"

"Plastic pellet gun and all."

"How the hell did that go to trial?"

"His daddy hired a high priced attorney who is trying his best to earn a couple years worth of retirement off of this kid's boneheaded attempt at criminal enterprise."

Ell shook her head and sighed. "Better make sure it's nailed down tight, and let me know if there any issues. We don't need some pricey suit messing up the easy ones."

"Yeah, don't you have your own 'pricey suit' battle coming up on the Bouton case?"

"Don't remind me. Fucking suits." Ell tapped him on the shoulder and headed further into the room.

Baker and Jones were absent, as expected, hopefully getting a couple hours in the bunks. The rest of the squad were honing in on their cases and barely noticed her presence. Rique gave her a nod as she wandered over to his desk.

"If you and I are taking point on this Jellic mess I'm going to need you to be my eyes and ears in here. Last time we pulled something this high profile, I got wrapped up and the squad was left scrambling. If I'm going to be running lead on a homicide I'll need someone making sure I don't get tunnel vision."

"We're big kids, L.T., we won't break the swing set while you're gone."

She glanced at the plate of frosted mini-doughnuts on the edge of his desk, snagged one, and let out a slight laugh, "You keep eating like this and your ass will be lucky to fit in the swings."

"Damn," he said putting down a half eaten doughnut. "Angel would be pissed if we couldn't use the swing."

"Jesus Rique, information and visuals your Lieutenant doesn't need."

Rique chuckled, "Next time leave my fucking frosteds alone."

"Deal, a little sugar isn't worth the torture of that visual."

He feigned pain placing a hand over his heart. "But seriously, Ell, we've all got your back. Every cop in here can manage on their own if this case gets crazy, and I'll keep an eye out for balls dropping. The media circus this is going to draw, especially on the heels of the Bouton mess and upcoming trial, isn't going to be pretty."

"Don't remind me," said Ell, the thought was enough to increase the throbbing on her temples.

"If we were smart we'd just hand this one off to Colonel Hot Stuff and sit back while the media storm rolls in, but..."

"Who claimed we were smart?" asked Ell.

"No one I've ever met. I'll roll through the pen and touch base with the crew, get all the actives on track. You go deal with the brass and make sure no one screws up our case."

Ell would have tried to come up with a bit of witty repartee but the growing headache, two hours sleep and ever present sexual frustration thanks to Rob's damn rules, made the effort required far too much. Instead, she smiled and whispered, "Thanks," before turning to make her way back through the bullpen and across the hall to her office.

She just managed to settle in and begin printing off the jurisdictional argument that she had been preparing when her office line rang. Checking the display she noted extension 145 – Commander Nuez. She took a deep breath before answering. She had hoped for a few hours to dig into the case before the fight for control began but clearly that wasn't going to be an option. Deciding to forego the handset, Ell punched the speakerphone key and tried to sound professional.

"Robbery / Homicide, Lieutenant Frost speaking."

"Good morning Lieutenant, this is Keith Dillon with the Commander's office. Commander Nuez requests that you make yourself available at oh nine hundred to meet with him and a representative from the Judge Advocate's office. The Commander also requests fifteen minutes with you in advance of the meeting. At a time of your convenience."

Checking the clock on her phone, Ell saw it was eight twenty-two. "At a time of my convenience, Keith? It's damn near eight thirty and you want fifteen minutes between now and nine. You do realize I'm a cop with an open, high-profile homicide and an entire department of other cops relying on me for leadership, right? So in what world is any of this bureaucratic nonsense convenient?"

Keith stammered, searching for a response but Ell cut him off before he could come up with anything more than awkward grunts.

"Never mind, tell the Commander I'll be in his office in fifteen with a recap."

She didn't wait for a response before disconnecting but immediately felt guilty. She enjoyed harassing the Commander's robot like assistant but it was usually just good natured ribbing. She'd taken her frustration out on him this morning and knew that wasn't fair. Fuck! She hated owing someone an apology, especially the robot. Unfortunately she hated guilt more and didn't need to add it to the pounding headache, exhaustion and growing frustration. She took one more glance at the clock, gathered her notes and decided she'd have to deal with Keith later. Right now murder and bureaucracy were fighting to monopolize her morning.

Normally she would have bypassed the elevator, opting to double time it up the stairs, but given how she felt and the fact that an empty car was waiting, she decided to give her legs a break. It took about twenty seconds to regret that decision. Before reaching the second floor, the lift came to a screeching halt. Emergency lights flashing.

"What the bloody hell?"

An automated voice came from the speaker embedded in the control panel. "Please remain calm. A maintenance technician has been notified. Approximate response time is twenty minutes."

"Pardon? Twenty minutes my ass!"

Ell pulled out her cell and dialled her partner.

"King of the Bullpen, how may I help you?"

"You can get your ass out to the lobby and break me out of elevator two."

"What?"

"Which part are you struggling with, Rique. Elevator two is stuck and I need you to come 'unstuck' the damn thing."

Rique made a conscious effort not to laugh but she could hear the jubilation in his voice.

"I'm pretty sure you'll need to wait for maintenance on that one, L.T. Even the King of the Pen's superpowers have limits."

"Maintenance is twenty minutes out and I'm due in Nuez' office in ten. Can your superpowers do math? Get me out of this fucking metal coffin."

"Ell, aside from going 'Die Hard' up the elevator shaft, I don't know what to tell you."

She didn't have time to argue but he had given her an idea so she hung up and hit speed dial two.

"Not that I don't love to hear from you but it's six thirty a.m. here, Ell." Rob's voice sent an unexpected shiver down her spine.

Punish me later. I don't have time for formal niceties at the moment. I'm stuck in an elevator at the precinct and need to know how to open the door."

"Call maintenance."

"Hilarious. You're the tech genius, so how do I hack this piece of crap so I can get out?"

"You don't. What car are you in?"

She could hear his laptop booting up on the other end of the call. "Two."

Seconds later the elevator let out three long beeps of surrender and the doors slid open. She was between floors but figured there was enough clearance between the roof of the elevator and the tile of the second floor for her to squeeze through.

"Thanks, my hero," she said in her best damsel in distress impression. Rob laughed.

"Whips an chains, can I go back to sleep now, please?"

"Get that beauty rest, we know you need it. Whips and chains back attcha." Ell smiled and disconnected the call.

She tossed her files through the opening and pulled herself up and out of the elevator, rolling onto the floor in front of a group of cheering crime scene techs.

"Bite me."

She grabbed her files, faked a bow and hightailed it up the stairs, bursting into the Commander's outer office minutes later, out of breath but on time. Keith gave her an odd look and seemed to contemplate what to say before motioning to the office door.

"He's expecting you."

Ell mumbled, "Thanks," gave the door a courtesy knock and headed in.

Commander Nuez began speaking without looking up. "Thanks for fitting this in. I want to make sure..." he paused, finally looking up and seeing the state she was in. Her hair was dishevelled, her eyes fighting to stay open and her blazer was stained with grease and torn slightly on the left side.

"Christ, Frost, what happened?"

She seemed confused and took a second to register that she looked like she'd just survived an explosion.

"Sorry sir, I got stuck in elevator two on the way up. Maintenance was going to be at least twenty minutes so I had to hack the system, open the doors and climb my way out."

"Or call and have me push this a half hour."

Ell stared at him as if the mere thought was foreign to her.

"Never mind, how'd you manage to override the doors?"

"I called in my I.T. slave."

"I thought Rob was at a conference in Seattle this week?"

"He is. You should really look into that man's security clearance."

The commander let out a laugh and shook his head.

"Ok, let's try to keep this brief so you have a few minutes to clean yourself up before the Judge Advocate gets here. I've reviewed the case files on this Jellic mess, though I must say I hadn't expected there to be much of a file yet. I was pleasantly surprised. I see you've taken over as primary here..."

"Jones and Baker stepped aside given that I'd cleared the scene and, since we figure this is bound to be high profile, it's probably best to have a ranking officer on the day to day. I plan to keep both of them in on it as much as possible."

"A good idea. Given that the Judge Advocate's office was breathing down my neck first thing this morning I have to assume they'll be fighting to take over. Your report indicated that jurisdiction is up in the air. Based on that, it's reasonable to assume the Department of Defense will be pushing hard to get us out of their way."

"Frankly sir, I'm not prepared to step aside. I've done some research this morning and I believe we have a pretty solid footing. Sanders puts the time of death between one and six on his preliminary report. Even assuming the earliest, the victim was a civilian at that time."

"Time of death is a finicky science, Lieutenant. They'll argue against it."

"They'll try. Even so, I've found precedent cases where PD jurisdiction has been granted when T.O.D. is undetermined but the victim is a civilian at the time of discovery."

"Is this really a fight we want to pick?"

"Your damn straight it is! This is my case Commander and there is no one more qualified to close it. I don't care what miracles Colonel Craig has performed in the last few months. This is mine."

Commander Nuez sat quiet for a moment, contemplating the options. "If you're willing to fight for it I'll back you up, but remember this isn't a county squabble. This is the Department of Defense. You better be willing to make some compromises."

Compromises, just what she needed to really fuck up an already difficult, high profile case.

"I'll do what I need to but I'm not dropping this one, Commander."

"And the missing girl?"

"I don't have much of a leg to stand on there. There was no foul play that we've been able to find. She's military so, as a missing person, it's not my case."

"And as a material witness or perhaps a suspect?"

Ell cursed to herself, she hadn't considered it. Her mind had been jelly this morning but even so, she should have come up with it.

"It's a good angle, and one we can use to get involved, assuming we hold on to the homicide."

"Ok, go get cleaned up and meet us down in Conference Three as soon as you're done."

"Thanks." Ell headed for the door but stopped short and turned back to the Commander.

"Oh, sir."

The Commander glanced up in response.

"Take the stairs."

Chapter Four

*E*ll hustled back down the stairs and through the halls to her office. She wasted no time ripping off the torn red blazer and replacing it with a black vest she had left in her bottom drawer some time ago. Grabbing a comb from the desk, she quickly ran it through her hair in a sad attempt to make it look presentable. Resolved that it was the best she could do in so little time, she prepared herself, mentally, and headed for what was sure to be a brutal meeting.

Ell steadied herself as she walked into the conference room. She wasn't one to stand on formality but immediately understood that that would not be an option in this meeting. Commander Nuez stood beside two very fit, very handsome and very formal men in full dress, military uniforms. Each filled them out well and Ell was impressed with the sight. She recognized Colonel Craig, but his companion remained a mystery. She wasn't overly clear on military insignia but given the number of medals, stars, and stripes on mystery man's uniform, she assumed he'd be in charge.

"Lieutenant Frost," Commander Nuez motioned to the

gentlemen. "I believe you know Colonel Craig, and this is General Costan with the Judge Advocates' office."

"General, Colonel." Ell nodded at each and all four took a seat around the large mahogany conference table.

"I'm not about to waste any time here. We both know that your young lady overreached her authority at the crime scene. That's not on you, Mr. Nuez," began General Costan, "but it leaves us a pretty cut and dry situation. I have a dead officer and a missing private. It's a military case any way you look at it. Now, if you'll simply instruct your subordinate to hand over the case files and any finding your crime scene techs may have, we will be on our way."

Ell did not take well to being discussed as if she was not in the room. Nor was the blatant misogyny welcome.

"Unless you look at the facts," she responded.

Commander Nuez cringed and the General's head snapped in her direction. "Pardon?"

"Facts sir. They're what we civilian young ladies use to make a determination in regards to our investigations. In this case those facts don't support your analysis."

The General returned his gaze to Commander Nuez. "I suggest you put your Lieutenant on a leash and remind her who she is speaking to. I think she's done enough to tarnish your precinct's reputation as of late."

Nuez knew better than to respond and let Ell continue.

"As much as I do enjoy a good leash," Ell winked at Colonel Craig, "I'm afraid that's for playtime and I have work to do. Now let's look at those facts, shall we? Due to a well publicized court martial, your dead officer ceased being an officer at thirteen hundred hours yesterday. Our medical examiner puts time of death between one p.m. and six p.m., that's thirteen hundred and eighteen hundred in case you need help converting. So, as I mentioned, if you look at the situation using the actual facts then it's a dead civilian and that, General, makes him MY dead civilian."

General Costan was fuming and about to respond when Ell cut him off. "I'm not finished. Now, I came into this meeting expecting to work out a compromise but, frankly, your boy's club attitude isn't going to work with me. If you're ready to stow it and treat me like an equal, hell I'd even settle for like a human, then perhaps we can work something out. Otherwise pack up your fancy medals, stow the stick in your ass, and stay the hell out of my way."

The General's ire was up but to his credit he managed to maintain control. Focussing his gaze on Ell, his voice laced with anger, he said, "Are you done with your tantrum, missy?"

Ell rose to her feet.

"If not for the respect I have for my Commander and my badge you'd be kissing concrete, not unlike your fellow officers last night, for that remark alone. I'll tell you what I am done with, your bullshit. If you want involvement in my case get an order from the district court, otherwise stay the fuck out of my face or I'll run your pompous ass in for obstruction."

As if unsure what to do, the General glared at Commander Nuez.

"Well son, are you just going to sit there and allow your employee to speak to me that way? Get some control over your unit and show me the respect I'm due."

"Commander," snapped Nuez.

"Excuse me?"

"It's Commander Nuez, not mister or son and as far as I'm concerned respect is earned, General. From what I've seen here, you've received exactly what you're due."

Colonel Craig sat quietly, his face stoic, but Ell could sense a slight grin. He was fighting to hide it but it was there.

The General's face grew red as he struggled to suppress his rage. Standing, he gathered himself and shot a burning look at Colonel Craig. "We're done here, Colonel, let's go."

"You may be finished but I have a discussion to complete."

"Colonel, your star may be on the rise, but I'd advise you to remember your place."

"I'm well aware of my place, General. I was assigned to this case, not by the J.A.G. core, nor by you. My orders come directly from the Department of Defense and unless there's been a promotion I am unaware of, you have no authority to override them."

"Son, you may be this week's shining star but you just crossed the wrong man. Enjoy your fifteen minutes of fame, you uppity little shit, because it's about to end in a blaze of regret."

General Costan pushed his way past the Colonel and exited without so much as a sideways glance.

Colonel Craig adjusted his uniform jacket and gestured to Ell's chair. "Please, let's attempt to solve this. I won't apologize for someone else's poor behaviour, but I will say that, from what I know of you, you deserve better. Let's see if we can get this off to an equitable and inclusive start, shall we?"

Ell fought to relax, the anger had given her a much needed adrenaline rush and it wasn't easy to put the brakes on. She took a couple deep breaths and settled back into the plush leather chair.

"So, Colonel, what exactly are you proposing?" asked Commander Neuz, giving Ell a moment to calm down and focus.

"I can't argue the science or the legal standing. Given what I have read, it seems both our sides would have a fair argument for jurisdiction. We could take the arguments up with the relevant parties, wait for a decision, and waste a shit tonne of time, energy and man power fighting for control. Or, we could come to a compromise here and now, focus that energy on catching whoever did this, and maybe find a missing young girl in the process. I do agree with one thing the General said, 'I'm not going to waste any time here.' because I don't believe we can afford to."

Ell thought that her initial assessment of the man from the night before may have been in haste. She was right that his confidence bordered on cocky but somehow he managed to hold the line and keep it in check. He was calm, but it was a forced, thoughtful calm. Beneath the surface he was running, his mind racing and his body just waiting to follow. It was something she often lacked. Something she envied. Composure.

"Here's what I suggest," he continued. "I'll cede the jurisdictional fight and let your team and your techs handle things unless you feel further resources on our end could help. In return, you bring me in on the investigation. Every step."

Commander Nuez looked to Ell, trying to gauge her response. "It's a fair offer, but it's Lieutenant Frost's case and who she works with is her call."

"I already have a damn good partner."

"But does he have my dashing jaw line?"

Ell couldn't help but laugh and the ease with which he delivered the line swayed her slightly. "Fine, I'll put you on the team but you take your lead from me. You follow my investigation and you report to me. Only to me. If I hear one mention of you going rogue on this or working some angle behind my back I'll shut it down faster than..." Stalling, she couldn't think of an appropriate metaphor. "Fuck... Well, fast."

"Faster than your wit perhaps?"

She smirked, but knew that it was the little touches that would help build a rapport and keep this partnership together. "You caught me on a rough morning so I'll let that one slide."

Commander Nuez seemed satisfied. "Will those conditions work with your superiors?"

"Oh, they'll despise it but I can make it fly. I have some credibility built up at the moment. If I recommend it as the best course of action, they'll let me run with it."

"And General Custard?" asked Ell to a chorus of snickers.

"Will flip his lid, but it shouldn't make much of a difference. The D.O.D. pretty much considers him a joke. Unfortunately, they're forced to respect the position he holds. Military honor and all that."

"Okay, let's try to keep the fall out to a minimum and quit wasting what time we have. Colonel, do what you need to and clear this with whoever makes the call on your end. You can work back in with Lieutenant Frost's team as soon as you have."

"I should be back by fourteen hundred," looking at Ell he smirked, "that's two p.m. if you need help with the conversion."

Exhaustion began to take hold as soon as Ell got back to her office. The adrenaline rush had helped keep her going for a short time but the crash was taking its toll. She checked the time on her phone and decided there was no way she could fit in a nap. Coffee it was, lot's of coffee. Even the precinct swill was going to have to do for now. She started to stand and then thought better, picked up her phone and punched speed-dial one.

"L.T., things are running like a poorly oiled engine in here but the crew's good for now."

"Thanks, Rique. Do me a favor grab what you've found on Claire Fenn and meet me in my office. We're going to be ramping up the search."

"Are we stepping on someone's toes or did you arrange to have it transferred to us."

"A bit of both, I'll give you the run down in five and do me a favor, bring a pail of that black tar-like coffee substitute that's brewing in the bullpen."

She could hear the shock and sympathy in his voice. "Seriously?"

"It's the lengths we go to for solid police work," she joked, though at this point she'd inject the caffeine straight into the vein if it were an option.

She sat back, resting her eyes, and nearly jumped out of the chair when Rique knocked on the door frame five minutes later.

"Damn, you look like you just spent a couple hours with Angel."

Ell laughed. "That bad? Well here's hoping the swill helps take the edge off." She took the cup from his outstretched hand and grimaced while downing a quarter of it. "Christ, is this getting worse? Who makes this crap?"

"I'm pretty sure Jones made that pot sometime last night. Your bravery knows no bounds, Frost."

Ell gestured at the world's most uncomfortable guest chair in the corner of her office but Rique shook his head and leaned against the wall.

"I'm not as brave as you, boss. I'll stand. What's the scoop with the missing girl?"

"Suspect, material witness? Take your pick, either way she's involved in the murder investigation and the murder investigation is ours."

"Really? The Judge Advocate let us take this one?"

"Not so much. The J.A.G. representative may have gotten a tad upset with my attitude, taken his ball and gone home. In my defense the guy was a grade A prick. I'm sure he'll try to kick up a shit storm but the Department of Defense has our backs, for now."

"Just like that? The D.O.D. just handed it over and has our backs?" Rique knew it couldn't be that simple.

"Well... we cut a bit of a deal with Colonel Craig. I'm bringing him in on this to work with us. He'll be reporting to me just like the rest of the squad."

Rique actually laughed, "Seriously? You're bringing in Colonel Cutie and you think he's going to just play ball with the civilians? How long till he bypasses you and takes our findings to whoever's pulling his strings? This is a bad idea, Ell. A first rate, bad idea. The military doesn't just give up control. They spy, they sneak and, when the time's right, they stab you in the back."

Ell knew he was right but everything about this morning had her on edge. "You don't think I fucking know that? What damn choice did I have? Tell me what choice I should have made here, Rique. The guy's a slimy military hotshot but he's also got a decent feel for investigation and people. If taking him on and fighting like hell to keep him from fucking us over is the only way to move this forward then that's what we do. We're wasting time measuring dicks and fighting for control while a killer moves on and a young woman is nowhere to be found. This power struggle crap had to get dealt with in order for us to keep going... So I dealt with it. Nuez is on board and Craig is certain he can bring the D.O.D. around."

"No shit, they love having a spy inside."

She was about to respond but Rique could tell she was at the end of a thin rope and held up a hand.

"You know I'm with you, Ell and I'll back your play here. All I'm saying is let's not turn a blind eye to where this could lead."

"Okay, then here's the deal. Your new job, on top of managing the rest of the squad and bringing me swill, is to keep an eye on the Colonel. Double check anything he touches and make damn sure you know who he's talking to and when. This is going to put a serious snag in our usual case rhythm but we don't have much of a choice."

"Manage the squad, have hot swill on tap and babysit the manchild. Oh yeah, these are the real reasons I became a cop. I'm your man."

"Thanks?" said Ell unsure if it was the right response.

"No, no, no, you're going to owe me a hell of a lot more than 'thanks' before this one's over. I'll make you a list."

"Okay."

"What the hell? Seriously Ell? No witty comeback, no life threatening beat down? You definitely need to drink some more swill, you're weird when you're tired."

"Bite me. So now that the crap is out of the way, what do you have on Ms. Fenn?"

"Not much. She graduated from Columbia University a year and a half ago with a two year legal assistant degree. She enlisted straight out of college, did six months basic training and has been with the J.A.G. core for just over a year. I couldn't requisition her full military file due to all the red tape but what I was provided indicates she has a solid record and not much notoriety since enlisting. Her recent history is about as clean as it gets but pre-College is where it gets interesting."

Ell's interest piqued, interesting usually pointed to leads and leads got her blood rolling.

"Five years ago, from what I can find, Claire Fenn did not exist."

"Pardon."

"This girl has all the right stuff, Ell. Social security number, driver's licence, passport. Hell she's even got a magic trust fund but all of it, even the cash, didn't exist until two days before she started college. She has no family, not even a long lost cousin that we can pin point, no minor record, hell she doesn't even have a social media presence prior to that day."

"So we've got a ghost."

"A ghost that's in the wind and that begs the question, does she want to be found?"

"Ms. Fenn just made the suspect list. Go get the case board updated and contact sleeping beauty one and two. I want them in on this. Put them on finding Private Fenn, Jones has experience with hunting ghosts. Colonel Cutie is supposed to be back by two o'clock sharp so I'm going to want to round table at that time and get our bearings."

"On it, and you should grab a damn nap in the meantime and save us all from having to put up with you."

Ell tossed him a smirk.

"The clock's ticking and I need to dig into the victim. The swill will have to do for now. Besides I've got my second wind."

"That's a caffeine induced high, Ell, and the crash is going to be brutal."

"Then I guess you'll just have to keep me supplied and fried until sleep's an option."

"Tar-Man at your service, my lady, I won't let you down. Speaking of down, how did you manage to get out of that elevator?"

"Wit and ingenuity."

"Ok, we'll go with that," he laughed as he spun out of the office and headed back to work.

Chapter Five

The remainder of the morning was a haze filled blur. Ell jumped between caffeine induced rushes and exhausting crashes but somewhere along the rollercoaster she found a rhythm. David Jellic's court martial proved to be interesting enough to keep her focused. Yet, despite his final few months, the life and times of David Samuel Jellic were anything but intriguing. Born into a military family, his father had been a serviceman and his mother a loyal wife with no job on record. The family had travelled around a lot in his youth, finally settling just outside Pittsburg when David was thirteen. His father served out the last ten years of a thirty year military career as the lead heavy duty mechanic on two Pennsylvania bases. At age nineteen, two days after his birthday, David Jellic signed on for a five year stint with the US Marine Corp. He did a small tour overseas in the early two thousands and was relocated to a local marine training and recruitment barracks as a Drill Instructor nine years ago. His record, or at least the version she'd been able to access, was clean until eight months prior. He had slowly risen to the rank of Sergeant and was considered to be a fair instructor. His promotions came slower than many, but they did come and Ell hadn't been able to find any major issues in his file until recently. He was your ordinary, mediocre, loyal soldier.

Then, eight months ago, he was arrested for leaking state secrets to a civilian reporter. The case files were still needed. She'd put Colonel Craig on unearthing them, partially to see what type of pull he actually had, but she had been able to gather a decent amount of information from the media reports on the case. Jellic had fought the charge and his attorney had been solid. Ell didn't know how but he had managed to reach an unheard of plea and in the end the charge was reduced to conduct unbecoming an officer. The sentencing hearing was held at noon the previous day and David Jellic was suspiciously absent. The tribunal ordered him dishonorably discharged in absentia and that should have been the end of it. It should have been. It wasn't. Now it was on her to find out why.

It didn't fit. The crime, the charge, none of it fit with the man as she understood him. And the plea? She'd seen deals cut in the past but this was the equivalent of a murder suspect getting a two week grounding and no dessert. It was too coincidental, something about the case was going to be at the heart of her murder. But where and how did either Fenn or Plante fit in? She hadn't found any crossover between Jellic and the roommates so why was he there. Why had the killer picked that location, and what was the message it was supposed to send? He had to have been staged for a reason. Humiliation? If so that screamed personal and personal didn't fit with her theory that Jellic's discharge was related.

There were too many unanswered questions and she wasn't going to come up with the solutions while her head was swimming in a mixture of ibuprofen and caffeine. She needed Lund's final report on the crime scene and made a note to contact Sanders on a definitive time and cause of death. Unfortunately those items would have to wait. Pulling herself from her chair she headed down the hall to procure some fuel from the vending machine. With a bag of stale chips, some rock hard Skittles and a pepperoni stick secured, she stumbled into the bullpen, poured herself another cup of liquid tar and collapsed onto the beat up sofa against the back wall.

The snap of the whip stung, sending a wave of relief through her as she fought playfully against the soft restraints pinning her arms tight across her back. Her arousal piqued, as every muscle in her body tightened against the pain. She was positioned awkwardly, her arms wrapped tight together, her ankles hogtied upwards towards her waist, face down and supported only by the silk sheet pressing against her chin. She screamed in ecstasy as the suede whip once again lashed across her ass. Her pussy began dripping, begging for more. She had wanted this, yearned to be taken. She needed it.

"Is that what you wanted?" he whispered from the darkness. "Is this why you fought so hard to have me by your side?"

Twisting slightly she looked deep into his eyes, struggled for words and finally, in a barely audible tone, said, "Please Colonel, don't stop, take me. Make me yours."

"Frost!" Rique's voice broke through, snapping her out of the semi-coma she had dropped into.

"Fuck, what time is it?" She sat up quickly, attempting to act normal but her heart was pumping much harder than expected. Her face was flush, mouth dry and the rush of adrenaline had her ready to fly into action.

"I told you the crash was going to be brutal. How long have you been out?"

"Well if you'd answer my first question, perhaps I could tell you. What fucking time is it?"

"One o'clock and based on the attitude, it wasn't long enough."

"Bite me."

"She keeps offering but never lets me follow through, oh the woes of the poor lonely cop."

Ell rolled her eyes and shook her head. "No words Rique, there are truly no words."

"Yeah, you're not the first woman to mention that. Anyway, I figured you'd want to rise and shine with a little time to prep before the all-star marine comes to rescue us all."

Ell's face flushed instinctively at the mention of the Colonel, luckily she'd already been a fairly dark shade of pink when she was jolted awake and it wasn't noticeable.

"Did you get the crew rounded up?"

"The lovely ladies are putting the finishing touches on some paperwork, they've transferred off a couple minor cases to clear their schedule and will be ready to roll in twenty minutes."

"Ok, I've got some notes on Jellic that I need to add to the board and..." Ell noticed the empty chip bag on the couch beside her, the Skittles and pepperoni having mysteriously disappeared. "Shit, has anyone eaten? We should probably order something. I don't see this one letting up before shift change."

"A couple pizzas oughtta do it. I'll make the call."

"Ok but nothing fancy. Cop food, meat, bread, sauce, cheese and something to wash it down with. If you need me I'll be working on the board."

It took about fifteen minutes to organize her thoughts and update the case board. With some time to spare she figured she could knock off a personal item or two and pulled out her cell.

"Thanks for freeing me from the metal prison. – E"

Rob's response came quickly.

"My first prison break, glad it was successful. Do I need to ask how or why? – R"

"Not my doing, the machines are rising up around here without the genius tech to keep them in check. – E"

"Stop breaking my precinct and take care of my cops, two more days. – R"

"Too long, I'm dying... but I've caught a live one so it should keep me distracted. – E"

"A live one? Work or pleasure. – R"

"Possibly both ;) but I was referring to a case. – E"

"Either way, play nice or I'll be forced to discipline you. – R"

"Stop incentivising me to do the wrong things. – E"

"But are they really that wrong? Gotta jet, super secret meeting of the robot overlord creation club in ten. – R"

"Make it a kind and generous overlord. Whips and chains, always. – E"

"Whips and chains, back atcha. – R"

The pizza arrived at ten to two and Baker, Jones and Rique followed the scent over to the case board. They looked at

Ell like lost puppies waiting for a snack but waited patiently before digging in. At five minutes to two, Colonel Anthony Craig breezed through the doorway and all eyes snapped his direction. The uniform fit well, focussing the eye in all the right places and the right places were very nice. The Colonel was well built and his square jaw and deep mysterious eyes added to the allure. Baker swooned and Ell shot her a glare, receiving only a girly giggle in return.

"Colonel," said Ell waiving him over and taking a quick glance at the clock. He was punctual, she'd give him that.

"Detectives Baker and Jones, Colonel Anthony Craig. He will be consulting with us on the Jellic case. Make him feel at home," shooting a glance at Baker followed by a sly grin, she added, "but not too much at home."

The smell of the pizza was driving Ell mad. She was running on tar and chips so she figured she wouldn't hold the vultures back any longer.

"I don't know if you had time to eat but we ordered in. You may as well grab a slice while we get down to it."

Ell popped open the first box and sent an evil glare her partner's way.

"What the hell is this green shit? Meat, bread, sauce, cheese. What in those ingredients is green."

"They're peppers L.T.," responded Jones, "and Rique obviously listened when I explained that no good pizza goes without peppers."

"What the hell happened to my cops? Seriously," she looked at the Colonel as he snagged a slice, "when did my cops become a bunch of veggie eating pansies?"

"The movement is upon us, Lieutenant," he responded. "Just be glad it's kale free."

Ell grabbed two slices, picked off the peppers and tossed them back where the slices had been. Sans peppers the pizza was glorious. Starvation may have had something to do with it but for a moment, just a moment, she was in heaven. As the rest of the team dug in, she began a review of her and Rique's findings in relation to Jellic and Fenn.

"Does this seem like too many oddities and coincidences to anyone else?" asked Baker. "Taken on its own, a ghost witness or suspect can happen. When you couple it with all the questions surrounding Jellic's case and then suddenly you find him dead in her apartment without any connection, there's no way it's coincidental."

"Agreed, but as you said, no connection," added Jones. "So how does it tie together?"

"We don't know enough about either situation." commented Colonel Craig. "We're too dark on too many angles to start hypothesizing."

Ell nodded, "And that's where you come in. The D.O.D. stonewalled me on both full files. Classified this, restricted access that. The standard runaround, but if they're serious about having you investigate this case then they're bound to open up the books for you."

"Did they mention what level of classification and restriction we were dealing with?"

"No, but you're their man on this, I have to assume they'll give you clearance."

Colonel Craig laughed. "Despite what you may think, the words restricted and classified have a purpose and they don't just mean from civilians to make their lives difficult. There are levels of clearance throughout the military, not unlike your own organization. Even if I'm the man running this investigation, I'm still only cleared to a certain level. Remember, my organization deals with national security, international security, and a whole slew of intelligence that not only is, but should be, protected."

"But..." prompted Ell.

"But I'll see what I can come up with. My clearance has been raised due to the situations I normally deal with and the men wearing five or more stars have grown to trust me. I'll need a few hours and likely a slew of phone calls and favors, but I'll see what I can get."

"You can use my desk," tossed in Baker quickly, causing Ell to roll her eyes and smirk quietly.

"Perfect, and you and Jones can take a run down to Columbia College and see what you can dig up on Claire Fenn. Someone there must remember her so let's see if we can nail down something about her pre-college days that may help."

Baker's flirtatious smile dimmed slightly as she put on a solid five second pout.

"Rique and I are going to go harass Lund and then swing by the morgue. The scene was somewhat self explanatory but Sanders has pulled off a couple miracles in the past so it's worth the visit."

"Colonel, coordinate with Rique to get your cell number on everyone's contact list and vice-versa. Let me know if I can do anything to help with the files, including kicking some military ass. Actually, make that especially kicking some military ass."

"Oh, I think you've done plenty of that for one day. Let me see if some carrot can get this job done before you break out the stick again."

Chapter Six

*R*ique met her outside the elevators on their way up to the second floor to check in with Lund and the crime scene techs.

"Shall we take the lift?" he laughed as she threw him yet another dirty look.

"I think the stairs will do, asshole."

As usual, the second floor was bustling with every spectrum of nerd and geek available. This was her man toy Rob's domain. Lord of the Geeks. The floor housed crime scene techs, I.T. techs and the precinct's new electronic crimes division. Walking the halls of the second floor used to feel like visiting a distant planet but Ell's technical knowledge was growing, thanks to Rob's ongoing presence.

"This entire floor is beyond me," commented Rique and Ell just smiled and laughed to herself.

Lund saw her coming but did not look up from whatever chemical crap he was studying when she walked in.

"Christ Frost, I half figured hell froze over. I've had this case for nearly twelve hours and haven't had your foot in my ass yet. I even found time for a two hour nap and a rushed sandwich in there."

"No wonder I haven't seen my file yet. King tech's been pampering himself while my murder investigation spins it's wheels waiting."

"Hey, I had the monkeys running scans and tests. My people can do their job without me breathing down their necks. I have some damn fine techs up here."

"I'm starting to think the department may not need him at all," she said to Rique with a wink, "Every time I talk to him someone else is doing the work."

"Delegation, my dear, the key to a great mans success. From the bags under your eyes I'd say you should learn to use it once in a while."

"Yeah, yeah, jib, jab, volley, spike. Let's skip it for now, where's my report on the Jellic scene?"

"You'll have the majority of it in the next two hours. There was a ton of blood on scene and not all the same type."

Ell's eyes popped open.

"I figured that would be a surprise. There were at least three different samples found, though we're still working to determine how much belongs to each. It's safe to say most of it was the known victim's but we have a decent sized sample from another male and a smaller amount from a female. The second male's going to have a nasty wound but there's only a smattering from the female. I'd say a bloody nose or small laceration."

"DNA?"

"Right now we're still trying to isolate the samples and ensure there are only three donors. We'll send anything we find in for analysis but it will be a few days even if we put a rush on it."

"Any other big ticket surprises you're holding back on, Lund? This is the type of information you call me about, by the way."

"Remove the foot, Lieutenant, my team's working overtime on this and I've got every man, woman and monkey on deck. But since you asked, the biggest surprise I can give you is nothing. As in, no evidence, no fingerprints, fibers, dirt, or trace. Nada. As clean as you could make it."

Rique did a double take. "What? No way, not with that scene. It was a disaster."

"Yes, but a very clean and well swept disaster from an evidentiary point of view. This, Lieutenant, is what's taking so damn long. Since I refuse to believe anyone could be this meticulous, we have resorted to some extreme testing on everything we pulled in, including all the rigging, gag and what not, because thus far, with the exception of the blood, we've found dick all."

"I don't get it, L.T.? A clean scene almost always means a professional hit but this was as amateur as they come. Rage, with a touch of planning but more emotion than anything else. We figured the perp had some pro bondage knowledge and came somewhat prepared but the on-scene tools that were scavenged from the apartment? The choice of location? None of this says professional hit."

"Except the evidence, or lack thereof," commented Ell as she mulled it over, trying to recreate the scene with this new information in mind. No matter how she came at it, the pieces didn't fit. She needed time to think it over and sort it out.

"Get me the report as soon as you can, though given what you're telling me it's not going to help much. The blood, however, may tip the scales so double time the monkeys on that analysis."

"What do you think we're doing up here, sipping Mai Tais and throwing orgies? We're on this and you'll have it as soon as we do. Now, consider my fat ass sufficiently whipped and let me get back to work."

She didn't need to be told twice. With her partner in tow, Ell hurried back down two flights of stairs to the parkade where her shiny Mercedes was ready and waiting. As they settled in, Ell glanced at her phone and noticed an unread email. It had come in four hours earlier and somehow she'd completely missed it.

Lieutenant Frost, I apologize for the late response but my day has been stacked. Detective Shaw informs me that you require a consult on your latest case of mayhem and debauchery. I've asked my assistant to set aside an hour between five and six. I'm sure the case discussion won't take that long but it's been a while since we last chatted and I insist we catch up.

Dr. Anne Grayson.

Dr. Grayson's insistence wasn't so much a request as a requirement. As the preeminent department shrink, if Anne Grayson wanted a chat you either chatted or risked a more formal request through your supervising office. She and Ell had built a solid rapport over the years and even though Ell was exhausted and honestly could not afford to spare the time, she knew it was just a burden she'd have to bear. She fired back a quick confirmation email and slammed the car into gear.

"Grayson has me slated for case review from five to six so we're going to have to make this quick. Hold on."

As the morgue came into sight, Rique found the courage to breathe without the fear of releasing a terrified wail. "I swear to Christ Ell, one day I'm going to run your damn license just to see if it's valid." Rique was white as a ghost, a standard skin tone after a ride with the Lieutenant.

"Pull up your panties and stop whining, we're here in great time and no one died on the way," she replied as she hung a quick right into an available parking spot across from the morgue and slammed on the brakes.

"Give me a minute. I'm not sure if that last statement is true yet."

"Keep it up and you'll wish it wasn't."

Upon entering the business like morgue facility, they were greeted by a cheery, twenty-something blonde in a short skirt and tight white blouse. It was a good choice and she filled out the outfit nicely. Ell heard Rique gasp slightly with a whispered 'Damn'. She smiled and shook her head.

"Mindy, isn't it?"

That's right, detective, and though it breaks my heart, I assume you're not here on a social call. Are you looking to speak with Davidson?" The flirtatious tone did not go unnoticed and on another day she may have had a more feral reaction to the beautiful young blonde. Unfortunately for Mindy, if Ell was at the morgue it was almost always a day like today.

"Yes, please let him know I'm here with Detective Shaw."

"No redhead today? A shame." Mindy gave a quick pout then picked up the reception phone and let M.E. Sanders know they were there to see him.

"You can head on back, he's in exam room three."

"Thanks," replied Ell as she and Rique headed down the hall.

"Damn, if I wasn't playing the loyal man."

"You'd be drooling all over a young blonde that plays for your same team."

"Seriously?"

"Seriously, and since when are you playing the loyal man? Is there something I should know about you and Angel?"

"Another time, L.T. Murder, mayhem and all that."

"Nice dodge, but this conversation isn't over, Shaw."

"Sanders," said Rique opening the door to exam room three just in time to force Ell to drop her interrogation.

Davidson Sanders stood before a corpse, looking as out of place as possible. His long silver locks hung down his back, lying neatly between his shoulder blades. His pants, a blue black leather leading up to a tight fuchsia dress shirt with the top two buttons strategically undone. An outfit that should never see the light of day yet Sanders pulled it off with style. He was an enigma.

"I see Mindy has managed to stick around longer than most of your assistants."

"That's the downfall of beautiful assistants that can't keep their hands off me... short tenure. As you surmised during your last visit, Mindy's tastes lie elsewhere. While part of me is significantly disappointed it has made for an excellent working relationship."

"You'll just have to find your extracurricular fun elsewhere. I don't know that nice is the right word given the location but it's 'refreshing' to actually be recognized on a return visit."

"I'd ask what brought you to my humble abode but I'm fairly certain that question is unnecessary. Your vic." He motioned to the slab before them. "I had half expected men in black suits to come busting in here and whisk him away in the middle of the night, given who he is and what I've read in the news. Since you beat them here, I can only assume you've managed to win some kind of power struggle today."

"Something like that. He's ours and I don't plan on giving him up."

"You may want to rethink that after you hear my report. Things with Mr. Jellic are not quite what they appeared at first glance."

"Oh goody, more mysteries," replied Ell sarcastically. "Give us the run down and please tell me you've nailed down the time of death."

"I wouldn't say nailed down so much as expanded from my original assessment."

Ell felt her heart skip a beat.

"What I didn't take into consideration on scene, couldn't have actually, was the fact that your boy here was severely drugged pre-mortem and had a drastic body temperature shift in the last hour and a half before death."

Ell was lost, drugs she could understand but a temp shift? It was a mild night and the apartment was well... an apartment.

"Care to extrapolate on that bombshell?"

"Best I can tell, the victim was frozen, nearly hypothermic

when he was initially strung up. The temp shift is wreaking havoc on nailing down the time of death because we don't know how or how quickly they thawed him. I can tell you the torture took anywhere from thirty to fifty minutes based on the deterioration of the wounds and the rate of skin retraction. He was alive through every gash you saw on scene, lived through the torture to the very end. What I can't determine is an exact time the whole thing began. Once I take the temperature into consideration, time of death could be anywhere from noon to nine and I'm leaning towards the earlier timeframe."

"Why's that," asked Rique.

"Well, this veers away from the pure science and into psychology but the only reason to freeze the body before you do something this horrendous is to throw us off and extend the possible time of death. Freezing actually worked against your killer, assuming the torture was done for information and not just psychotic kicks. By taking the victim to a near hypothermic state the killer would have overwhelmed his nerve centers."

"Making the torture much less effective," finished Ell.

"Bingo. So why work against yourself? The only logical reason to do it is to deceive the M.E. and if you're looking to do that then odds are you're also looking to push the possible time of death as far as you can away from the actual. So it's likely your killer hit early and froze the body to stop us from narrowing things down."

"Possible, assuming the torture wasn't for kicks."

"And that's where the cause of death comes in," continued Sanders. "A surgical strike across the carotid artery and no, it wasn't a mistake. It was a pinpoint slice held off for the finale and responsible for most of the blood on scene. The torture would have been bloody but those cuts were designed to inflict maximum pain and minimum damage. This one," he ran his finger across the victim's throat, "this was designed for a quick and painless finish. It was mercy, Ell."

"Torture for kicks and then a mercy kill? Not likely. Whoever did this was after information and most likely got what they needed. They finished him off quick, easy and bloody because it was the best option they had. A quick surgical strike, however, not unlike the freezing, the gore would throw us off the true motive."

"Again, that feels professional, L.T. The freezing, the torture, a surgical kill, it's hitman one-oh-one." commented Rique.

"Yeah, so why the fuck does a pro show up semi-prepared and have to scrounge the apartment for bits and pieces? Every piece that adds up seems to have one that contradicts it. It's like we're playing with two damn puzzles tossed together in the same box. This does, however, emphasize one point. The biggest piece we're missing is a motive and if Jellic was frozen then tortured for up to fifty minutes before they killed him, there was a damn solid reason behind it."

Chapter Seven

$\mathcal{T}$he ride back to the eleventh precinct was nearly as frightening as the one before it, but Rique was able to drown out the fear with a new piece of the puzzle to chew on. More and more the evidence was pointing to a professional hit but, even if you ignore the inconsistencies there were two major concerns. Why Jellic, a nobody drill instructor from a small training barracks who had recently been discharged and who the hell had the skill, time and motive to pull it off?

"It's just not playing," he commented as Ell flew them through the streets towards the precinct. "No matter how I look at this, the professional angle doesn't play. There is too much that doesn't fit the profile and too many outstanding questions."

"Maybe that's why it's a professional hit?"

"Run that by me again?"

"Whoever this is, they've gone to a lot of trouble to throw us off our game. An immaculately clean scene with little to no physical evidence. Freezing the body to extend the time of death window. These were intentional. They've made it a goal to confuse our investigation. So perhaps the household items used, the apparent lack of motive and the poor choice of location were all part of that process. Toss in just a touch of amateur to cover up the true crime."

"I could buy the household items fitting that theory, assuming the killer had scoped the place out and, knew they were available, but not the lack of motive? There's a motive here, the lack is on us for not finding it yet. The killer may be covering up to keep us away from it, but it's there. Besides, if this was a hired professional, they wouldn't concern themselves with covering up a motive because the motive wouldn't be theirs. Hell, half the time they don't know or care what the client's motive is. The money clears, the target dies and none of it comes back on the mystery man who has no connection to the victim."

"It's another awkward piece that just won't jam into place but we'll run the theories with the rest of the team and see what, if anything, pops."

The car literally caught air as they descended the ramp into the precinct parkade.

"Jesus Frost, what's this thing worth? Ninety G's, maybe more? You'd think you'd baby it a little and keep the damn thing in one piece."

"Cars are like partners, if you baby them they get soft and pansy like. You need to beat on them every so often to keep them tough. Besides, I paid the something something G's to make sure she could handle a little abuse. She likes it this way, don't you baby." She ran her hand seductively across the dash and Rique squirmed in his seat.

"Never again, do not ever let me see that again."

As he reached to open the door he found it locked. He pressed the unlock switch, the door unlocked and then immediately locked again. Looking over at Ell, her finger on the switch, he raised his eyebrows. "Seriously? Am I being punished, Lieutenant."

"Punished, no. I'm sure you get enough of that on your off duty time. I believe we have an interrogation to finish."

"I've seen your technique, Frost, you'll never break me."

"Rique, honestly, is there something you want to talk about? Keep in mind this lady you spoke of being 'loyal' to is one of my oldest friends. My oldest friend, my partner, and frankly I don't have a clue what's going on."

"It's pretty simple really. Look, when two adults like each other and enjoy playing together, they..."

Ell laughed and cut him off. "Fuck you, asshole."

"I don't know what to tell you, L.T. It's a thing and I'm rolling with it. Talk to her, she may have more insight for you but from my end, I'm invested. I'm enjoying it, so I'm doing what I feel is right and to me that means loyalty."

"And is she in that same place?"

"I don't know. Hell, I don't even care. I'm just being true to myself here."

"You will." Rique gave her a confused look. "Care," she emphasized, "If she's not in that place and you find out, not through a conversation but some other means, you'll care. You'll care a lot."

"And?"

"Talk to her you stupid shit. Have a grown up conversation about who each of you are, both apart and together. Discuss what the hell is going on and see if you're in the same place. Angel is a bright person but if you spend all your time together naked and sweaty she won't have any more insight than you do as to where the two of you are heading."

"Talk's not really my strong suit, Ell." Rique puffed out his chest and put his fists on his hips in a superhero pose. "I'm a man of action."

"Jesus," she shook her head with a slight smirk and unlocked the doors. "Get out of my fucking car before you make me sick."

Rique was quick to take the offer.

"And either pick up a damn phone or sit down with that girl, you pansy ass," she hollered as he made a beeline through the parkade towards the doors.

Confident that she'd embarrassed her partner enough, Ell migrated the topic back to the case as they double timed the precinct stairs. Rique cut off on the first floor, heading back to Robbery / Homicide but Ell kept going for three more flights on her way to Dr. Grayson's office. The earlier nap, if it could be called that, had helped but the fatigue of a sleepless night was settling back in. That said, even imminent death wouldn't get her back in an elevator any time soon. She swung around the corner and into the reception area with five minutes to spare.

"Lieutenant," acknowledged a young man behind the desk. Ell knew she was supposed to remember him but couldn't come up with a name. "The Doctor will be with you in just a moment. Please have a seat."

After four flights double timed a seat sounded like a fine idea. Ell plunked down into a hard leather reception chair and sat staring at the young man.

Brock? Brian? Brandon? She was sure it was a 'B' but couldn't place a name to the face.

True to his word, within five minutes he returned, summoning her back to Dr. Grayson's office.

"Thanks... uh," Ell paused awkwardly, hoping he would

step in and offer his name. Instead he stared at her absent-mindedly so she just shook her head and repeated. "Thanks."

'People,' she thought. There were days she could do without them.

The office, if it could be called that, gave off a similar vibe to that of the doctor herself. Ell considered it a forced comfort. Plenty of natural light brought in through a large picture window, lush carpet and fancy artwork adorning the walls. Unlike most offices, it had no desk but rather two leather armchairs and a dark corduroy couch. 'Oh, that couch,' thought Ell, remembering the soft, caressing feeling of the foam molding around her. That couch was something special. It was a couch of dreams, possibly the world's most comfortable couch. It was the antithesis of her guest chair. It was an evil construct, having drawn her into many long winded confessions of fears she refused to acknowledge. It was a tool, just like the rest of the décor, and one the doctor used well. 'Witchcraft,' she thought. 'It has to be witchcraft.'

"Ell, I hope James didn't have you waiting long," said Dr. Grayson from one of the leather armchairs as she walked into the room.

The doctor refused to use titles. "Names," she had preached, "help to form bonds." Speaking of names, 'James?' she thought. It wasn't even a 'B'. Where the hell, was her head today?

"Thanks for seeing me, Doc. I know it was short notice." She glanced at the couch, the amazing, evil couch, and opted for the second armchair. 'Let's see her work her witchcraft without her tools,' she thought.

"Ell, we discussed this. Anne, Anna, even Mrs. Grayson if you must, but we don't use titles in this office. In here, we relate, we acknowledge who we are, and we own that."

"Yeah, sorry Anne," she said rubbing her hands over her face and taking a deep breath. "It's been a long day."

"Don't tell me, you've been on this straight through since I was emailed? The timestamp said Rique had sent it out at just after three this morning."

"Yeah, a couple hours prior to that. It was a late night and long day. I managed an hour of downtime around noon which helped to shake the pounding in my temples but I can't seem to get my head into it today. The edge, the one that I rely on to find the missing pieces, to fill in the gaps of the puzzle, it's just not there. In fact, there's not much of anything there, it's like I'm numb and, frankly, it's scaring the shit out of me." Ell stopped, 'Why was she saying all this? What brought on the spew of emotional crap? Fucking witchcraft,' she thought.

"How have things been? I know they've been busy, stressful and successful on a professional level, Ell, but how have you really been? Personally?"

"I've been..." Ell started, as if by instinct and then stopped herself. "Before we start digging in to my psyche and all the fucked up truths that make me... me, can we do a once over on this case? It's a cluster of mixed signals and we can't get a handle on the profile. Nailing down the victim's situation is confusing enough given the security run around we are getting, but this perp is a complete enigma."

"Whatever you need Ell, this is your meeting." Doctor Grayson pulled out a manila file folder from the small end table beside her. "I took the liberty of reviewing the case notes earlier today. A gruesome scene that, I assume, raised some pretty intense emotions for you."

Ell squinted and cocked her head to the side.

"Oh, come on Ellison. Bondage, suspension, all the tools of 'pleasure', from your perspective, perverted into weapons. This is the second time in as many months that you've ran across it. We may not have 'talked' lately but I can assume the Bouton case and now this, have left a mark."

The use of her full name, something reserved for only special people and circumstances should have pissed her off, but it didn't. In this room, with Dr. Grayson, it just felt normal. She hadn't considered her own reaction to the scene. Could that be why she had been on edge all day? Could that be the reason for the numbness? 'Fuck, what am I doing?' she thought.

"Yeah, we'll do me later, Anne. Lot's to discuss. I'm a giant ball of fucked up. Right now I need to focus on the case."

"Sorry, professional hazard. I dig into what I see. I have a pretty good picture, based on the crime scene report from Lund."

"Wait, you have the crime scene report from Lund?"

"A preliminary, I requested it this afternoon and he sent it right over."

"Whatever spell you used there, you need to teach me."

"I like to think I have a persuasive personality."

'Scary, witchy personality,' thought Ell letting a slight smile slip out.

"In my line of work, it's helpful. As I was saying, I have a pretty good idea of the scenario so why don't you run your thoughts past me and maybe, together, we can gain some insight on those missing pieces you spoke of."

"Ok, so our initial impression was that the perpetrator had some professional skills. Not in the torture and killing but with the suspension and bondage. It was well executed. They used professional strapping and wrapping. Every strand was flat and tight to reduce friction and avoid any possible issues if the victim struggled. They knew what they were doing on that end. The torture and kill looked too messy for a professional killer but there was knowledge there... intent. Some of the tools were brought with, specialty items like the suspension hook, but a lot of it was scrounged from the apartment. You expect a pro to be prepared."

"It was poor planning. Or rather, partial planning. I see your point, that's not what you would expect from someone with a lot of experience in torture and murder."

"But, that's where our recent discoveries contradict the scene. Lund's report indicates no evidence was found with the exception of the blood. That screams a professional, well planned hit. Rique and I just paid a visit to the M.E. and he confirms that the torture and murder, despite the appearance, were performed by someone that knew exactly what they were doing. They froze the victim to throw off the time of death, picked exact pressure points to inflict the most pain in a short period of time and selected the killing strike with precision to ensure maximum blood loss and a quick end."

"Helping to contaminate the scene," finished Dr. Grayson. "It appears to be a highly skilled professional who only partially planned for the event?"

"Yeah, and that doesn't fit. It just doesn't happen. Not with pros. Sure, things go wrong and they need to scramble, adjust the plan, but they always have a full plan to begin with and they prepare for it."

"So, an unprepared professional, spur of the moment perhaps? Let's say the job was in place and a plan was underway but something changed, that scramble you spoke of, and the job had to be dealt with immediately. Could that cause the anomalies we are seeing?"

It was something to stew on. It still didn't quite fit but it was a step towards an explanation. Ell needed to think about it.

"It's... close. It's still not the perfect fit but it's a hell of a lot better theory than I've come up with. I need to circle back at it once my head's clear. There's something else there. I just can't put my finger on it."

"Perhaps the best thing we can do to help you find your answers is to work on clearing out the issues holding you back. Ridding that numbness you spoke of."

'Well shit,' thought Ell. 'I walked right into that one.' She resigned herself to the inevitable, rationalizing that it may actually help.

With a deep sigh, she said, "Ok, where do we start?"

"Why don't you tell me how you've been doing since the Bouton case, aside from this case and today."

"Honestly, I've been good."

"Good?"

"Don't get me wrong, that case was a disaster. It touched on some dark subjects that many people don't want to face and, as you know, it crossed into some very personal territory for me. But, in the end, I found something. Something in me that's been missing."

"And your social life? I understand that case tied in closely with your friend Angel and..." she paused unsure what to call him, "and Sebastian."

"Not my favorite few days. Things between Angel and I are still a little strange. We're working through it but there are issues on both sides and it's put a strain on what we had. I figure time and persistence will help. As for Sebastian, he and I are good, we've talked a couple times since then and there's no friction."

"Talked?"

"Yes, I'm not using his services anymore."

"Really, now that's interesting."

Ell hated it when she did that because it meant she was about to be forced to bare her soul on everything related and still Dr Grayson would never, not even upon threat of death, reveal why it was interesting. She'd just look Ell in the eye with a calm smile and ask, 'Why do you think it's interesting?' Half the time Ell wanted to yell 'I DON'T', but instead she was left frustrated and feeling ever so slightly self-conscious. So instead of asking why, Ell decided to turn things sideways.

"Weird, I don't find it interesting at all."

"Tell me, why don't you find it interesting, Ell?

She couldn't help herself, Ell burst into laughter.

"Ok, fine, I do find it interesting. I just wanted to bypass the whole 'why do you think it's interesting?' dance we do every time I'm here. Half the time I don't have a clue what you find intriguing in the things I tell you or what epiphanies about my psyche they help you reach. In this case it actually is interesting. Interesting, frightening, amazing and utterly confusing. I haven't seen Sebastian because I haven't needed to. I've... well I guess I've found someone."

Dr. Grayson prided herself on her professional approach but the surprise in her eyes was unmistakable.

"Someone who shares your affinities?"

"For the most part, yes. We don't see eye to eye on everything. But I think that's normal, right?"

"More normal than you know. So you've decided to settle down to a monogamous relationship?"

"Oh, hell no. At least, I don't think so," she replied, realizing that she hadn't really put much thought into whether or not that was where things were headed. The two of them had never discussed it because they both knew that wasn't who she was. "But I've found something special, and different, so I'm open to exploring options I've long since disregarded."

Ell, knew this was going to lead to more questions and she wasn't sure what she could or should share. In the past she had always been brutally honest with Anne Grayson, it was what made their 'chats' successful but now she had to consider Rob. He worked here, knew Dr Grayson, and while he wasn't required to go through mandatory sessions like the officers in the building, Ell knew they were friendly. Talking about their relationship here also meant outing him to a friend. It was a line she didn't come against often but one she hated. He'd given her something precious, his trust, and for some reason she felt obligated to protect it. To Ell's surprise and delight, Anne didn't pursue it any further.

"So, things have been, good?"

"See, that's what I said, if you'd just taken me at my word we could have saved all that time and explanation."

"Yes, but we'd have bypassed all the juicy gossip," she laughed. "So now tell me what's different. What makes this case send your mind for a loop and bring forth this numbness you mentioned?"

"Doc... sorry... Anne, if I knew that I wouldn't be here. I'd be busy wrapping this damn thing up."

"The crime scene?"

"Gorier than most but not the worst I've seen. Not even the weirdest."

"But, not unlike Bouton, the killer took something important to you, something special, and perverted it."

"Yeah, and I know what you're getting at. It pisses me off, but it shouldn't have me in knots like this. As you said, I've dealt with that before... recently."

"So what IS different? How'd you get past it all during the Bouton case? What are you not doing this time?"

"I don't know. I just worked the case. I focussed on the leads. I coordinated with my team and we brought the bitch down."

"This new..." Dr. Grayson paused, realizing that she didn't know the gender of Ell's new partner and, with Ell, it wasn't obvious. "Man?"

Ell laughed, "Yes, it's a man."

"So this new man, when did all that start?"

"Technically, just after I wrapped up the Bouton case."

"Technically?"

"Well, it had been building for a while. We knew each other, casually, and as we started spending more time together it just kind of... grew."

"During the case?"

"Yeah."

"You, Ellison Frost, found time during the Bouton case to become romantically involved with someone."

"It wasn't like that. We were working the case and things just evolved."

"Working the case? This is someone involved in the Boulton case?"

'Well fuck, how the hell did that just happen?' thought Ell. She was sure she'd bypassed the mine field and yet somehow she now found herself with her foot flat on the pressure switch. She wondered if this was how it felt to be on the other side of the interrogation table.

"Oh, for fuck sake, it's Rob, okay."

"Rob," Dr Grayson thought for a moment before something clicked in her eyes. "I.T. Rob? Wow. Excuse me while I sit here stunned and jealous."

Ell smiled, she'd have laughed but she honestly didn't know if what she'd just done was 'acceptable' in relationship circles.

"Ok, sorry, let's back burner the million questions I have about that for another time. So if I have this right, during the Bouton case you were also in the midst of building a budding romance with the hot I.T. stud you were consulting with?"

"Yeah, we spent a lot of time together discussing the case and things just went from there."

"You had similar interests."

"Yes, that case, how we found the body, it opened up a lot of discussion. We were able to connect and talk it all through. It gave us a way to discuss ourselves, our passions, the bondage and submission. How the case tied in with us personally. It's how we solved it. Those discussions helped break it all down."

"And this one? Have you discussed it with him?"

"No, he's out of town and won't be back for a few days."

"Oh my god, Ellison. I've forgotten how frustrating you can be when it comes to relationship basics."

"What?"

"Ok, but listen closely, YOU MISS HIM! He's your fucking rock, Ell. Someone that knows you, your dreams, your pleasures. Someone that can relate to how you feel when you see the things that you crave become perverted for evil. I imagine we'd have had this conversation, though a much darker version, during or after the Bouton case had he not been there. In fact I watched and waited, almost sure that you'd fall apart at some point and need to discuss it. I was genuinely surprised and elated when it didn't happen. Now I know why."

"So I need to talk to Rob, that's your advice? It seems a little basic."

"You need to talk to someone. Someone you can be honest with who can relate or, at the bare minimum, not judge you. For a few years, that's been me. I believe this is the happiest I've ever been to be replaced."

"Umm, thanks, I think."

"I'm here if you need me, Ell, but I have a feeling that's not going to be as often so long as you have him. My advice? Call him, talk this case through and lean on him to gain the composure you need. Go solve this thing and when you're done with it you and I are going out for a drink."

"A drink?"

"Yes, a drink. It wouldn't be right to dish about your sexy new boy toy in a professional setting."

The thought of 'dishing' sent shivers down Ell's spine but the truth was, aside from Angel and Rob, there wasn't another person alive that knew her as well as Anne.

"Drinks it is." Ell rose and headed back out into the craziness of the real world.

Chapter Eight

C olonel Craig was hovering outside her doorway when she returned to her office.

"We have a meeting in forty minutes."

"I'm going to need a few more details than that, Colonel. Who with, where and perhaps even a why?"

"I've been digging into the Jellic court martial as you requested, and the entire case makes no sense from start to finish. From what I've found there was no evidence on the initial charge. I'm not just talking about a circumstantial case, I'm talking nothing. There is no way anyone should have levied the charges against him and certainly no reason for an attorney, even a fly by night low level J.A.G. hustler to have taken the plea deal. So I began wondering why a high priced attorney such as Jenson Dover rolled over and that made me question how and why a lifelong military man with little to no savings, managed to procure the illustrious Jenson Dover as his attorney? Since I couldn't find any ties between the two I figured we should question the man himself. We have an appointment at the law office of Janz, Sullivan and Dover in forty minutes."

"This is your plan? Go ask Dover?"

"Seems the easiest route to the answer," replied Craig unsure what she found so humorous.

"Janz Sullivan and Dover are one of the most expensive and sought after defense firms in the city. What do you think the odds are that they will be willing to break client confidentiality to help us?"

"Lieutenant, I'm not naïve, I realize they're going to cover their own asses and hide behind privilege so long as they can. As it turns out, in the civilian justice system the rule of privilege has few exceptions, however, while ours is a civilian case, the files we will be requesting were part of a military preceding. A system with substantially more exceptions to the privilege ruling."

"So this meeting isn't about getting the information but rather figuring out if we have a valid means to do so?"

"That was the thought."

"And I'm along for what, eye candy. As a military officer you're going to have more pull here and you'll certainly have a better feel for military case law."

"Perhaps but I figured you'd be pissed if you missed out on the opportunity to rattle some big wig defense attorneys. Besides, I understand you're a force to be reckoned with in the interview room and I would love to see these pompous bastards sweat a little."

"Ok, so eye candy and entertainment. I can get behind that. You said forty minutes, give me ten to get my files together and meet me in the parkade. I'll drive."

"Better make it five, we're cutting it close as is."

Ell just laughed and winked. "Trust me ten minutes will be fine. As I said, I'm driving."

The Colonel reluctantly agreed. He didn't get the joke but Ell knew he soon would.

Once he was out of the office Ell pulled out her cell.

"Hey stud, what time is it there? – E"

"Just after 4:00, why? – R"

"Why is right, why is it 4:00 there and 6:00 here, what possible use is there in fucking with the time? – E"

"Are we having this conversation again? – R"

"No, I'm just making sure you know my feelings on it. – E"

"Well aware, is this why you texted me???? – R"

"No it's just a nice side benefit. What time are you done with creating a technological world of wonders for us all to be enslaved within? – E"

"Wrapping up at 5:30, no panels tonight. – R"

"Ok, I need about thirty minutes of your time tonight if possible. – E"

"Oh the things I could do in thirty minutes, my dear. But the distance may limit my options. – R"

"If memory serves, you've done more with less and trust me... memory serves because I won't forget it. Unfortunately this is a professional request. – E"

"Does my Lieutenant need something hac... legally circumvented? – R"

"No, well maybe, but not yet. I just need to talk it through. I've been told it will help. – E"

"Told? – R"

"Grayson, long story, I'll fill you in tonight. Talk to you at 6:00 which is fifteen fucking minutes ago. See, I told you this time shit was stupid. – E"

"I'll be here. Take care of my cops. Whips and chains. – R"

"Whips and chains back atcha. – E"

Ell hit send on the final message as she rounded the corner on the last set of stairs heading into the parkade. Colonel Craig was waiting at the base of the stairwell.

"I wasn't sure what you were driving."

"The shiny silver wet dream in the corner," replied Ell gesturing to her S550.

"Fuck, either the police department is overfunded or you civilian cops are overpaid."

"Oh, if only either of those two statements were true. Hop in and don't forget your seatbelt."

To his credit, the Colonel did not frighten easily. He did, however, keep his head on a swivel as she bolted across three lanes of traffic at a speed rarely seen on metropolitan roadways. He put on a brave front but Ell could sense a noticeable relaxation once she put the car in park.

"And ten to spare, told you we'd be fine."

"Perhaps if you'd let me know we'd be competing in the Indy 500 along the way I wouldn't have doubted you."

"It's so much more fun this way."

"That, dear Lieutenant, depends on which seat you're riding in."

"And here I thought it was just the Metro PD that was full of pansies. I didn't realize it was the armed forces as well."

"I'll make you a deal, hand me the keys on the way back and we'll see who the pansy is."

The thought of letting him take the wheel of her baby almost made her sick but she fought it back. "I have a counter offer for you. If you can make one of these fancy lawyers spill something juicy, I'll take you up on that deal."

The Colonel smiled, confident with maybe just an edge into cocky. "Challenge accepted."

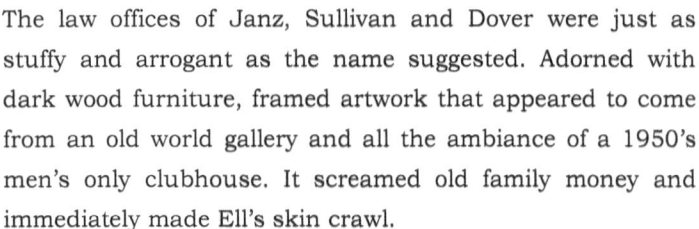

The law offices of Janz, Sullivan and Dover were just as stuffy and arrogant as the name suggested. Adorned with dark wood furniture, framed artwork that appeared to come from an old world gallery and all the ambiance of a 1950's men's only clubhouse. It screamed old family money and immediately made Ell's skin crawl.

The receptionist, a scowling brunette straight off the pages of skank weekly, looked up at them with a glare as they entered.

"Names?" she demanded.

"Lieutenant Frost and Colonel Craig, we have an appointment with Jensen Dover."

"As to what business?" she asked, the condescending tone dripping off her tongue.

"See this," Ell slammed her badge on the raised desk between them. "This means I'm here on my business. And what that is, is none of yours."

"Jesus, cool your jets lady, I need to know what case the time gets billed to."

"If you don't pick up your phone and let Mr. Dover know that Colonel Craig is here you'll be able to bill it to your case for obstruction."

"Fucking cops," she muttered but Ell let the comment go.

As the receptionist called back to advise Jensen Dover that they were there, the Colonel leaned in beside her.

"Was that really necessary?"

"Necessary? No, but it sure was fun. I'm eye candy and entertainment, right?"

"I'm going to regret that."

"No, but those around you may," she winked and took a slight step back, allowing him to take the lead as they were approached by a tall, slender man with perfectly coifed white hair and a suit worth more than her monthly salary. She recognized him from the Jellic case files, though Mr. Dover appeared less than all powerful in person.

"General Craig?" he asked.

"Yes, my associate and I would like to ask a few questions about the..."

"Yeah, yeah, the Jellic case. It's just about the only reason you boys come around here. Let's take this somewhere more private."

He led them through the halls back to a luxurious office the size of a small condo. The room was setup to impress with a continuation of the dark wood furniture, deep brown, leather chairs and a desk large enough to hold a small arsenal of electronics. The smell of furniture polish and expensive cologne overpowered them as they entered.

As soon as the door was closed, Mr. Dover headed for his desk and, not waiting for a question, he began, "Look Colonel, I'll tell you what I told your D.O.D. colleagues last week. I have no intention of letting the terms of this deal go public. Jellic's untimely demise hasn't changed that. If anything it's strengthened it." The last phrase was whispered under his breath and both the Colonel and Ell had to strain to hear it.

"Mr. Dover I think you have the wrong impress..."

The attorney cut him off. "Trust me, I get it. Your goon squad made it perfectly clear two weeks ago that we were to settle and the information we were in possession of needed to remain buried, so that's where it stays. I don't need you boys waltzing in here every few days with a damn reminder. Jellic is dead and as far as I'm concerned all this crap is behind me. I'm taking that nice windfall you boys provided and disappearing. I just need to wrap up the cases already on the docket. Tell whoever is pulling your strings that Jensen Dover is not an issue. I know how to tow the company line and keep my damn mouth shut."

Colonel Craig was about to say something when he felt Ell's hand on his elbow. He glanced at her and she shook her head slightly.

"You do that, Jensen, but don't leave town just yet, we don't want you raising suspicions," she gave him a steely look and gently guided the Colonel out of the office and back down the hall.

Once they were out of the building he turned to her, "What the hell?"

"The guy is a ticking time bomb of information but if he realized who we really are he'd be halfway to nowhere before we were back at the precinct. Right now I have nothing to hold him on and no way to make sure he stays put. This way, he'll be working to clean up his final few cases and giving me the time I need to get a warrant for his files and possibly his ass depending on what we find in there."

"All we have is his ramblings indicating that the D.O.D. may have strong armed a deal out of a defense attorney, it's not much for a warrant."

"We have much more than that," said Ell hitting a button on her phone.

Jensen Dover's voice came through crisp and clear. "I'm taking that nice windfall you boys provided and disappearing. I just need to wrap up the cases already on the docket."

"I never enter an interview without recording it. I'd have informed Mr. Dover of such had he given me a moment to introduce myself. As it stands, that sounds an awful lot like a defense attorney being paid off to me. Judges tend not to like that sort of thing."

As they approached the S550 she tossed him the keys. "Kind of a bullshit way to win a bet but I'm true to my word," turning to stare him in the eyes, she added. "Any mark you leave on her I'm going to duplicate on you, got it?"

"She's in good hands Lieutenant, she's in good hands."

Chapter Nine

*T*he ride back was not nearly as frightening as the thought of another person being in control of her baby. In fact, Ell had to admit that the Colonel could drive. He was quick and aggressive but in control. Not reckless in the least. Her mind began to wander as she pondered how those traits would carry over to a more intimate setting. His strong arms pinning her to the seat of her baby as he took control, forcing her to reveal her most intimate desires. The lust gripping her as his lips traced their way across her throat. Her arms and body pinned in place, unable to stop him, unwilling to try.

"Frost?" he said for a second time and she snapped out of the trance.

"Sorry, what?" she asked trying to shake the cobwebs free and come back to reality.

"I asked if you enjoyed the ride?"

'That's not the ride I want and need right now,' she thought but responded, "Sorry, I dozed off there at the end. It must not have been very exciting."

"Yeah, well sadly there are no marks on your 'baby' so your revenge will have to wait."

"Your loss Colonel, I get the feeling you may have really enjoyed a nice ass whipping."

With a very obvious lure at her entire form from head to toe, he responded. "I am honestly not sure if I'm elated or disappointed."

"Well, you keep thinking about that and let me know when you figure it out, stud," she replied as she strolled away leaving him smiling at her from the edge of the car.

Ell pulled out her cell on the way to her office, scrolled through for the right contact and dialed.

"Ell, business or pleasure," D.A. Jason Stranik answered the line.

"Stranik, you wouldn't know what to do if I actually said pleasure."

"Perhaps but I think I'd have one hell of a good time figuring it out."

"Another time," she responded in a quiet alluring voice. "Right now I need a warrant."

"Ok give me the details and twenty minutes for a cold shower, damn."

"Jensen Dover, I need a search and seizure for all files related to David Jellic and the Department of Defense. I also need a material witness hold order for the man himself."

"Jensen Dover, as in bigwig attorney Jensen Dover?"

"One and the same."

"Ell, no judge in the city is going to give you a warrant for an attorney's files. There's this little legal clause called privilege that they tend to take seriously."

Ell tapped a few buttons on her phone, "I just forwarded you an audio clip. Take a quick listen and let me know if this meets one of the privilege exceptions."

She could hear Dover's voice in the background followed quickly by Stranic, "Jesus Christ."

"Honestly, Ell, this is going to depend on the judge we get. Privilege is in place to protect the client not the attorney, you'll get your witness order no problem but client files are a tricky line to cross. I need to consider who my best option is to take this argument to. Give me an hour and if you don't hear back, wait longer."

"Thanks, and Stranik, if possible, try to keep this quiet. I don't want the witness order to get back to Dover before I can serve it. He's already on edge and ready to disappear."

"No promises but I'll do what I can."

The line went dead just as Ell rounded the corner to her office. She quickly checked the time, 7:18 p.m. She had just over forty minutes until her call with Rob, with no time to head home first she wandered back across the hall for a tar refill.

The bullpen had started to clear out, a few of her cops were just packing up and others settling in for the evening. Jones, Baker and Rique were huddled around the case board in discussion.

"L.T.," called Rique, we were just going over the notes from Colombia and I was filling the 'B' squad in on Lund and Sanders' reports.

"That 'B' better stand for 'best' and not the other term I'm thinking of," commented Jones with a glare.

"I was thinking bodacious," responded Baker with a slight giggle and a flip of the hair that sent shivers down Ell's spine. What she wouldn't give for twenty minutes in a locked room with her red headed playtoy.

"So what's the scoop on Columbia? Did we find a link to some sort of history for our missing Ms. Fenn?"

"Not really," replied Jones. "Campus records have her attending for two years, four semesters, with solid grades in the top ten percent of her class and little to nothing on friends or family."

"We spoke with all of her professors," said Baker. "Three had vague recollections of a student fitting her description during the years in question, the others couldn't place her. We are told that that's fairly standard in these large colleges. Faces come and go and the profs only remember those that really stand out."

"You'd think top ten in your class would stand out. So we are still dealing with a missing ghost?"

"We did manage to pull something out of her records that may or may not be a lead. The college requires a medical emergency contact on file for all students. Claire's contact was a Jennifer Dalton of Jacksonville, Florida. We are trying to track her down."

"Could be a lead, tug it until you know where it goes, in the meantime I have Stranik working on a warrant for Jellic's attorney and files." Out of the corner of her eye she saw Colonel Craig approach and settle in beside her. "I figured you would have headed home."

"You're still working. I'll rest when you do."

"Just what I need, another hero. Ok, I'm going to let you fill in the kids on the details of our *oh so fun date night* while I go take care of some shit. Short version is, if this warrant comes through tonight I'm going to want to take the attorney and his files right away. Our goal will be to keep it as quiet as possible so I need you four to work out the plan and get everything and everyone prepared to execute it."

"Really?" said Rique, "The queen of control is letting us formulate the plan without her? Do you have a hot date, L.T.?"

"Something like that, but I'll do my best to make it a fast and satisfying quickie. Like I said, I have shit to deal with."

"Definitely a date," winked Rique.

"Fuck off, get to work and make sure the damn plan is solid." Turning quickly to avoid the laughter and ribbing she headed back to her office to make the call.

"Lieutenant, five minutes early. Either you couldn't wait to talk to me or your case is running smoothly."

Now, with a moment to relax, the sound of his voice sent a calming chill throughout her.

"Well it damn sure isn't the second one. This case is a cluster fuck. How's the conference going?"

"Just about ready to take over the world and I think I may have found some interesting new toys for the precinct."

"Don't fuck with my cop shop, I'm just finally getting used to all the gizmos and gadgets you've installed in the last year."

"I didn't hear you complaining when your desktop was upgraded."

"A necessary evil. Someone in the department had to have one that ran."

"And run it does, so what's with this call, Ell. Grayson?"

"Fuck, ok, first off if you're going to be pissed at me please wait till you're back here, I don't want to deal with it over the phone."

"Ok?" he said with a nervous tone.

"I may have, kind of, possibly outed you to the good Doctor."

"What?"

"I had to see her on this case and you know how she is, dog with a bone and all that, she flipped it around on me and started doing her whole shrink thing. Asking questions about me, my life, blah blah blah. Next thing I knew she had me cornered and I had to tell her about us."

Rob laughed, "Ell, I didn't expect you to keep us a secret. It's not like we are running around hiding in closets. Half the precinct suspects something is going on."

"Yeah but this is different, Grayson knows me, as in the real me, all my fucked up shit, all my crazy proclivities, what gets me off. I've given her some pretty nasty details in the past and now that she knows we're together? She's not stupid, she can do the math."

"And?"

"What do you mean and? And I just outed you."

"Christ Ellison, I'm not hiding. I don't go around advertising my desires but I'm not ashamed of them. Grayson's a good, professional woman. I trust her. I assume you do as well."

"Well, yeah. I've been telling her some pretty deep secrets for years."

"Then what's the issue?"

"Fuck I don't know, this wasn't just my secret. I don't know all the rules to this shit."

"Ell, it's fine. So what did the doctor have to say?"

"That I need to talk to you about this case."

"Because?"

"She thinks you're my rock or some crap. You clear my head, or talking does, or... shit I don't know, Rob, I'm just supposed to talk."

He laughed at her frustration.

"Ok, take a couple deep breaths and talk. We'll see if the good doc is onto something."

"This one messed me up and I don't know why. All morning my head was screwed. I couldn't focus, I could barely feel, I was numb. Worst of all, I couldn't figure out why. Hell I got stuck in a damn elevator and had to be rescued by someone a thousand miles away."

"My pleasure, by the way."

"Yeah, my hero. Anyway this case is..." she paused searching for the word. "Well, it's fucked. The victim was a former marine, recently former, as in discharged anywhere from two hours after to six hours before his death, so it's a jurisdictional nightmare. We found him in some completely unrelated property suspended and bound, tortured and killed. Whoever did this knew ropes, knew wrapping, knew the game and it's fucking with my head."

"Because, like Bouton it hits too close to home."

"Kind of. That's what Grayson said. I don't think this one is going to tie in as closely as Bouton but it's still pissing me off. This is my life, my pleasure that they are perverting. They're stealing the safety away from something I treasure."

"Sounds like a solid reason to make them pay. You know, if murder and torture aren't quite enough."

She took a deep breath and realized that for the first time today her body had relaxed. The chat with Anne Grayson had began to clear her head, but this, ranting with Rob, released more stress than she had imagined possible.

"Thank you."

"For what?"

"Being you, just being you."

"Well I can't avoid that so there's no reason to thank me. Now tell me more about this case."

She did, and it helped. They ran through the probabilities, the issues and the glaring confusion between professional and amateur.

"I think Anne may be on to something. A pro with a pushed timeline or something that's gone wrong."

"It's Anne now is it?"

"Well she's not my doctor. She is a fiery little one, though, I wonder if your stories had more of an effect on her than you know."

"The two of us are supposed to get drinks at some point so maybe I'll dig into that and let you know."

"Drink's? Ell, even your friends have to drag you kicking and screaming for drinks."

"It was her idea, she wanted to 'dish'. Honestly, when I agreed I didn't know if I had a choice. The woman is a bloody warlock."

Rob started laughing, "God I miss you but I should really let you get back to your case."

She reluctantly agreed, "Yeah murder and mayhem to solve and avoid. Only another day and a bit, right?"

"That's all and then we can have a little discussion about what you owe me for freeing you this morning."

She was more than willing to pay any and everything he wanted.

"Whips and chains," she said, sad to be hanging up.

"Whips and chains babe, but remember the rules, El-lison, no self pleasure. If you want some relief you need to find a willing plaything."

With that the line went dead and Ell whispered to herself, "Yeah, I think we can arrange that."

Chapter Ten

$\mathcal{T}$he call came in at 8:32 p.m. and Corporal Jon Strand wasted no time contacting Colonel Craig. Ell was just wrapping up in her office when she heard the bullpen flying into commotion. Rique nearly ran into her as she crossed the hall to investigate.

"L.T. it's your missing girl. The roommate just received a ransom demand.

"Where?"

"Phone call to the apartment at 8:32 p.m."

"Contact Lund and make damn sure he had a trace on that line," she hadn't thought to double check with him earlier but it was standard procedure in a missing person case. Calling across to the bullpen she said, "Jones, Baker, you two haul Craig's ass with you and try to keep up, Rique, you're with me."

Her partner made an audible groan. "Oh, suck it up. I need you coordinating en route. What did I tell you Colonel, pansies, the whole lot of them."

Rique resigned himself to his fate, checking in with Lund as they headed for the car.

"Lund says kiss his ass this isn't his first rodeo and of course he has a damn tap and trace on the line. He has the call flagged and is running it now. Depending on where it originated from, it could take a few minutes. He'll send me the recording as soon as he has it."

Thank god her team was competent, where was her head, not double checking or ordering the tap was a rookie mistake.

"Hook into the Bluetooth and queue it up as soon as you get it. I want to hear this bastard's voice. Patch in Jones and Baker, we need to coordinate on the way."

Rique dialed Jones and routed the call through the car's hands free system.

"Jones, put us on hands free so we can run this through on the way," commanded Ell.

"Hands free?" laughed Jones, "This is a piece of shit department issue vehicle. I don't think the feature is even an option."

"Well put me on speaker phone, turn down the damn stereo and remind me to speak to requisitions about an upgrade when I need some fun."

"Ok, we're on speaker but I'm pretty sure we're about six cities behind you right now."

"Use the gas Jones, vertical pedal, right hand side. Ok, so we are going to be neck deep in this hostage situation when and if that warrant comes in. I need you and Baker to take lead on that op. Coordinate with Stranik and keep me in the loop. As of right now, kidnapped girl trumps dead guy. I don't want any balls dropped on the Jellic case but our priority is bringing Fenn back alive. Who knows, maybe we'll get lucky and kill two birds with one bullet."

"Stone," said Baker.

"What?"

"It's kill two birds with one stone."

"Why the hell would I use a stone when I have bullets?"

"Recording is in, L.T." said Rique avoiding an explanation.

"Run it and keep this line active."

Rique hit a few buttons and the recorded call streamed through Ell's speaker and Jones' phone.

"Hello?" Ell recognized Corporal Strand's voice and assumed he had stayed over with the roommate once crime scene had cleaned and cleared the apartment.

"Two point five million delivered to Jalsedin Bay pier 145 by 8:30 a.m. or the freaky little bitch takes a long swim with the native wildlife." The voice was modulated, disguised and unrecognizable.

"Hello, who is this? Is Claire alright? Hello?" there was a slight panic in the Corporal's voice.

No answer came and the call disconnected.

Ell told Rique to run it again. This time she was focusing not on the caller but anything else that was there. She swore there was a second voice in the background, a voice or a noise. Something.

Tell Lund to isolate the background, fade out the caller and send me the file. Oh, and see what his tech monkeys can do with the modulation on the caller's voice. He hid it for a reason, let's find out why."

She beat the second unit to the apartment by at least five minutes, gave the car a slight tap on the front quarter panel and headed in. Thankfully tonight's entry was far easier than the previous one.

"Lund has a slew of tasteful curses for you about not

telling him how to do his job and advises we will have the modified recording you requested shortly."

Ell hurried up the stairs, took a couple deep breaths to calm and center herself and knocked twice.

Corporal Strand's voice boomed from within, "Who is it."

"Lieutenant Frost and my partner Detective Shaw."

The Corporal opened the door, his sidearm safetied but drawn. "Where's the Colonel?" he asked as they entered.

"A couple minutes behind us with two fellow officers. Is everything alright here? No follow up to the call, nothing un-expected?"

"Everything is a long way from alright, Lieutenant, but no, there's been nothing since the call. Liz is a mess, she had just started to relax and now this. We got back here about an hour ago and were packing a few things so she could come crash at my place, she didn't, doesn't, want to stay here. It's messing her up. What the hell is going on?"

"At this point we are still trying to determine that. We have a tech team analyzing the call to check for validity among other things. This mess hit the news quickly today and Claire's name is out there so it could be some crank try-ing to get his rocks off by scaring people."

"Or it could be legit?" he asked, a slight waiver in his voice.

"It's too early to tell. I'd give it fifty-fifty."

"Fuck, she's a good kid, Lieutenant. We had a falling out but she's a good kid and doesn't deserve this."

"No one deserves this, Corporal, but if it is a hostage sit-uation then the ransom demand is a positive."

She could see his confusion, "No one gets rid of a hostage with the money still in play. That gives us until 8:30 a.m. and, in these things, time is everything."

The others arrived on-site and Ell had Jones and Baker start canvassing the neighbors.

"Rique, go see what, if anything, you can get out of the roommate. In the meantime, Corporal, I need a complete recap of your day."

He immediately looked to the Colonel for confirmation, Colonel Craig nodded. "Give her the run down, son."

His report was thorough and professional with accurate timestamps and emotionless, factual detail. It made Ell wish some of her detectives had been forced to go through basic training.

"Thank you, Corporal. At ease," said Colonel Craig and he made his way across the room, taking a seat on the sofa.

"Once my partner is finished with Ms. Plante the two of you should probably head out and avoid the apartment for a day or two. Can you make that work?"

"Yes, ma'am."

Ell cringed. "Lieutenant, or Ell, or sir if you must but please, not ma'am."

"Yes, sir."

The formality felt just as weird but it was acceptable.

"We should place someone on them, at least until morning. I'm assuming he's going to feel more comfortable with a military escort than a couple cops. Any suggestions?"

"Honestly, the Corporal can handle himself and would be insulted at the suggestion."

"I'm not as concerned with his level of insult as I am with keeping him breathing."

"Put a cop on him, he won't like it but he'll brush it off as civilian formality and he'll be less likely to try and ditch them given the opportunity."

"Corporal, I'll be placing a plain clothes officer with you and Ms. Plante for the evening," she said, not giving him a chance to refuse. "It's just a precaution but my Commander would have my head if I didn't. He'll keep his distance but he'll be within sight."

He understood the issues with the chain of command and nodded, reluctantly accepting his fate.

"Well played," commented Craig.

"I've watched my share of war movies, Colonel. I know what gets you boys off."

He shook his head and laughed, whispering to himself, "I'd like to see that firsthand."

Ell, catching the statement, leaned in close and said, "I'm a little busy right now but come see me later."

For a confident man the Colonel embarrassed easily. Having not thought she would hear him, his face turned a dark pink when she responded. He composed himself quickly, straightened his uniform jacket and excused himself to the hall just as Rique returned from the bedroom.

"No help, Ell. The girl's a mess."

"Ok, I want this phone line forwarded to my cell. The Corporal will be taking care of Ms. Plante and I'm going to roll out a plain clothes officer to stay with them. At a distance," she added ensuring Corporal Strand heard her. "Pick someone you trust and have them outside in fifteen."

Baker and Jones came back into the apartment, having canvassed the remainder of the floor.

"What happened to Colonel Cutie? He looks nervous as hell out there," asked Jones.

Ell almost broke but managed to keep herself composed. "No idea, did your slutty little partner get to him?"

"Hey!" responded Baker. "Sultry! And, to my regret, I haven't yet had a chance to wrap my finger, or legs, around the poor Colonel."

"Awe, the sad life and times of Detective Jamie Baker. What did you two find out?"

Baker smirked at her, "Everyone's in total freak out mode after last night but they have nothing new to report. No one saw or heard anything out of the ordinary."

"A guy's bleeding out on your neighbor's floor, being tortured for answers in a place like this and no one hears it. How is that even possible, Ell?"

"Just add it to the list of shit that doesn't add up in this case, Rique. It's a long and distinguished list. There's not much else we can do here so let's get this place cleared out and seal it up for the night. You two," she waved at Jones and Baker, "call Stranik and find out where the hell my warrant is."

"Already done and he stated, and I quote, 'Tell Frost to get off my ass and let me do my job.' ," replied Baker.

"I hope you promptly defended you Lieutenant's honor."

"Oh, oops."

Ell smiled, "Ok, get back to the eleventh and get that plan finalized. I assume Dover is out of the office by now so see if you can find a way to track his movements and be prepared to move when the call comes in. Rique and I will wait for the lovebird's escort and meet you back there."

They were on their way out the door, when she called after them. "And don't forget the Colonel, I only have two seats."

Chapter Eleven

She wasn't back in the precinct for more than three minutes when her email chimed. Lund had managed to remove the voices on the ransom call and enhance the background noise.

"About time," she muttered. "Rique, Jones, Baker, and whoever the hell else is still on this case, follow me," she called into the bullpen on her way to her office.

The five of them crowded into her closet sized office and huddled around her desk as she pulled up the file on her computer.

"Ell, we could have picked a bit larger space to do this," commented Rique.

"Find me one with a Xonar DSX sound card and Bose Companion speaker system and we'll move." The four of them looked at her as if she was speaking a foreign language and she finally understood how Rob felt on a daily basis.

"The sound is good in here," she said, slowly as if to emphasize each word.

She hit play and they all listened to the odd recording of white noise mixed with a muffled voice.

"Can you loop that?" asked the Colonel.

Ell clicked around for a moment and then restarted the recording on a loop. On the fifth run through, Colonel Craig held up a hand. "Did you catch that, it's right while our perp would be talking but it sounds like someone gagged in the background. Help, grand fox? Something like that. Run it again."

"Definitely help," said Baker. "Land rocks? I can't make it out."

On a hunch, Ell pulled up a map of the Jalsedin Bay docks. The ransom demand mentioned a pier in the area and she was betting their perp wouldn't want to go too far out of the way with a hostage in tow.

"The Sandbox," she said. "It's a closed down club out on Pier 14. It was under renovations last year and the developer ran out of cash. I'll lay odds she's trying to say Sandbox."

For a moment there was complete silence.

"Rique, I need everything you can find on the location, owners and building in twenty minutes. You two," she waved at the girls, "Get SWAT and hostage rescue on the line and organize a conference room. I'm going to contact Commander Nuez and get this rolling. Colonel, you may want to do the same on your end of things."

"This is a civilian op. If it's okay with you, I think I'll wait to report in until it's over."

Ell shrugged and everyone raced off to deal with what needed to be done leaving Ell alone with Colonel Craig.

"Any specific reason you're leaving this one up to me and my team?"

"Call it a hunch for now."

'Yeah a hunch,' she thought, 'and nothing at all to do

with the little tidbit of information Dover let slip about the D.O.D. paying him off.'

She picked up the phone, checked the time, cursed the fact that she had to call the Commander at home just after 10:00 p.m., and dialed.

"Hello?"

"Commander, sorry for the late hour."

"Do you sleep, Frost."

"Honestly, I'm not sure if I do anymore. It's been a while."

She gave him a quick update on the ransom call, the leads and the pending operation. He gave her the go ahead, said he would coordinate from his end and to call with an update once it was over, regardless of the hour.

Twenty minutes later Ell was cordoned off in a mid size conference room with twenty four cops from various departments. She was starting to gather everyone together for the briefing when Jones flagged her down from the doorway. She headed over and stepped outside for some privacy.

"So how important is the attorney?"

"Pretty damn important, why?"

"I just received word from Stranic, he's secured a material witness order. Apparently the search warrant's a no go unless we can find something else. The judge said that the attorney's possible criminal actions don't offset the rights of the client, dead or not."

"Fucking bureaucrats."

"Yeah, what you said but it got me thinking. If we can get this shyster in a box with the threat of charges over his head, maybe leverage an 'accidental' leak about his cooperation with the authorities, he's bound to roll on whoever is pulling his strings."

"Agreed, do you know his whereabouts?"

"I had a black and white do a quick drive by on his house five minutes ago. The lights are on and someone's home. My records indicate that his wife left him four years ago in a nasty divorce and there are no kids on file so I'm betting good money that's him, tucked in for the evening."

"How many do you need to do it right."

"If we want quiet, smaller is better but it's a big damn house in a high priced neighborhood. I need at least six of us to properly secure it on entry and the neighbors in those areas are damn nosey. With a team that size I'm not sure we can do it under the radar."

"You need a distraction."

"It wouldn't hurt but even a distraction in the area to pull away the snoops is bound to draw some outside attention to the attorney."

"No, you need a city wide distraction, like perhaps a high profile, live on Channel Six, police raid on a possible hostage situation."

"No way, L.T. We may," she emphasized, "be able to run these ops simultaneously but you can't risk your breach for mine. There's a girl's life on the line and if the perp gets wind of your op it's over. She's dead and they're in the wind."

"Who said anything about risking my op?" responded Ell with a sly smile.

Ell pulled out her cell before reentering the room, found the number for Cindy Shepard and hit dial. Cindy was a top notch reporter with the Chronicle. One Ell trusted and had built a pretty decent rapport with in the last couple months.

"Hello, this is Cindy."

"Shepard, it's Ell."

"Lieutenant, I've been meaning to call you in search of the truth on this Jellic matter."

"Yeah, I think we could all use a bit of that. Right now I've got something else going on and I need a favor."

"You know the deal Ell, you scratch mine, etc. etc. So what's up?"

"I'm willing to barter a little on this because I may be putting your neck on the line. I need the name and contact for an onscreen reporter with some pull. Someone that can get the airwaves flooded on short notice and someone you are not particularly fond of."

"What's popping Ell, if you have a story I can get it circulating."

"Trust me when I tell you that you want no part of this one. I just need a contact with some juice. The less you know the better."

Cindy could read between the lines and was starting to get concerned. "Is this gonna come back to bite me in the ass, Ell?"

"I'm not going to lie, if word gets out that you gave me the contact it could, but I promise that word won't come from me. I'll do what I can to keep your name clear.

"I'm firing you Donald Worther's contact info via text. He's one of the lead reporters for KYA News and he definitely has the pull you're looking for. The guy's a misogynistic prick so there's no love lost here. When you finish whatever the hell you're doing, don't forget who your friends are."

"If and when I have a newsworthy story you'll be my first call."

"That's not good enough, Ell. I want an exclusive on this

Jellic debacle. You and whoever you're liaising with from the Department of Defense."

Ell smiled, Cindy was a good solid reporter, she always treated Ell and the department right, but she knew when to push for what she wanted.

"I can't speak for the D.O.D. but I'll do what I can on my end. As soon as I have a suspect in the box, I'll give you thirty minutes."

"Sounds like a deal."

"Whatever you hear tonight, stay away from it. Let the rest of the field cover it as they wish but go out, get a drink and take the night off. Thanks for the name."

True to her word, the contact information for Donald Worther was waiting in Ell's messages before the call ended.

"Christ Ell, you're going to burn your reputation if you do what I think you're planning," said Jones.

"Only if they figure out I set it up. I need a landline and a decent tech that can reroute an outgoing call to cover our asses. Give me five minutes."

She headed to the small office across the hall and pulled up her messaging app.

"Hey sexy, I need to spoof an outgoing call to make the caller ID appear different than it is. Is there anyone in my time zone that could pull it off? – E"

The response came moments later.

"What line are you placing the call from and where do you need it to come from? – R"

Looking down at the extension in front of her she replied. "Our precinct line 2855, I need it to appear as if the call originated from Central PD. – E"

"Should I ask why? – R"

"Probably not ;) – E"

Rob was quiet for about forty seconds.

"Okay, you're all set. Calls from that extension will trace to Central for the next forty minutes. – R"

"Seriously, I didn't need to beat a trace but damn, you just earned yourself a very special reward. – E"

"Oh? Don't think I won't collect on that as soon as I'm back there. – R"

"Whips and chains .– E"

"Whips and chains back atcha. – R"

Ell headed back across the hall to brief the team and outline the basics of each operation. Timing was going to be key and she wanted all teams in place and ready to breach when the signal came.

Baker and Jones would be heading up the breach team on Fourteenth Street and securing the attorney while Ell led the team at the Sandbox. Both locations were troubling to breach with multiple exits and maze like interiors so each team would need to coordinate scouting in advance. It wasn't the most complicated operation she'd organized but it had enough moving parts to cause problems. All it took was one error and things could go horribly wrong.

The teams loaded up and headed out at 11:14 p.m. leaving a reluctant Colonel Craig behind to handle the phone call that would set everything in motion.

The Sandbox had been abandoned for years but the area around it still housed a number of businesses. The late hour helped to cull the traffic but they were still forced to setup the command post, a non-descript black cargo van, three blocks from the building and move in slowly and silently in order to avoid detection. Ell and Rique would be held up in the van and remain out of the fray until SWAT had given the all clear and secured the site. She had wanted to be in on the breach but running two simultaneous operations negated that opportunity. Instead, they had secured both lead SWAT officers with a night vision camera that sent a live feed back to the van. Both Jones and Baker wore similar gear, giving Ell a solid picture of both operations as they went down.

The teams scanned both properties with heat signature cameras as they settled in and waited. Jones reported a single signature in the upstairs bedroom while the team at the Sandbox reported only a faint signature in a rear office. The report put Ell on edge. They were expecting multiple signatures at the Sandbox, assuming the hostage would be well guarded. She immediately began rolling through the entire scenario in her head. Had she misinterpreted the ransom tape? Were they at the wrong location? With both teams on alert and little time to waste she shook the doubts out of her mind. You roll the dice you have and if they come up snake eyes you ante up and roll again. She picked up her cell and sent General Craig the go message.

"Make the call. – E"

The next few minutes felt like an eternity. Ell sat, staring at a monitor and attempting to block out all the possible scenarios that could cause either breach to go sideways. Finally, her phone beeped to indicate an incoming message.

"The bait is set. – C"

The next step was out of their hands, the timeline from here on out would be set by the speed of the media, a factor out of her control.

It took fourteen nail biting minutes but the monitor to her right finally flashed and cut to a "Breaking News Scene" as a video feed from a news chopper filled the screen with a shot of an abandoned warehouse on the north end of town.

Ell pressed the button on her earpiece microphone.

"Team One, repeat Team One, green light. Go."

On the monitor, from the choppers eye, she could see her secondary SWAT unit spreading quickly to surround the abandoned warehouse as a news anchor rambled on about a hostage rescue in progress. She gave it thirty seconds, hoping the coverage would draw other media outlets like moths to the proverbial flame, then, again, she hit the button on her earpiece microphone.

"All teams, repeat all teams, green light, Go."

The barrage of monitors before her lit up with movement as both the Sandbox and Dover teams leapt into action. As expected the breach, bind and extraction by the Dover team took just over forty seconds and Baker and Jones executed it with flawless precision. The witness was rushed through the home, out the back and into a dark SUV quickly and quietly. Baker stayed behind to ensure any damage or evidence of the breach was cleaned and corrected while the remaining officers blended into the shadows of the neighborhood and disappeared.

The operation at the Sandbox, however, did not proceed as precisely. As the teams breached, front and rear, Ell heard a loud explosion and saw a bright flash of light on one monitor before the feed was lost entirely. The SWAT team scrambled, reacting quickly and modifying their approach. One of the two wireless camera feeds came back online and Ell's heart dropped. There were at least two members down and others scurrying to secure the area.

Calls of, "Clear," could be heard throughout the building followed by a frantic call for Lieutenant Latner, the lead SWAT agent and man with the only working camera at the time. Latner rounded a corner towards the back office where the faint heat signature had been detected and the image became clear. A young woman they would later identify as Claire Fenn could be seen naked, face down, bent over and restrained to a folding pommel horse. Metal shackles and silver chain encased her wrists ankles and waist restraining her movement. A tight black leather hood had been pulled down over her eyes and nose. A thick metal collar circled her neck, a silver chain, recently broken free, dangled from the edge of the collar. The floor around her was littered with the tools of torture. A series of blades in varying sizes, canes, scalpels, a black leather flogger, a bull whip, and two bare wires clamped to her nipples resting on the edge of a gas generator. Her sides, chest, arms and face were littered with slices and her back bore the faint marks of flogging. As soon as the all clear was called, two SWAT members rushed to her aide, followed shortly by a series of paramedics and then finally Lieutenant Ellison Frost.

Once on scene, Ell received a full report from Lieutenant Latner. Aside from Claire Fenn, the building was empty. No other bodies, alive or dead, had been found on-site. The rear door had been rigged with an undetected pressure plate attached to some form of high explosive. Latner suspected C4 but suggested that Lund's boys would have a more detailed report on it.

Two SWAT agents were down, however, their protective gear had taken the brunt of the blast. The paramedics were confident that both would survive, though it had been touch and go for a few moments. Claire Fenn had been unconscious when they found her. She appeared to have significant blood loss, was suffering from slight exposure and had been rushed to St. Pete's hospital for follow-up. Ell suspected the psychological impact would be far more long lasting than the physical.

Having done all she could to catalog the scene, she handed it over to Lund and his crew, took a step back and damn near collapsed onto the concrete street. Tears raced down the side of her face uncontrollably as she was hit by a flood of emotions. She sat there, alone in the dark, struggling for control, and stared at the ground beneath her as the tears dried and she was overtaken by nothingness, a numbness that could not be broken.

She grabbed her phone and made a quick call to Baker and Jones who had just placed Jensen Dover in a cell and were now coordinating with Colonel Craig. She gave them a quick update and told them to get some rest and re-group at 7:00 a.m. Pulling herself to her feet, she stumbled her way to a nearby squad car and caught a lift back to the precinct. She called Commander Nuez with an update on the way, not a pleasant call to make but the Commander thanked her and reassured her that the injuries were not the fault of her or her team. It was a nice gesture but she knew she would carry the responsibility for some time. She always did.

She stumbled through the halls of the eleventh precinct and considered driving home and getting a decent nights rest. After some thought, she opted not to waste the forty minutes travel time and, instead, crash in one of the bunk rooms that were setup for just such an occasion.

Chapter Twelve

T he pain washed over her. A calming, settling pain. A loving, seductive pain, as the leather tips of the red suede flogger snapped against her back. She was begging, pleading to be taken. His lips brushed across her neck, his left hand cupping her breast, lightly pinching her nipple.

"Is this what you need, can you feel it, pushing the numbness aside."

"Yes, oh god yes. Please, harder," she moaned as he entered her fast and hard from behind. Driving into her as his nails slid slowly across her back, the flogger once again snapping against her ass sending shockwaves of ecstasy rumbling through her spine. He grabbed her hair pulling hard, forcing her neck up and back as he continued to push deeper, harder. She could feel the orgasm building as a cold sharp item touched the skin of her throat. She was on the edge, her entire body beginning to tighten when a sudden rush of excruciating pain flooded her system. True pain, not something the body could convert to pleasure but searing, screaming pain. Blood gushed from her throat covering the silk beneath her as she tried desperately to scream. Fighting to maintain control *she let loose a terrible wail as laughter, hideous laughter filled the room.*

Ell bolted awake, the horrible laughter still reverberating in her mind, sweat pouring from her body and soaking the sheets beneath. Taking a moment to gain her bearings she cursed into the air, "Fuck!" and took ten slow, deep breaths trying to lower her heart rate. She could feel the adrenaline pumping through her and, instinctively, she knew sleep was no longer an option. Checking her phone she noted the time, 4:58 a.m, less than four hours was going to have to suffice. 'Well that's almost double what I got yesterday,' she thought with a slight laugh as she pulled herself out of the bunk, heading for a shower.

Ell let the scolding hot water wash over her, slowly dragging the fear and stress with it, and by the time she was done she nearly felt human again. The two hours free time prior to her team's arrival went quickly. She updated her case notes, sent Commander Nuez a detailed report on the operations from the evening before and checked in with the hospital on the status of both the victim and the wounded SWAT members. The two officers had minor lacerations and concussions. One had required surgery to remove a piece of metal shrapnel from his abdomen and the other had required a series of pins and screws in his left tibia. Both men were stable and would require time off for recovery, but they were doing well and in good hands.

Claire Fenn had regained consciousness, was extremely

dehydrated and experiencing some minor pain from the various lacerations. She was doing well considering what she'd been through. Ell would need to interview her as soon as possible, however the attending physician had requested she wait until later that day. A uniformed officer had been placed outside her room and was instructed that only the medical team be permitted access for now.

She was reviewing an update to Lund's crime scene report when Colonel Craig poked his head in her door.

"Please tell me you haven't been here since last night."

"Here, but not here," she emphasized. "I crashed in a bunk on-site rather than heading home."

He looked down at the guest chair but given the shape it was in, thought better and continued to stand.

"And how are you holding up? I heard you had a couple men go down last night."

"They'll survive, I talked to the hospital earlier and it's nothing some time and physio won't fix. We saved the girl, secured the attorney and no one died. I'm calling it a win."

"But no one is in custody and there are no additional leads on who we are looking for."

"No, but we're closer than we were and we now have an eye witness who may be able to clue us in as to who and why. Not my best evening but far from my worst. Did you update your contact at the Department of Defense."

"It seems in all the shuffle and exhaustion it slipped my mind. I'm sure I'll get to it later."

Ell saw through the statement.

"Do you want to discuss it?"

"If I did I may be admitting to something other than exhaustion and a bad memory."

"And how long can a bad memory hold out before some-one on the other end starts sending out reminders?"

"Hopefully, until after we've had a chance to sit down with the attorney and get some answers."

"Well, if you need some probable deniability I can start shutting you out of anything useful, on paper."

"Let's hope it doesn't come to that because, honestly, if it gets to that point then we'll have hit on something big and…"

He trailed off but Ell understood, he was already struggling with loyalties and if this case somehow flipped back on some area of the D.O.D. or military it would put him in a very difficult position.

"I want to give Dover a couple more hours to stew in isolation before I question him. Apparently he was screaming for an attorney on the way in, I don't know if he contacted one last night but he was given the opportunity. We can hold him and question him on the material witness order for now, but unless we can flip him on something quick or scare him into cooperating, I have the feeling that he has the money and clout to get it squashed."

"In the meantime?"

"Homework and harassment. I was just looking over the final tech report from the Jellic scene. There's no new evidence and the final tally was three distinct blood samples found on-site. The victim, an unknown female which will likely match Claire Fenn, and an unknown male. According to Lund's estimation the unknown male lost about a quarter pint so it wasn't a pin prick but it wasn't lethal either. I'm wagering that's our perp's. They're running DNA nationwide but won't see results for at least another twenty-four hours. His team is still working on both the scene and items from last night. I'll rattle his cage on that later this morning. He did send me photos of some of the items recovered and one in particular looked unique. A silver collar with evenly spaced black diamonds and a long silver chain."

"Not your run of the mill item and not something most people would wear."

"Not publicly."

"Pardon?"

Ell almost laughed, she often forgot how naïve some people were about submissive behavior.

"It's a collar and leash, Colonel. Something one buys for that special someone."

"A bondage toy?"

"More a submissive toy, the collar has an element of bondage to it but it's not about restraint so much as owner-ship and loyalty. This one is a little more formal than a play-time model. It's probably ceremonial."

"I don't even... I'm a relatively open minded guy, Lieuten-ant, but you're speaking a different language."

To really explain the symbolism and meaning of a collar to him she would need to educate him on a lot more detail on a dominant/submissive relationship. Instead, she circled back to something Rob had once pointed out to her.

"First you have to wrap your mind around the fact that we're not just talking about something sexual. This is a relationship structure. Think of a collar as a wedding ring used in dom/sub relationships. It symbolizes the union. Since most people in these types of relationships have to be very discreet in order to avoid stereotypes and bigotry, the collar is usually set aside for intimate moments.

Those, however, tend to be soft leather or suede. Something as intricate and jeweled as this would be used for ceremony."

"There are ceremonies?"

"A collaring ceremony, it's basically the same as a wedding ceremony minus the clergy. Two people expressing their love for one another and exchanging vows to honor and protect. Instead of a ring, they use a collar."

Ell could see him battling his conservative nature but the explanation was simple enough and didn't upset too many moral beliefs so acceptance was easy to find.

"Since I don't think I have ever seen one of these for sale I assume they're a specialty item."

"Very and that means..."

"We have a decent chance of tracing it."

"There are only a few high end jewelers that would put any effort into a collar. It's not a quick sell and most are done strictly on commission. We don't know how or where our perp got it so we'll start local and expand if need be."

"So where do we start?"

"Honestly, I'm not sure. I don't have a magic database of collar manufacturers. I'm going to make a couple calls and try to put together a list. Where are we on a true version of Jellic's court martial?"

"The official file has been heavily redacted and thus far I haven't been able to find anyone who has seen an original version. Whoever redacted the file has high end clearance but that's all I know so far. I'll keep digging while you make those calls."

Once he was back across the hall, Ell pulled out her cell and paused. There was a time she could make this call without a second thought but now things just weren't the same with Angel. She took a deep breath and hit dial.

"It's seven a.m. Ell. Seven in the fucking morning."

"Good morning to you too, Angel."

"There's no such thing. There's good afternoons, great nights and shit fucking mornings. This is the reason I sleep through them and you, you of all people, know this."

"I hear you whining but I also know you were probably up two hours ago playing slap and tickle with my partner before his shift."

"I was up two hours ago. Still up. Still up from a damn fun night, though my Latin playtoy wasn't around. His evil bitch of a boss kept him working for damn near forty-eight hours straight."

"That wench!" replied Ell in mock support.

"Not the word I'd pick but it'll work. So why, for the love of all that is holy, are you waking me up at this ungodly hour."

"I need some information?"

"Yeah, I figured no one was dead since you let me banter. Or at least no one I know. Is this business or pleasure?"

"Business but it ties in with pleasure. I'm trying to ID a silver collar, jeweled, fancy, and probably ceremonial."

"Is this the Jellic case?" Ell could hear a bit of panic in her voice and knew Angel was worried it would involve someone in the lifestyle.

"Yes, but it seems community adjacent."

"Send me a photo and give me fifteen minutes to put together a list of possible local sources. This one is free but if you ever call me before noon again I'm gonna take it out on your partner's pink ass."

"He'd probably love that."

Angel broke and let out a laugh. "Yeah, me too."

"Thanks Angel and..." she paused for a second. "Let's make time for a coffee or something this week. You know, catch up."

"Deal, but skip that damn coffee. We need a night of tequila and whisky."

"Damn straight girl, it's on."

She hung up, feeling slightly better about life in general as a little bit of stress melted away.

With a few free minutes on her hands she began composing a text to Rob, just to touch base and update him on the events of the night before. She glanced at the time, remembered that he was two hours earlier and thought she better not. Instead she pulled up the crime scene photos from the night before. She wanted a closer look at the setup.

The photos themselves were taken after the removal of Ms. Fenn but she had a couple screen captures from the night vision video that helped her get a feel for the position of the victim. The lacerations had caused blood pools to form around the pommel horse. Ell wondered if any of the blood came from their mysterious male donor and made note to ensure Lund ran sample comparisons. The scene was gory and not the best thing to be focusing on with an empty stomach but she reminded herself that the victim had survived. That in itself was a small miracle given the amount of time between the abduction and rescue. She continued to stare at the photos. Something about the scene seemed odd but she couldn't put her finger on it. She was still racking her brain when an email popped up from Angel Demarco.

She pulled up the email. Angel had narrowed the list of

local possibilities to four high end jewelers and one custom artist that specialized in 'alternative apparel'. Ell did a rudimentary search on each, checked through some online portfolios looking for similar work and, for a moment, wished she had time to shop.

Shutting down her search and making note of the business locations, she headed across the hall to check in with her team. Baker, Jones and Rique were already huddled around the case board making updates based on the discoveries in the last twenty-four hours. Colonel Craig was mysteriously absent.

"Well don't you three look like rays of sunshine."

"With all due respect, Lieutenant. Bite me," said Rique taking a large swig from a to-go cup.

"Is that coffee? As in actual, non-tar, drinkable coffee?"

"It may be," he responded suspiciously and maneuvered it out of her reach."

"You're dead to me, Rique."

"What else is new?"

"Well, since you asked. Those of us that drug our asses in early this morning have been working the case and, conveniently, have a nice list of errands for you zombies."

"One of the items recovered from the Sandbox last night was a custom silver collar. Shiny, jeweled, just your type, Rique."

He gave her a friendly smirk and let her continue. "It's a unique item with very few possible manufacturers. Thanks to my partner's plaything, I have a list of four possibilities in the area."

"You talked to Angel?" asked Rique, setting his coffee down on the table in front of them.

"Yes and oh the gossip we had. It was business you moron. As I was saying, four possibilities and I need two of you to start running them down. Dealer's choice on who goes."

"Shopping for shiny jewelry? Count me in," smiled Baker giving her red locks a flip to the side and flashing a subtle wink that send chills down Ell's spine. Ell paused and regained her composure.

"It's not a shopping trip, it's a damn case."

"Yes sir, Lieutenant sir. Purely business, no fun allowed. I copy that," Baker gave her a quick salute to cap off the sarcasm.

"One of you go babysit the cheerleader and make sure she doesn't end up broke. I need whoever's staying behind to keep pushing on Ms. Fenn's former identity. Track down that damn emergency contact and find out who the hell she is. I'm interviewing her this afternoon and I'd rather not go in blind."

"I'll handle the background," said Jones. "I already have a start on it. There's no use someone taking over now and spinning their wheels. I received a message from one of the professors we spoke to yesterday indicating they may have found something that could help us. I figured I'd take a run back out to Columbia and see what it is."

"Sounds good, if anything pops, let me know," she shifted her gaze to Rique. "Jewelry shopping with a beautiful redhead," said Ell as she started to walk away, "Looks like this is your lucky day, Rique."

"Yay me," he replied reaching for his coffee and noticing that it was gone. He snapped his gaze up just in time to watch Ell stroll away, cup in hand.

Chapter Thirteen

*B*y nine o'clock she had thoroughly harassed Lund about the crime scene report on the Sandbox, finalized her full update for the Commander and was beginning to wonder about Colonel Craig's mysterious absence. As if by fate, just as she began to get concerned, she caught a glimpse of his rock hard, uniformed figure turning the corner into the bullpen. Before she could go check in with him her desk phone began ringing. She checked the display, Ext. 0356 – Holding. Smiling, she knew what the call would be about before she picked up.

"Frost here."

The voice that followed was frustrated yet professional. "Lieutenant, this is Jerry Kohl down in holding. You're material witness has ask that I inform you that you are, and I quote, violating his god damn rights and he'll see you rot in a cell for it."

"Having a fun morning, Jerry?"

"Oh, it's been a blast as usual. This one is a bit more uppity than the standard drunks. He's been tossing some fine legaleeze in with the curses. The pompous rich ones are always the worst."

"Unfortunately, that pompous rich ass is going to be with us a while. Did he contact an attorney?"

"No, get this, when I offered him the opportunity to do so he replied that he, and I quote again, didn't need some damn shyster stealing his cash. He could deal with this in propria persona, whatever the hell that means."

"I'm pretty sure it means he's a dumbass, Jerry. I'm going to let him stew for another thirty then I'd like him brought up to interrogation room two."

"You meant interview two, right. He is a witness."

"No, I meant interrogation. I don't think Mr. Dover will be a witness for long once I get him in a box."

"Will do, Lieutenant. In fact, it will be a pleasure."

Ell hung up, spent about twenty minutes reviewing her notes, and headed across the hall in search of the Colonel. She found him huddled over a file at Baker's desk.

"Anything important?" she asked.

His head snapped up in surprise. "Honestly, I don't know yet. It's another redacted file on Jellic but seems to have a few differences compared to what I've been previously provided."

"Where'd you get it? Or do I want to know?"

"Probably best if we ignore that question for now."

"For now," she said though every atom in her body wanted to interrogate him until he broke. "I'm about to have a nice little chat with our guest, Jensen Dover Esquire. Care to join me?"

"Oooh fun, am I good cop or bad?"

"Bad, but I thought maybe we'd play bad officer worse cop on this one. Turn up the heat and get the bastard more afraid of us than whatever the hell he's wrapped up in."

"You should let me take a shot at him for a couple minutes before you come in. Right now he thinks I'm working for whoever he's afraid of. I can play that up for a few minutes and he may slip up again. If he does you can use it to drive him into the ground."

Ell considered it. She wouldn't be able to record Dover in the interrogation room without notification so anything the Colonel got out of him would be questionable in court, but if it opened the door to something she could press on, some further leverage, it could be worthwhile.

"Ok we can play it your way but I'm keeping a close eye on him. If I see him shutting down I'm taking over."

She checked the time, decided Dover had stewed long enough and the two of them headed down to interrogation. Ell told the Colonel to give her a moment to get settled into observation and signal Officer Kohl to leave before he entered. She slid into the small room next to Interrogation Two, turned towards the one way mirror and nearly dropped as the sight within the room hit her square in the chest. Both her witness and Officer Kohl lay still in a growing pool of blood. Ell grabbed her phone, calling the main entry desk as she ran back into the hall cornering into the interrogation room.

"This is Lieutenant Ellison Frost, secure code 873496. The precinct has been breached. Shut it down. Full lockdown on my order. And get an EMT team to interrogations, stat. Officer down. I repeat, officer down."

"What the he..." began the Colonel as she opened the interrogation room door and he got his first vision of the gory scene within.

Ell raced through the pooling blood, checking for signs of

life. Jensen Dover was gone but officer Kohl still had a faint pulse. The blood was warm and still flowing from the gash in his neck. Ell ripped off the bottom five inches of her blouse and used it as a makeshift bandage, applying pressure to the wound and trying to slow the blood loss. The in house EMT arrived within minutes, relieved her and went to work on blocking the wound and stabilizing the man for transport.

As soon as she was relieved Ell bolted down the hall still covered in blood, half her blouse missing. She flew past her office and through the corridor to the main entry. As expected the precinct had been locked down, armed officers at every entry and exit. The procedure took less than three minutes.

"You, you and you." Ell pointed to three officers she recognized but did not know. "I want everyone in this building with the exception of those manning doors rounded up into Conference rooms A through F, if they don't fit keep adding letters. I need two additional officers you know and trust to verify and clear each room once you have gathered personnel. I want this building cleared within the next twenty minutes, if anyone gives you any crap you let me know immediately and I'll drag there asses out personally. If that person is Lund, feel free to shoot him on-site. Go."

Ell grabbed the nearest phone and dialed extension 145.

"This is Commander Nuez' office. Keith Dillon speaking."

"Keith it's Frost, no time for shit I need the Commander immediately.

"I'm sorry Lieutenant, the commander is in a meeting at the moment and..."

"Keith you have ten seconds to get him on this line or I will personally pull that robotic brain out through your ass. NOW!"

Ell did not get a response just dead air for a moment followed by the Commander's voice. "Frost, why does my assistant look like he's about to cry?"

"Sir, we are in full lockdown, the building has been breached but is secured. Officer Kohl is down and in critical condition. Jensen Dover is dead. I'm performing a full sweep of the building and moving all occupants to Conference Rooms A through whatever. The bodies were discovered within minutes of attack. The perpetrator may still be on-site."

"Jesus Christ, what do you need?"

"Right now, a small miracle couldn't hurt. Assuming the on-site EMT can get him stabilized, Officer Kohl is going to need transport and someone needs to notify his wife, girlfriend, boyfriend, whatever. We have teams in the field that need to be notified that the station is in lockdown, mine included. I need someone in dispatch to get the message out without pressing the panic button."

"I'm on it. Unless you find a nut job covered in blood," she looked down at herself and the humor of the statement was not lost on her, "I assume you'll be interviewing everyone you're rounding up?"

"That's the plan."

"Then the union needs notification and a union rep will need to be present."

"That's just what I need, more suits in my way," she shook off the annoyance. "I'll also need access to all surveillance in the last hour."

"I'll deal with it, check your computer in five minutes and I'll get someone from the union here asap. How long to clear the building?"

"I have three officers rounding up anyone present and two clearing behind them. I gave them twenty minutes."

"To clear six floors and a parkade? That's a little optimistic, Lieutenant."

"Well this way they'll hustle their asses. I figure it'll be closer to forty. The staff's not going to like it."

"With an officer down they can suck it up and deal with it. Let's find this son of a bitch."

Ell headed back to her office, running into Colonel Craig along the way. "What the hell?"

"We are in full lockdown. No one in or out until I can clear this building. I have surveillance footage on its way but I'm not optimistic. Someone with the balls and skills to walk into a precinct and do this would have known we'd be watching."

They headed into the bullpen and she quickly washed the blood off her hands and arms before heading back to her office where she rummaged through a drawer and found a clean, non-torn blouse. Without a second thought, she began to strip down and change. The Colonel's eyes went large and he quickly turned his back.

"They're boobs Colonel, I'm guessing you've seen some before." He ignored the comment. Given more relaxed circumstances she'd have laughed. Looking down at herself, her dress pants still stained in blood, she resigned that this was the best she could do. She sat down, found a link in her email to a series of surveillance videos and began combing through them. As expected it was useless. From ten minutes before she found the bodies until she locked down the building the tapes were completely dark. No video, no snow, no timestamp.

"Figured as much," she motioned the Colonel around her desk to take a look and watched as fear crept into his eyes.

"Are these usually time stamped?"

"Yeah, bottom right, why?"

"Shit, I've seen this, Ell. Actually I've used it. The software's called CleanSlate. It's something we use for extraction ops. It's what I used in Columbia. There's a slight purple hue in the bottom right, where the timestamp would be. It's a telltale sign of the software."

"Military software?"

"Not exclusively, it's a private firm with military contracts. I don't know if CleanSlate was a specific contract or if it's open market. I just know we use it."

Ell pulled out her cell and dialed Rob's number.

"Well, if it isn't my favorite wake up call."

"I don't have much time and I'm putting you on speaker phone." She set down the cell and hit the button. "We're looking into a security breach. What do you know about a software called CleanSlate?"

"I know it's a damn fine piece of code, can take over most surveillance systems, locally hosted or off-site, in under twenty seconds and it is damn near undetectable."

"Is it publically offered or strictly military?"

"Neither, it's sold privately to very specific, well vetted, organizations. Some are military, some civilian, almost all are law enforcement related."

"Any chance there's a copy that leaked outside of those channels."

"No, and that is a definite no. There are sixteen copies worldwide, only those sixteen will work, ever. Copying the software is not an option as it's setup to connect and verify with a private server daily. If the system isn't verified every twenty-four hours it is effectively deactivated until verification can be achieved. It's a security system that cannot be duplicated or bypassed. It's the most sophisticated anti-piracy algorithm available."

Ell was starting to get a bad feeling, "And you know this because…" she prompted.

"I wrote it, or at least the anti-piracy tie-in to the code. It was a nice little side contract with the developer, GenData Group. In fact I was able to retain ownership on my portion of the code and license its use."

"Well yippee, your beautiful software was just used to put an officer in the hospital and one of my key witnesses in the morgue."

Rob's apparent pride disappeared quickly, "I'll send you the sixteen names right away."

"Anyway to tell which of the sixteen were active today?"

"It's possible. If I can get access to the encryption server then I can identify which organizations had the software online. I'm going to have to sweet talk GenData for access but it should be doable."

"I can have a warrant in under an hour if you need it."

"Let me try to talk my way in first. I have a pretty good relationship with the company and warrants tend to muddy those waters."

"Thanks," without thinking about who was in the room she added, "whips and chains."

"Whips and chains back atcha. Take care of my cops."

Colonel Craig grinned but wisely said nothing. Ell's mind, occupied, hadn't thought twice about the slip.

"A handy source."

"He's the local I.T. slave and conveyer of robot overlords. I need to monitor the sweep and start prepping my interviews. Any chance you can take the list of companies when it comes in and find me someone other than your organization that could be responsible for this?"

"Gladly."

She thought about sending him back to Baker's terminal, but knew the searches would be quicker and smoother at hers.

"What's your security clearance level, Colonel?"

"I'm not sure what you're asking?"

"Your level, classified national secrets and so on?"

"Some."

"That sounds higher than mine, use this terminal and don't make me regret letting you do so."

She left him to it and got the distinct impression he was watching her ass as she walked away.

'Wishful thinking, Ell. Get your damn head in the job.'

The union rep was a pain in her collective bargaining ass. It was like attempting to question a ten year old with their mom in the room. No one wanted to say anything without permission and the entire process took twice as long as it needed to. About half way through, with another forty-five officers and employees left, each growing more frustrated by the minute, Ell needed a break to clear her head.

Stepping out of the interview room she was flagged down by one of her patrolling officers.

"Sir," he said, knowing better than to call her ma'am. "We have a problem on two."

She knew immediately, but hoped she was wrong. "Please tell me it's a perp."

"Not exactly."

"For fuck sake, didn't I tell you to shoot him? I'm sure I said shoot him."

She picked up a nearby phone and called Lund's extension. When the line picked up she didn't wait for a verbal answer. "God dammit, Lund, stow your damn ego and do what the officers tell you. I have a precinct on lockdown and need to clear the building."

"Yeah and I have five tests on your damn crime scene running, two of which have been on the machines for three hours and will be fucking worthless if I have to scrap them and drag my ass downstairs for a useless fucking roll call."

"Look, it's protocol, it sucks but we're going to have to accept the lost time."

"Do you think I killed a witness and slit Kohl open, Frost?"

"You know I don't."

"Ok, so I'll tell you right now, I didn't see shit, I didn't hear shit, I don't know shit. Can we skip the interview and let me go back to finding your damn killer."

"Lund you're a pain in my ass, and not a fun playtime pain. Finish your damn tests. I'll have the officers clear the rest of the floor."

Ell hung up and shook her head at the officer. "Leave him there but clear the rest of the floor and lock it down."

With a deep breath she headed back into the interview room and signaled the union rep to bring in the next one of her colleagues that she had to formally rake over the coals.

Two hours, ninety-eight interviews and two cups of tar-like black liquid later, she had nothing. The building had been swept with no signs of anyone unexpected. None of the interviews turned up any useful information and no one seemed to pop as involved. The only positive note was that the EMTs had been able to save Officer Kohl and he was now in stable but critical condition at St. Pete's. After a quick chat with Commander Nuez, Ell gave the all clear and ordered the building reopened. Lund and five additional crime scene techs descended on Interrogation Room Two but, as with the previous scenes, Ell didn't expect them to find anything of consequence.

Ell, defeated, headed back to her office and found Colonel Craig deep in research.

"Your I.T. man came through with a list of five organizations with active software in the last eight hours."

"Five?" it was better than sixteen but Ell found it very disturbing that five organizations found a use for this particular software in such a short time.

"It gets better, I was running down the list of users and your boy wasn't kidding when he said GenData was picky about who they'd sell to. It's a high-end list of US and ally acronym organizations. One interesting item did stick out, however. The US military has two licenses. One belongs to Unit Alfa Delta Oscar. That is the extraction unit I worked with in Columbia and Peru. The second belongs to Unit Hotel Lima Alfa. A unit that I have yet to find any substantial information about. I don't just mean it's above my clear-ance level either. Aside from being on this list, I can't find any evidence that it exists. It's a ghost."

"Let me guess, it was also active today."

"You ought to be a psychic."

Chapter Fourteen

*J*ones called in with a quick update, letting Ell know that the medical contact had been a dead end and had never heard of Claire Fenn. The professor, however, had found an attendance record from her final semester. While her transcript indicated she had taken his course, an optional study in contract law, his records had no indication she was ever in attendance. Ell told her to gather what she could and head back. She wanted to see the record before questioning Ms. Fenn.

She fired Rique a quick text telling him the precinct had been given the all clear and to let her know when he and Baker were back in house. She wanted to sit down and brainstorm before jumping into yet another line of investigation. This case was expanding, two dead, two injured and no idea where it was going next. She needed to regroup and start pulling things back in before they spiraled out of control.

"Give us twenty. Just wrapping up. – S"

Twenty minutes, too much time to stew. Ell knew that was what she'd do if she stayed in her office so she headed down the hall and jetted up the stairs to the second floor.

"Lund was back in his office with a new set of samples and items from the most recent crime scene. They were stacking up on this case, but this one was different. This one was in their own house.

"Don't, Frost. I don't have time for your crap. We literally just got this shit back up here."

"I know, I just wanted to check on those tests you were running when all hell broke loose."

"Oh, blood analysis and prints off the items on scene at the Sandbox. Bad news is only your hostage's were found in both cases. All the blood can be attributed to her. There were prints on some of the toys, a couple blades, the flogger. All hers, though there were a few smudges and partials we can't match due to quality."

"Do you have any good news to go with the slew of bad?"

"We were able to analyze the explosive. It was pentaerythritol tetranitrat or PENTA. Basically C-4's little brother. It's not an easy product to get your hands on. It's mostly used by the Finish military but can be found state-side if you know where to look."

"When you say little brother you mean not as powerful."

"It's a rough scale and it all depends on how much we are comparing but, yes. On a general scale of explosive force it's more directional and less potent. This particular load was set-up beside the main hallway. It was powerful, but the core of the blast was positioned to blow upwards as opposed to out."

"You're losing me."

"This was setup to harm, possibly maim, anyone foolish enough to trip the pressure plate but it wasn't optimized to kill. If properly aligned that device could have taken out the entire back side of the building."

"Really? Our perp hasn't been reluctant to kill up to this point. Was it just a sloppy install or messed up device?"

"I won't rule it out but it's unlikely. As I said PENTA is more directional than C-4. It's something you choose when you need that control. Maybe it's all they had and maybe they screwed up the install but..."

"That's a lot of maybes for someone we believe to be a pro. That's the problem here, always just one or two little things that scream amateur but way too much saying pro to make it true."

"You could be dealing with a team, one pro and one apprentice."

"That would explain this issue but not the apartment. There is no way the top end of the team would let the bottom go into a torture situation without all the tools."

"Shit, you're the detective; I'm just running numbers and chemicals up here. The figuring out shit is on you."

"Thanks Lund, and I mean that, thanks."

"You want to thank me, stay off my ass while I run the labs on this latest batch and stop finding me fresh crime scenes."

"Your mouth to dog's ear."

"What?"

"I said, your mouth to dog's ear."

"Jesus, God's ear, Frost, God's ear."

"Does this look like a fucking church. Besides, how the hell do we even know if God has ears?"

"Just go away, Frost. Please."

With a smile, she turned and headed back out and down the stairs. Fifteen minutes well spent.

Sitting around the case board, having just received a full update on the precinct lockdown, breach and security tampering, her team remained speechless.

"There are the inquisitive minds I rely on."

"Jesus, Ell. It's just so un-damn-heard of," said Rique.

"And risky," added Baker. "I know this perp is good but even for a pro this was a huge risk. We picked up Dover less than twelve hours prior which means they had no time to prepare. They were confident they could beat the cameras but without time to study the precinct they didn't know what type of additional security they were walking into."

"Apparently they knew enough. But that brings up another question. How'd they know we had Dover?" asked Jones. "We kept the pickup quiet, covered our tracks and kept him off the scanner and the books."

"Even with the best operation there is a paper trail," commented Colonel Craig. "That's how we locate hostages in the remote areas of countries like Columbia. Someone always leaves bread crumbs to follow, even when they do their best to cover their tracks. In this case there was plenty out there. Your D.A. had been working on the material witness order and warrant through most of the day yesterday. Those requests and inquiries leave evidence. The order itself leaves a paper trail. Then there were about two dozen officers involved in the double operation and another seven or eight that would have seen Dover at the precinct last night or this morning." He could see the disdain in their reaction to the possibility of an inside job. "I know you don't want to look at fellow officers but I'm just trying to point out that there were plenty of crumbs to latch onto."

Ell couldn't shake the feeling that the entire mess was still too sloppy. "So, let's assume the killer knew we were pulling Dover in as soon as we knew it. That gives them what, fourteen hours to plan and execute this strike. It's still not enough time to do it right, which means they're running on instinct and fear. They had to take him out before we talked to him, otherwise they'd take their time and do this once they had all the information. Our shift changes, security layout, etc. The only reason to rush it was to make sure he didn't talk and still, even rushed and with little planning, they were in and out in less than fifteen minutes."

"Were they?" asked Rique. "Are we sure of the timeframe?"

"The bodies were still warm and spewing hot blood when I found them and I had the building locked down within two minutes. Unless they can walk through walls they were gone by then."

"Ok so that covers out."

"What are you talking about?"

"You said they were in and out in less than fifteen minutes. We've established they were out within minutes of the crime but do we actually know when they came in?"

"The security footage went dark approximately ten minutes before I found the bodies. We assume they cut the cameras just before their entrance."

"Makes sense," said Jones, "If you're packing that kind of hardware it would be crazy not to use it to cover your entry."

"The timeline is too tight." said Rique, "They had to gain entry, and we know they didn't come in through the front, locate Dover who had just been moved to interrogation, an odd place for a witness, and do it all without being seen. Even for a pro with preparation that's tight."

"I'm starting to think nothing is too tight for this perp," replied Ell trying to rub the frustration out of her temples. "It's like they get off on the risk, on making things more difficult than they need to be."

Baker shook her head, her red locks swaying side to side. "Does anyone else feel like we're spinning our wheels here? Every new crime scene adds more questions and supplies us with less evidence."

"Yeah," replied Ell with a defeated sigh. "So we need to stop spinning assumptions and go back to what we know as fact. What did you find out about the collar?"

Rique looked at Baker then answered, "All five jewelers were taken by how intricate the insets were and the craftsmanship of the piece. None would cop to making, selling, or seeing it. I get the impression they would have claimed it out of pride alone if it was theirs."

"So it was another bust."

"I don't know if I'd call it a bust, Detective Baker managed to order three beautiful custom pieces and three of the five jewelers were able to provide us lists of artists they felt could be the manufacturer based on the, and I quote, complexity and subtle nuances of the piece. There are about twenty in total, unfortunately none are local."

Ell gave Baker a raised eyebrow and got the feeling she was going to end up in some new silver restraints, clamps or pins someday very soon. The thought brought a heat to her skin as her mind began to wander and long for something, anything enjoyable. "Ok, I want you making calls and running those twenty down. Start with any names that show up on multiple lists. Jones, shoot me a copy of that professor's attendance data. I need to review it before I head up to the hospital to question Ms. Fenn. The rest of you, grab a bite, find a thread and start pulling. If something unravels I want to know about it immediately."

Ell took fifteen minutes to review the documents provided by Jones. The attendance records were not very informative. They were tracked only five times throughout the semester at random intervals. It was interesting that they did not include Claire Fenn's name but not overly suspicious. Setting them aside she grabbed her coat and headed for the door.

St. Pete's was a twenty-five minute drive from the precinct, standard ambulance response time was sixteen minutes, Ell did it in fourteen and a half just to prove that she could. The blood stains on her slacks had dried but she still managed to garner a few sideways glances and at least one nurse that asked if she needed assistance.

She had checked in with admitting, Claire Fenn was on floor six in unit 612. Before heading up she made a quick detour through a large white corridor to the ER. A handsome young man in his mid twenties sat at the ER admitting desk finalizing some routine paperwork. Ell laid her badge on the counter in front of him and flashed a genuine smile. "I'm wondering if you can give me an update on Officer Jerry Kohl, he was brought in earlier this morning with major throat lacerations."

"One moment, please," he rolled further behind a plexi-glass barrier, picked up his phone and made a call. Ell could not make out the conversation but when he rolled his chair back to the main desk he said, "Someone will be with you shortly, ma'am."

The word spiked an involuntary anger but Ell recognized that the man was just trying to be polite so she slid the badge back in her pocket and said, "Thanks."

"Lieutenant Frost," she heard from behind her to the right. An older officer in full uniform waved her to the side. She recognized him from Central PD but struggled to pull his name from the far reaches of her memory. "Officer Danuski, right."

"That's right. Jerry and I were partners for four years before he transferred to the eleventh. When I heard what happened I took the day and rushed over. I've asked the hospital to let me know if anyone is inquiring, just in case. I don't know what happened, no one is talking about it, but when a cop goes down in his own station, well, I figured I better put some precautions in place."

"A good plan, I can tell you that Officer Kohl wasn't the target and we don't believe him to be in any imminent danger but precaution never hurts. How's he doing?"

"He's still out but he's stable. He's had something called an anoxic brain injury, basically he's in a short term coma. The doctor said it was touch and go when he arrived. He's lost a lot of blood and drastically cut the oxygen to his brain. They don't know when he'll come to. It could be tomorrow, it could be next week but the doctors are optimistic. They tell me this type of coma rarely lasts. Another thirty seconds on the floor bleeding out and well..."

She could see him fight from welling up, trying to maintain the manly cop appearance.

"Stay with him, it will mean something when he comes around."

Ell rested a hand on his shoulder, a brief gesture of solidarity and then headed back down the glowing white corridors in search of a stairwell. She passed three elevators along the way but couldn't bring herself to use one. At this rate she'd be able to skip leg workouts for a week. She said a quick, "Thanks," that the building only had six floors and headed straight over to check in with the nurses for unit 612.

After a quick flash of the badge they sent her down two more halls to room 61253. A uniformed officer sat beside the door, his head slowly twisting, monitoring the halls. She could tell he was at full alert, a rarity for someone on a basic door watch. It was a boring but important job. One this officer seemed to take pride in.

She pulled out her badge as she approached.

"Officer... Smitts," she said taking a look at his nametag. "How's the patient?"

"Alive, sir. Aside from that you would need to ask the doctors. I have not been in to see her. My orders were to restrict access to medical and police personnel and I can't do that from inside."

"Any visitors?"

"None that saw her. Aside from the doctor at seven a.m. and two nurses at six a.m and eleven a.m. there has been no entry, sir."

"Any attempts?"

"Yes, sir. A young woman and a military officer. I informed them that Ms. Fenn was unavailable and directed their medical questions to the nurse's station."

"Jon Strand and Elizebeth Plante?

"Yes, sir, those were the names they gave."

"Thanks. I'll need fifteen or twenty minutes with Ms. Fenn, feel free to take a break, stretch your legs, grab a coffee. Whatever you need."

"Thank you, sir but I'm good. My shift change is in two hours and eleven minutes. I will be fine until my replacement arrives."

'Rob's robotic overlords are replacing my officers,' she thought bringing a smile to her face as she strolled past him into the room. Claire Fenn sat on the edge of her bed staring out a sixth floor window at the city below. Her wounds were stitched and beginning to heal and now, without the blood, Ell could tell she was a well toned and fit young lady. Her five foot seven stature was offset by strong muscle tone and defined features. Her jet black hair was cropped at the shoulder, shorter than in the photo Ell had seen at her apartment. The shorter length accentuated her jawline and gave the woman a more serious look.

"Ms. Fenn, my name is Lieutenant Frost. I need to ask you some questions about what happened."

Her eyes were steel, emotionless orbs. Perhaps a form of dealing with the trauma she'd endured.

"Okay."

"Why don't you tell me what you remember and I'll ask questions to help fill in the gaps if possible."

"I," she paused, "I was relaxing at home. I don't know when it was. I've lost track of time. I know I had the day off from work. I was relaxing at home and there was a knock on the door. We rarely get company and my roommate, I have a roommate, anyway, Liz was working so it was odd. Like I said, company is rare. I didn't think much of it, opened the door and there was this man. He was wearing a baseball hat and had a mask. Like a cowboy thing, a... bandana pulled up to his nose. Before I knew what happened he hit me. Hard," she said pointing to the purple bruise below her right eye.

"Did you recognize this man?"

"No, I could only see his eyes but he... well he wasn't familiar."

"Go on, he hit you..." prompted Ell.

"Right, I must have blacked out for a second. When I came to I was in my bedroom. Strapped to the bed. I still had my clothes on but I was tied, you know, spread eagle, tied to the four corners of the bed. Something was over my eyes and I couldn't see. I couldn't move. I tried but I couldn't. I heard screaming from the apartment, screaming and begging. I can still hear the howls," she trembled visibly as she struggled to get through the story.

"It seemed like hours, hours of screaming and then nothing, dead silence. I was sure that whatever had happened, I was next. Someone came into the room, he was laughing and I could smell the blood on him. I could actually taste it, you know, that iron taste. I started to scream and he laughed harder. He untied me, pulled me to my feet, still blindfolded and led me out of the room. I didn't know where we were going, what he would do to me. I couldn't see but I made a lunge to my right trying to get free. I slipped and went down hard. I'm not sure what I hit but my head took a nasty smack. Just before I blacked out again I heard another scream. Not like the others. It was closer and louder."

Ell watched her struggle with the words, as if she was

fighting to get them out. Her eyes, however, never changed. They were stunned and distant. It was disconcerting.

"When I came back around I was naked, on my knees and tied over something. I think it was suede. It was soft. I couldn't move or see. There was something wrapped around my head. It was tight and uncomfortable."

This was how she had been found, stretched over a pommel horse, restrained and hooded.

"I don't know how long I was there. I kept blacking out and when I'd wake, sometimes it was quiet, but only for a while. Only until the pain began and once it did it didn't stop. Not until I blacked out again. I screamed. I tried to scream but no one heard me. He said no one would hear me. He laughed and said I was his now."

"Claire, I know this is difficult but I need to know. Did he rape you?"

"No. there were times I wished he had, just to escape the pain, but he didn't. He just kept, well, I don't even know the word."

'It's torture,' thought Ell. 'The word you can't find is torture.' Her response confirmed the medical records but Ell had to ask.

"Then, somehow, by some miracle, I woke up here."

"Is there anything you can tell me about the man, Claire, anything at all?"

"I don't know, it's all, it's all so hard. He was tall. Not giant but taller than me, six footish, maybe. He had dark hair cut short, trimmed to about a half inch on the sides. The hat covered the top so I didn't see it. I don't know what else. I only saw him for a minute before he hit me."

"Would you be willing to sit down with a sketch artist? It

may help. Sometimes you don't realize how much you actually saw."

"If it will help."

"Okay, I'm going to try and organize that for tomorrow morning. If the doctors still have you admitted we will do it here otherwise I will set it up at the eleventh precinct and have someone come get you. Just one more thing and then I'll stop pestering you. When you went missing we started to run a background check..."

Seeing where she was going Claire cut her off "Oh, you're wondering who Claire Fenn is?"

"More, who she was. You seem to have appeared out of thin air the day you signed in at Columbia."

"Yeah, well Claire Fenn has a good history, good times in college, a decent career and no background to run from. Jane Sandusky of Winterset, Iowa had a lot more baggage. A violent ex, two dead parents and not a lot of career prospects. When she was twenty-one her then dirtbag, abusive boyfriend got into a bar fight with some young man that made eyes at her. He put said young man in the morgue. When the D.A. offered her the opportunity to get out of Iowa with a new name and fresh start in exchange for testimony that she probably would have given freely, she took the deal and Claire Fenn was born."

"This dirtbag boyfriend, does he have a name?"

"Jonas Petruk, he should be doing fifteen to life somewhere right now."

"Thanks for clearing it up. I don't want to drag up painful history but it was a hole so we needed to fill it."

"I just... I just really want to go home. Has anyone contacted Liz?"

"We've been in touch with her. She and Mr. Strand were by to see you earlier but for your protection we were restricting access. If you'd like, I can let them know they can see you now."

"Yeah, thanks."

"Thank you. I may have more questions for you later but for now, get some rest and heal up."

"That's exactly what the nurses keep saying."

Ell felt sorry for the woman. It was difficult to imagine what she had been through. It was a scar that would never heal. On the way out she let Officer Smitts know that Mr. Strand and Ms. Plante were approved to visit. He nodded to the affirmative, his eyes continuously scanning the halls. Everything about the moment gave Ell the chills. The robot overlord cops were unnerving as fuck.

Chapter Fifteen

*O*nce she had settled back into her office, Ell began updating the file and took a few moments to reflect on the conversation with Claire Fenn. The question that reverberated in her mind was why? Why, drag Jellic to that location? They hadn't found any link between him and either Claire or Liz. There was no reason to use that particular spot. It wasn't secluded, soundproofed, or even a half decent location for torture and murder yet it was specifically chosen.

Why take Claire hostage? It wasn't to silence her or he'd have killed her there and then. The ransom sounded good at first but that didn't fit either. He waited at least twenty-four hours to make the call and did he really expect to be paid? If so, by who? Claire had no family, no nest egg of her own and the roommate certainly wouldn't have been able to put together two point five million dollars. No, she was certain the ransom was a ruse, but that left the reason for taking her a complete mystery and brought on more questions.

Why torture her? She wasn't raped, wasn't questioned yet she was continuously tortured. For what? Just to hear her scream? Ell knew there were people out there who would revel in it for just that reason but they were literal psychopaths, eratic, manic and sloppy. This guy was meticulous, trained and careful. It didn't match. Like most things in this case it didn't add up.

She couldn't reconcile it. No matter how she spun it around it just didn't fit. Feeling the frustration growing and ready to take over, she sat back and forced herself to let it go.

'I need a distraction,' she thought and picked up the phone to call Scribbler. Denise Cue, or Scribbler as the squad referred to her when she was out of earshot, was the best sketch artist in the city.

"Hello?"

"Denise, it's Lieutenant Frost, I hope I didn't catch you at a bad time."

"I'm just wrapping up for the day, what's up."

Ell checked the time, 4:23 p.m., 'Must be nice.'

"I have a witness in this murder, kidnapping, second murder and attempted murder mess I'm working."

"Is this the hostage rescue from last night?"

"Yes my witness is the hostage. She's been through hell and only got a quick glimpse at the demon that took her there. I was hoping you could work your magic fingers and calming voodoo to coax an image out of her."

"I can work it in tomorrow morning. Can you have her down here for nine?"

"At this point I'm not sure. She's currently under care at St. Pete's. If she's released tonight, yes. Otherwise, is there any chance you can do it there?"

Ell knew how much Scribbler valued her swanky lounge

when it came to putting a witness at ease in order to pull an image together. She figured it was a bunch of crap just to get the sweet gigs, but who was she to argue with results.

"I can, but I'm going to warn you now, a hospital is going to have a serious negative effect on my accuracy."

"I know but let's call a spade a spade, Denise, your half assed is twice as good as the next guy's best. I'll work with what you get me. Speed's more important on this one."

"I appreciate the compliment but I'm no Picasso."

"Well, I certainly hope not, you can't tell what that fucker's painting. Nine a.m. at St. Pete's, I'll let them know you're coming and update you if the location changes. Thanks for working this in."

"We all do our parts, Lieutenant, and sometimes it makes a difference."

Ell disconnected and had not even released the handset when the phone rang. Surprised, she answered without checking the ID.

"Lieutenant Frost speaking."

"Well, aren't we formal today," came the unmistakable baritone of M.E. Sanders."

"You caught me in a slow moment, what's up?"

"I figured you would be down here inquiring about Mr. Jensen Dover sometime today, probably just as I was shutting things down. I thought I'd save you the trip. There's nothing there but what it looked like, a sharp knife drug across the jugular from left to right. Based on the angle and depth of the wound the safe money is that he was attacked from the front. That makes your killer right handed or at least ambidextrous. It should narrow your suspect pool by about ten percent. You're welcome."

Ell laughed, "Every bit helps. Have you seen the medical report on Officer Kohl?"

"Yes, it was sent over about forty minutes ago, he's stable but hasn't regained consciousness."

"How do his wounds match up with Dover's?"

"Similar though not as deep, officer Kohl was standing at the time of the attack whereas, I speculate that Mr. Dover was seated. The killer could not get the same leverage on the officer so the wound is similar but slightly shallower. It's probably what saved his life. Well, that and a very talented and on the ball first officer on scene."

"More like late and lucky but we can agree to disagree. So aside from the slight depth difference, we're talking about the same knife and style?"

"Damn near identical. It had to be the same attacker and the same weapon. Both cuts were made with a six inch knife with a thick tapered blade, to be precise."

"A standard issue hunting knife?"

"That or something similar."

'Maybe a military survival knife,' she thought.

"Any defensive wounds?"

"A large gash on officer Kohl's right forearm and some bruises on his left inner thigh. It looks like he tried to fight back. Dover had three slices on his palms which are likely defensive."

"Thanks for the call, and saving me the trip. I owe you."

"Feel free to pay me back via a good word to that fire-cracker red head under your command."

"The one young enough to be your grand-daughter? Ten minutes with her would put you belly up on that slab of yours and I'd be out my favorite M.E."

"I've been belly up on that slab before and if memory serves it wasn't half bad."

"Christ Sanders, imagery I did not need. Consider that payment for the call."

The next hour was spent updating the case board and checking in with her team. Jones advised that while Ell was gone D. A. Stranik had contacted her. Jensen Dover's untimely death, when coupled with the tape Ell had of him discussing a possible payoff in relation to the Jellic case, had finally been enough to convince Judge Stower to sign off on a search warrant. She and Detective Baker had executed the warrant, wading through a barrage of pompous attorneys who swore they would have their badges and threatened legal action while they did so. The detectives were just starting to review the files.

Rique had feelers out for the most likely sources in relation to the collar but had yet to hear back from the majority of possible suppliers. Ell took the opportunity to get him digging into Jane Sandusky. She gave him the details of Claire Fenn's history and asked him to check out and verify the story. She had no reason to doubt it, but it always paid to verify a witness statement if possible.

Colonel Craig had been digging through the second Jellic military file he had received. As with the first it was highly redacted but he was comparing the two in hopes that something new would surface. He kept his head down, buried in the file while she checked in with her team and a few other officers in the bullpen.

Ell had been back in her office for a little over ten minutes when the Colonel stuck his head in. She waved him in and watched as he took a quick look behind him and then calmly shut the door.

The last time her office door had been closed with her inside immediately sprung to mind. A wild flurry of skin and hair as Jamie Baker had forced her down onto her desk, cuffed her to the corners, tore her clothes off and began to devour her. The memory brought back a rush of ecstasy. It washed over her as she stared at the General. She could feel the wetness of arousal as her mind ran with the possibilities. His voice broke through her fantasy and the slight waiver in it pulled her back to reality.

"I think I may have found something. To be honest, I've been sitting across the hall for the last twenty minutes trying to convince myself I'm wrong. That it's just a coincidence."

"In my experience it's never a coincidence. Not when you want it to be. What did you find?"

"The file I located, the second Jellic file, is basically the same as the one provided to you. From what I can tell there's nothing added and nothing missing but the redactions are different. Neither is more or less thorough, but certain phrases redacted in your file are included in mine and vice versa. It's all pretty standard, except this."

He slipped a sheet of paper across her desk. She had seen it in her copy of the file. It was a highly redacted report outlining Jellic's initial statement to the J.A.G. officer first assigned to investigate the potential charges of treason for passing state secrets. From what Ell could gather it was a fishing expedition and over the course of their conversation the prosecutor had been throwing out the code names of classified projects and attempting to gauge Jellic's reaction. All the information on the actual projects had been redacted but you could see the pattern and understand the questioning based on what was available. The copy Colonel Craig had just handed her was identical to her own with the exception of two words. Unit H.L.A.

"Again, I've never heard of Unit H.L.A., nor have I been able to find any information on it," said the Colonel. "What are the odds we would come across both Unit Hotel Lima Alfa and Unit H.L.A. in the course of this investigation and not have it mean something?"

"Son of a bitch."

Ell had been in a decent mood, slightly frustrated but content. This hit her like a wall of stress.

Without another word she picked up her handset and dialed 145.

"Commander Nuez' office, Kieth Dillon speaking."

"Keith, it's Frost. I need ten minutes with the Commander."

"Certainly, Lieutenant Frost, I can schedule you in for 9:45 tomorrow morning."

"Today Keith, preferably now."

"I'm sorry Lieutenant but the Commander is fully booked for the rest of the day and must be out by six p.m sharp this evening."

"Keith, think back on our long relationship. Have I ever called for a meeting with the Commander when it wasn't a god damn emergency? This isn't a request. I will be up there in five minutes. Make sure he's free."

She hung up and swung her gaze up at the Colonel. "You need to give me twenty minutes. Please, just wait until I'm back in this office."

"Ell? You know I have to report this. I can't sit on it. Not something like this. Not if your investigation is heading towards military personnel."

"You'll agree to keep your damn trap shut for twenty minutes or I'll drag you outside and cuff you to a fucking pole. I need time to get ahead of this before the D.O.D. tries to steamroll over me and shut down my investigation."

She could see the internal struggle playing out on his brow. She understood. It was a big ask, and if the roles were reversed she wasn't sure what she'd do.

"Twenty minutes," he resigned, "but after that, fuck, after that I don't know what I'm doing."

He was struggling with something that she understood, honor and loyalty. Honor for the dead, for himself and for the truth versus the loyalty to his unit and to the core. On those rare occasions where the two demanded conflicting actions it could literally tear you apart. She couldn't help him because, frankly, she didn't know what the right path was.

She walked up to him, looked him in the eyes and could see the pain flooding through them. Her hands cupped the sides of his face as she rose up on her toes and embraced his lips with her own. It was soft, deep and unexpected but it was one hell of a kiss.

"Thank you," she whispered and headed out the door for the stairs.

She bypassed the elevator without a second thought and within minutes she strolled through the outer door of the Commander's office.

"Keith, I hope you cleared his schedule," she said as she strolled past him.

"Lieutenant if you'll wait one..."

She ignored his pleading, pushed open the Commander's door and headed in, unannounced. Commander Nuez was at his desk, alone, waiting with his hands folded in front of him.

"What took you so long? Keith urgently interrupted my meeting and escorted Sergeant Dorns out in a panicked rush at least thirty seconds ago."

"Stairs," was her only response.

"I suppose that's the safer bet given recent events. One day you'll need to tell me how you get him to react like that," the Commander nodded towards his door, "He's highly efficient when he needs to be."

"Threats, sir, I use good old fashioned threats."

"So what's the emergency, Lieutenant?"

"This Jellic, Fenn, Dover mess is about to become even more of a shit storm and I felt it best to get you up to speed before your phone starts ringing."

The Commamder's eyes went dark and he nodded for her to continue.

"Our investigation has led us to a line of inquiry that is going to be difficult to pursue, not simply because of what we are pursuing but because it's going to reopen the jurisdictional issues."

"Jellic may be up in the air, so is the Fenn case given her standing in the core, though the tie to the Jellic matter helps, but Dover? That is a civilian in a civilian location. No questions there."

"Yes, but as a civilian, pursuing this lead is going to be next to impossible."

"Spell it out for me."

"I assume you are up to date on the case files?"

"Yes."

"Good, the breach in security this morning was aided by a security bypass software called CleanSlate. It is sold and monitored privately by GenData Group. They have a very sophisticated vetting process and a highly secure anti-piracy algorithm. Currently there are sixteen copies in existence all with civilian law enforcement, military, or government agencies. There's a lot of acronym based organizations on the list."

"And they're confident that another copy isn't out there. A copy or clone?"

"I spoke with the genius behind the anti-piracy algorithm and he assures me that, as of right now, it's foolproof."

"These guys can be pretty cocky, how confident are you that he's not just covering his ass?"

"Pretty damn confident because if he is I'm going to boot it right back to Seattle when I see him tomorrow night."

She saw the realization in his eyes. "You're joking, right?"

Ell shook her head.

"Rob built the software used to breach our precinct?"

"The antipiracy code it uses, yes. It was a side contract and apparently a great deal, yadda yadda."

"You don't think…" he let the question hang in the air.

"No, oh hell no. In fact it's worked to our benefit as he was able to sweet talk GenData into providing access to a private tracking server. He gave us a list of systems online today, one of which was a phantom organization within the US military referred to as Unit Hotel Lima Alfa. Neither my team nor Colonel Craig has been able to find any information on them."

"You said 'one of', which means there were others making this a pretty slim lead, Lieutenant."

"It was a slim lead, this morning when we discovered it, and it was placed on the back burner until ten minutes ago when Colonel Craig brought me a second copy of Jellic's redacted file. Same file, different redactions and this one had a previously unknown reference to a Unit H.L.A. It was one of the classified items he was accused of leaking."

"And the issue becomes how do you investigate a military organization without tipping off the military?"

"That's not an option because I have a dedicated military officer sitting in my office graciously providing me twenty minutes to discuss this matter before he has a duty to report it to the Department of Defense."

"Son of a bitch."

Ell was taken aback, it wasn't often the Commander cursed and, for some reason, it felt far more vile and effective when he did.

"Yeah, that's what I said."

"I figure you have forty-five minutes until the D.O.D. descends on the eleventh precinct to shut us down, confiscate our files and take over. At which point, I'd bet good money the entire case gets neatly buried and forgotten."

The Commander picked up his phone and rubbed his temples, pausing before dialing. She could tell he was struggling with what he was about to do. With a deep breath he dialed.

When the other party picked up he said, "I need all remnants of a case file wiped from our records, backups included, and transferred to Lieutenant Frost's home unit. We have twenty minutes and I need it done well, there can't be a record of the transaction. Is it possible?"

The Commander paused then continued, "Thanks, enjoy

the conference and if you get a chance be sure to see the Space Needle."

Ell sat slack jawed, "Did you just..."

"Yes, but that only takes care of soft copies. You need to gather your team and your files and get them off-site. We won't be able to stop them from scooping up the physical evidence but there wasn't much there. I can get Lund to misfile a vial of each blood sample before they swoop in to clean us out."

"The collar?" said Ell without realizing it was out loud.

"What?"

"There was a silver jeweled collar found on the victim at the Sandbox, it's a unique item and my team is running down the manufacturer. We need to protect it and to preserve the chain of evidence."

"Evidence often gets placed in the wrong box. It's a big storage area after all. I'll take care of it. Go get your team and yourself out of here."

"The Colonel? He's waiting in my office."

He hit the speaker button on his phone and dialed Ell's extension. It rang four times and went to voicemail. He hung up and tried again. On the fourth attempt the line picked up.

"Hello?" came an apprehensive voice.

"Colonel Craig, this is Commander Nuez. If possible, I would like to have a quick discussion before you make the call I know you are about to make. I'm not going to try and stop you but I'd like your input on what I can expect to follow. Can you give me ten minutes?"

"Yes, sir, ten minutes will work, where would you like to meet?"

"My office should do, I will send my assistant down to escort you up. In fact, you can make the call from here once we've talked."

He disconnected the line, called Keith and asked him to find and escort the Colonel, then he turned to Ell and said, "Go do what needs to be done. I need to phone Lund before the Colonel gets up here. Get your team and get gone, you're now all on official 'stress leave' while I deal with the fallout. Use the time well."

She knew what he meant and intended to do just that.

Chapter Sixteen

It took fifteen minutes, some dodged questions and, eventually, a harshly worded order to ensure her team, their files, the case board and all other research materials related to the case were secured and out of the precinct. While packing her own personal files she noticed that Colonel Craig had left the page from the secondary Jellic file on her desk. She felt as if she was betraying a confidence but apologized to the air and slid it in with the rest of her files.

There weren't many options for a secondary location and the Commander had instructed Rob to transfer everything to her home unit so she resigned to the lost privacy and let the team know they would be setting up in her suburban two-storey brownstone. The invasion was a pain in the ass but necessary. Granted the home was big enough but it was a home, her home, and not a place she wanted to share with three other people, even her team. With her single desktop computer and very limited office space it was going to be awkward and would make running this case twice as difficult, but when the only other option was to bend over and take what the Department of Defense was dishing out, she'd take it. She preferred a little foreplay and a lot more satisfaction if she was bending over.

"Shit, L.T. living the high life," commented Jones as they walked into the now fully renovated Victorian home. Ell had forgotten that, with the exception of Baker, her team hadn't seen the house. The thought made her realize that she and Jamie would be working here, together, for the next few days. She had found it easy to compartmentalize their affair when in the working atmosphere. Seeing her now, smiling coyly as she sauntered through the private space made Ell realize that this was going to be far more difficult. She was already fighting off the urge to haul the feisty red head into the bedroom for some much needed stress relief. What she'd give to nestle back in between her thighs and run her tongue across her sweet lips.

"Frosty home, Frost," commented Rique snapping Ell out of the thought and earning a groan from the other two women.

"Ok, let's set some ground rules. First, no puns," she glared at Rique, "I'm setting up in the office. We can clear the furniture out of the way and use the living room for the case board and a round table space. The three of you will need to find a decent area in the kitchen or den to work out of. If you make a mess in my damn kitchen, clean it up and if I catch any of you scrounging through my drawers or snooping through my room you had better be prepared to be my fucking slave for the remainder of known existence. Tech is going to be tight. I have an old laptop that can be setup and shared if needed, otherwise scrounge what you can find and keep everything off the department network. We're on our own here."

"Never pictured Lieutenant Ell Frost as the Rebel leader but I'm in, let's take down this Empire," said Baker, garnering odd looks from the other three.

"Seriously," she prompted. "Star Wars? Rebels? Empire? Does none of this ring a bell?"

"No clue," replied Jones.

"Star what," asked Rique casting a glance at Ell.

"Not really," said Ell, "but we can go with it. We're the Rebels, they're the Empire. Let's just get to work and nail them down before they 'strike back'.

Jones and Rique let out a suppressed laugh as Baker looked at the smiles crossing all three of their faces.

"Fuck you all," she laughed and they went about setting up the case board and files in a reflection of what they had taken down before they fled the precinct.

The collective shit hit the fan about an hour after their evacuation. Commander Nuez had contacted Ell and advised that she and her team should steer clear of the precinct for a couple days. Colonel Craig's call had triggered a chain reaction through the military command structure and landed a squad of J.A.G. representatives on-site. They were now combing through anything they could find. The Commander had fought to keep them out, but they had gone over his head and the mayor and chief of police relinquished control of the case with nary a fight.

Ell had seen it coming. The real shit storm was just beginning to build. Once the J.A.G. reps figured out that they had wiped every bite of data on the case, the serious questions and accusations would begin. In the meantime, while the Commander kept them busy trying to find someone's head for their platter, Ell and her team would dig and hopefully something would pop.

Part of her wanted to reach out to Colonel Craig, to explain, but she knew she couldn't. 'Honor and loyalty,' she thought. 'We all have our own boundaries for each.'

By the time they had setup, began running through the files and ensured they would be ready to resume the investigation come morning, the clock was just ticking past nine. Ell told them to head out and regroup at their new base of operations at seven-thirty. Baker looked at her with a questioning glance as they filed out but Ell shook her off. As much as she would love to spend a night entwined with the gorgeous young woman, she needed to set some boundaries, for now. Besides, she couldn't remember the last time she actually got to sleep in her own bed. A hot shower and a solid seven hours sleep sounded damn fine.

Chapter Seventeen

*E*ll had just stepped out of the shower, dried her hair and slipped into a white silk robe when the doorbell rang.

'What the hell,' she thought as she made her way down the stairs to the front door, grabbing her service pistol off the dresser along the way. She took a look through the peephole and saw the firm, muscular form of Colonel Anthony Craig waiting on her doorstep.

'Son of a bitch.' Turning and seeing the case board and files in clear view she called out. "One second, I just got out of the shower," and ran over to close the French doors that separated the living room from the hall.

Gathering her composure, and forgetting what she was wearing, she pulled open the front door.

"Colonel?" she feigned surprise.

"Lieu... Lieutenant," he stumbled catching a glimpse of her tight silk robe, the water causing it to hug her body and increase the allure. "Sorry, did I catch you at a bad time?"

Ell looked down and suddenly realized what she was wearing. "Shit, sorry, I literally just got out of the shower."

"No apology needed, trust me, the outfit is... flattering."

Part of her wanted to pull him inside. She was, after all, standing in the doorway talking to him in a wet white silk robe. It wasn't hiding much from him or the neighbors. The fact that her home now housed all the information that his organization was searching for made the decision a little more difficult. She'd forgone modesty for the job in the past but Mr. and Mrs Swetsky in the bungalow across the street may not appreciated her need to do so. With a quick look down at her all but naked form, she shook her head and stepped to the side.

"Christ, get your ass in here before I give the neighborhood children a free show."

"It's not a bad show. Honestly, they'd probably appreciate it."

Ell smiled at the compliment. "Momma Swetsky may think different."

"Then Momma Swetsky needs to live a little and learn to enjoy the sites while they're available."

She closed the door behind him leaning back against it and pressing her tits and core tight against the silk without realizing what she was doing.

"Did you come here to banter and flirt or did you have something else in mind."

He was struggling. She could see it in his eyes. The struggle of a man unsure what path to take.

"Honestly the banter is a little easier to cope with and the view sure isn't making it difficult."

"But?"

He took a breath and tried to focus, "But, I came to apologize. I know you can't and won't understand, but I didn't have a choice. I had to make the call. I didn't want to do it. I knew where it was likely to lead, but I have a sworn duty. Like it or not, I had to call it in and report."

"Look, Colonel."

He burst into laughter, "Sorry, the title was just so out of place. We're standing in the foyer of your beautiful home, you're draped in wet white silk which may as well be transparent and still you use my formal title. I think as long as I can see that you have a fondness for hearts," he pointed to the heart shaped nipple ring pressing against her robe, "we should probably stick with Tony."

Ell smiled, "Well then, Tony, I get it. Trust me, I get it. I have bosses, a chain of command and loyalty to the job. I know that, occasionally, that means we have to do things we don't like. Things we're not proud of. It's hard to fight against that. The only question I ask is, was it done for a good reason? I can't always say yes and I'm sure you can't either, but we strive for a lot more yeses than nos and hope we can deal with the fallout personally."

"I can't help but think this one fell into the solid no category. The D.O.D. passed this back off to General Costan with the J.A.G. core who promptly sidelined me and informed me he would be in touch to discuss what, if any, role I would have in the investigation. I hear his team descended on the precinct rather quickly to seize everything you had."

"That's what I heard," she replied trying not to look him in the eye.

He nestled her chin between his index finger and thumb, raising her eyes to his. "I'm sorry, Ell. I never wanted you off the case."

"I'm pretty sure when I showed up at that apartment the

other night you would have much preferred I bow to your superiority and walk away."

"Yes, and I'd have been just as wrong then as the D.O.D. and J.A.G. are now. I've watched you work this case, seen the dedication not only in yourself but in your team. If I was to hazard a guess, I'd say this is likely the first time you've been home since you got the call on Jellic."

"You wouldn't be wrong. It's not always like this. Usually the job is the job, but occasionally a case comes along and it bites at something inside you. It takes something from you and you can't let it go until you've won that piece of yourself back."

"I'm sorry to have taken away that opportunity. It was the restraint wasn't it?"

"Sorry?"

"The restraint, the way in which the victims, Jellic and Fenn were found, that's what bit into you. That's what hit the personal note."

"I..." Ell straightened up dropping the alluring pose, unsure how to respond. "In a way, yes, it was a perversion of something that holds a special place for me. How did you know?"

"It was just little things like your knowledge of the tools, the collar, the lifestyles they are used in. It wasn't just a kinky sex toy to you. Then there was the way you said good-bye to your I.T. friend."

She raised her eyebrows.

"Whips and chains? Not a standard greeting. I assume the two of you are a couple."

Ell should have been put off, embarrassed. In the past she had hated to explain anything about her personal life but lately, probably thanks to Rob's openness, she was becoming more comfortable with the conversations.

"Couple is probably not the right term, we are... well we are what we are. Intimate, connected, and there for one another. We provide what the other needs."

"And the kiss you laid on me before all this went to shit? How is he going to react to that? Or this, for that matter." He gestured at her drying but still semi-transparent robe.

"He'll probably want details. We're together, intimate and connected but we're not...." she paused, looking for a suitable term, "exclusively committed."

She could tell he was struggling with the idea. The military taught, almost forced, conservative belief structures. It helped in organizations where order was a necessity.

"Doesn't intimacy and connection go directly against that concept?"

Ell reached out for his hand. "If we're going to have this conversation, let's take it somewhere more comfortable."

She hadn't thought the scenario through, immediately realizing that she couldn't take him to the living room or den as each was strewn with case files. With few other comfortable options she led him to the master bedroom and took a seat on the edge of the bed.

"If I'm going to talk intimacy I may as well do so in the room designed for it," she said as an off the cuff excuse.

It was intended to cover her only option but she could tell the idea had him a little flustered.

"Tell me, Tony, do you have family, siblings perhaps?"

"Sure, I have two younger sisters."

"Perfect, I'm going to try and explain my concept of intimacy and connection and I think you'll understand it without much effort if we do one simple thing."

"What's that?"

"Forget about sex."

"You just brought me into your bedroom while wearing that robe and you're asking me to forget about sex? That's a tall order, Ell."

She laughed, "Forget about sex in regards to the explanation. You have two sisters, would you say you love them, that you would do anything to see them happy?"

"Sure, they're family."

"And do you talk to them, not just superficial conversations but meaningful ones. Do you help them come to terms with things that are bothering them?"

"Sometimes. Not always but occasionally."

"That's intimacy, Tony, and you experience it with more than just a single person. Now, I bet you also have a few good friends. Friends that have the same interests as you, who love the things you love."

"Of course."

"And that is connection and again it is not held for just one person. Now, finding those items, intimacy and connection, within the same person, it's rare, and definitely something to be treasured, but it's not wholly unique. If you were to have common interests with your sisters, the connection we just spoke about, do you think either would be upset with you over your relationship with the other?"

"I'd certainly hope not."

"So the only real issue is sex. We are hardwired to think sex should be monogamous but the way I see it, sex is merely an extension of the intimacy we just discussed."

"I suppose but people are far more likely to get jealous of a lover than a friend. It's almost as if it's a built in trait."

"It is, and it's a battle you fight if you want to live the lifestyle I do. I've come to realize that jealousy is never about the person you are with or even the one you are jealous of. It's about ego. It's about insecurity. Jealousy is fear, fear of losing the intimacy we share with someone or fear that our intimacy and connection cannot match what they can or do have with another. So, do we ask our partner to change in order to quell our fears or do we face them, accept them and focus on our individual relationship as opposed to others?"

She could see him thinking, trying to understand while fighting against years of knowing otherwise.

"It's not something everyone can do, or wants to, but once you let go of jealousy life becomes full of possibilities. You and your relationships become the center of your focus and you open yourself up to growth and experiences."

"I think I understand. It's still odd as hell, but I get it. So you and... Rob is it?" she nodded. "You're free to see others."

"We're all free to do what we please, Tony. Rob and I want to see each other happy, whether that is together in our relationship or apart in others. What we do outside of 'us' can't have a negative effect on that relationship because it's separate. It will never affect how we feel for one another or what we have. We both know that and therefore we are free of fear."

She could see he understood but was still fighting an internal battle. "Jesus, what time is it? I should let you get some rest."

"It's later."

"Pardon?"

Her hand slowly caressed his thigh.

"I told you I was busy and to come see me later. The time, Tony, it's 'later'."

She could almost hear the clutch in his throat as he fought against his basic impulses. Her hand slid up, gently running across his hardening cock, past his belt and up his chest. Her eyes locked on his as she pushed him backwards, laying him flat across the bed. Leaning in, her lips brushed across his neck. She nibbled gently, remembering that she would need to calm some of her impulses in order to give him what he craved and needed. Her lips met his, devouring him as her hand worked open his belt and slipped beneath the edge of his pants. She gently gripped his shaft, feeling him hardening with each soft stroke. The want and lust she had been actively suppressing pushed forward taking over her very being. Letting the robe slip from her shoulders, her skin warm and soft, yearning for his touch, she began slowly unbuttoning his shirt. With each button her lips followed down the newly discovered flesh. Nibbling gently and resisting the urge for a full on assault.

Her body was racing, her pulse nearly loud enough to hear, her desire begging to take over yet she fought for restraint. Fought to ensure the pleasure would last. She could tell she wasn't the only one fighting that urge. She knew that drawing things out would increase the frustration but make the final release so much more pleasurable. It was rare for Ell to be on this side of events. To be controlling the pace, but she knew that, for now, Tony needed her to lead. For him, the boundaries were still unknown. He would be hesitant to push them.

His hands caressed her back slowly moving across her skin, a tingling sensation as the soft touch brushed through her. Her pulse racing as they moved around her sides cupping her tits. She continued to free his chest from the shirt as her lips worked their way to the edge of his belt. A sudden snap of pain flinched through her as his fingers clamped down on her rock hard nipple. "Harder," she moaned as he pinched it between his thumb and index finger. She could feel his hesitation and continued to beg, "Please, harder, take me, make me scream."

He increased the pressure and Ell felt the rush of pleasure she had been seeking. It was a minor release and she knew this would be a night of minor releases, her partner unsure as to her threshold and too worried to push.

Coming down from the high she had just received she quickly pulled at his waistband, freeing his now rock hard cock and wasting no time engulfing the tip between her lips.

She teased him, running her tongue gently across the shaft, flicking the tip of his cock as his body begged for more. The tease was something that would drive her former partners to their edge and she was always grateful for the punishment it brought on. Tony fought the urge to force her, though his fingers did tighten, pinching her nipple again and giving her just a taste of what she wanted, what she needed. Her mouth instinctively slid down his shaft, her throat opening to take him in. She could hear him moan, feel his arousal grow with each stroke. She desperately wanted to finish him, to taste him, but knew there was so much more to come. She slid off of him, ripped his pants the rest of the way off and was about to straddle him when his strong firm grip enclosed her left wrist and swung it around and upwards behind her back.

Within seconds he was standing, spinning her to face the bed and forcing her, face first into the mattress. She fought, playfully with her pinned arm as she could feel the juices beginning to flow down her inner thighs. His grip tightened slightly as his cock slapped against her clit. "Is this what you wanted, what you needed?" he asked as his hand connected with her ass and his cock began to fill her.

She growled in response, "Yes, please, fuck me, take me, make me yours."

His cock continued to drive deep and hard as the sound of flesh on flesh grew louder, his hand continuing the assault on her ass, driving her passion forward to a point where she could no longer take it. Her body quivering as the impact of the climax took over. He slowed his strokes, waited patiently for her body to ride out the orgasm and just as she was beginning to settle he began again.

This time the climb to the peak of arousal was fast. Having barely caught her breath Ell screamed in joy and satisfaction as a second climax rolled through her body.

She could tell he was close as well, his motion not slowing this time as she clenched and writhed around him. Out of instinct, while the pure rush of pleasure washed over her, she fucked back against him hard and fast. At the last possible moment she felt him pull free, screaming as he covered her back in cum. Her own juices flooded the bed as she continued convulsing, collapsing flat against the sheets.

She smiled, knowing that it had not been easy for him to stop and pull out of her, nor necessary. He collapsed onto the bed, as she rolled over, knowing she would need to do laundry before using the bed again. She leaned in, kissing him softly and resting her head on his chest. "Thanks."

"Christ no, thank you. I hope it was satisfying, I don't really understand everything you enjoy. I was forced to improvise."

"You improvised well, though the ending, while noble, wasn't really required. I should have said something."

He laughed, "Really and when would that have come up? Would that be standard conversation during a multiple homicide investigation or perhaps you were thinking of having the chat between orgasms?"

"Well, definitely not the latter. That may have been the quickest succession I've ever had."

"Really?"

"Definitely, my partners tend to tease and draw them out slowly. The build up is torture but often worth it. This was a very nice alternative."

"Very nice is good enough for me."

They laid in silence, holding each other as they drifted off, satisfied and relaxed.

The light was dim, nearly dark but the screams were vibrant and clear. She could hear them in the distance, begging for the torture to stop, begging for their lives, but she could not move. Could not react. She was pinned, not by restraints but by fear, fear of losing yet another, fear of seeing her pleasure once again perverted to a source of evil.

She was fighting hard against the fear, fighting to release her body from what held it when a warm, soft hand rested gently on her shoulder and suddenly everything changed. The light grew, pushing out the darkness, the screams, so twisted and painful became those of passion, of pleasure. She could feel the fear drift away and her body relaxed, drifting with it. She glanced over her shoulder and Rob smiled back at her. A secure, loving smile that set everything at ease.

Chapter Eighteen

*I*t was just after four a.m. when she woke to find Tony sitting pensively on the edge of the bed. She reached out and ran a hand across his back unsure what was on his mind.

"So, I'm guessing the J.A.G. representatives didn't find much at the precinct and from the looks of things, you have no intentions on letting this case go."

'Shit,' she thought. "How..."

"I went to grab a glass of water and took a wrong turn into what, I think, used to be a living room. It appears very similar to the precinct bullpen at the moment."

"Like I said, I still have to win that piece of myself back."

"How do I not report this, Ell. How do I let it slide?"

She sat up and grabbed his chin, turning his eyes to hers.

"If you want loopholes I can give you them. It's not your job anymore. J.A.G. has pulled you off of it and the D.O.D. doesn't expect a report. But, you're not looking for loopholes. You're looking for both moral and ethical justification for fighting against your loyalty. At the end of the day all I can ask is, what do you feel is the honorable thing to do? Not for yourself and not for me, but for David Jellic, for Claire Fenn and, god forbid, even for Jensen Dover? I can't tell you what that is, not for you."

"Fuck!"

"Tony, if you need to call this in, pull out your cell and make the call because if you leave to think this over, I guarantee there will be nothing here by the time the J.A.G goons come to search."

"And if I don't?"

"Then I work this case. Me and my team crack open whatever dirty secret the D.O.D. wants to put a lid on and we take down whoever's responsible for two murders and countless other crimes."

"With me?"

"If you want in, you've more than earned a spot at the table, but you have to realize what that choice does to your career. Once you're in, you're in. I won't give you the option to make this choice twice."

She could see the fight in his eyes. He was hurt, not by her but by an organization he believed in.

"When do we start?"

"The team will be here at 7:30 a.m., there's no reason not to get another couple hours rest in before making ourselves presentable."

"I don't know if rest is possible. I don't often toss a budding career and lifelong dream in the trash. How about a warm shower, breakfast, coffee and a conversation? I think maybe it's time we got to know one another."

Ell looked down at her naked body, still covered in sweat and juices from the night before, and nearly burst out laughing at the truth hidden in the comment.

"That sounds like a damn fine idea."

The warm shower, even when shared and fighting for the jets, was a close second for the most glorious feeling of the past seventy-two hours. Surprisingly, breakfast easily came in third. It turned out Colonel Craig was an excellent cook and had managed to whip up a couple vegetable omelets with rye toast and a side of greasy, salty pig, Ell's favorite side for any breakfast. She had balked at the thought of vegetables interrupting her enjoyment of pig and eggs but after a few minutes of hesitation and a well timed comment or two, to save face, she found the omelet quite tasty.

The two of them discussed their lives, though that was mostly their work as each lived their job far more than anything else. Ell gave him a full rundown of the Bouton case, how she met Rob and what all of that had meant for her. How it had changed her life. The Colonel tried to reciprocate with stories of his own, having to gloss over much of them due to national security classification. It made Ell realize just how difficult that would be. The struggle involved in knowing those types of secrets, and not being able to do anything or discuss them with anyone. She was beginning to understand how much his loyalty to the core truly meant to him and how deeply his decision to help her would affect him.

By seven they had cleaned up, finished an entire pot of freshly ground dark roast and settled into the living room around the case board. They were just beginning to review notes from the previous day when Rique, Baker and Jones arrived. Ell answered the door to find all three waiting on her front porch. "Jesus, did you three all catch the same cab?"

"Carpooled," said Baker. We thought the neighbors may get nosey if we were all parked out front." She didn't mention that the neighbors would be familiar with her white Challenger but Ell knew it was true.

"Speaking of which, what's with the Range Rover in the driveway?" asked Rique as he slipped off his shoes.

"About that..." said Ell.

"That would be mine," replied Colonel Craig rounding the corner from the living room. The three stared at Ell, shocked and confused.

"The Colonel's here," she deadpanned.

"No, shit," said Rique.

"Look, I don't want to get into the specifics right now," she glared at Rique hoping he'd get the picture and hold off on the interrogation. "Colonel Craig will be seeing this through. He had a chance to report us earlier and he didn't but all that shit aside, I trust him and that should be good enough for any one of you."

Rique held up his hands in a surrender motion. "You're the L.T., L.T. If you say he's in that's all I need."

As he passed her he whispered, "For now."

Baker looked at Ell, then the Colonel, then back at Ell and smiled. 'Fuck,' thought Frost, realizing that Baker had just made them. On her way past she whispered, "I wanna play too."

"Get your shit setup," commanded Ell, ignoring them both. "I want to review where we are and who's on what leads." Her phone began to ring. "Grab a coffee and get settled, we round table in ten." She pulled out the phone, didn't recognize the number and picked up.

"Hello?"

"Lieutenant, it's Denise Cue. I wanted to touch base before I headed for the hospital this morning. I understand there was some jurisdictional dick wagging yesterday and you're currently on personal time. Do you still need me to go see what I can get out of Ms. Fenn?"

"Thanks for checking in, Denise, yes, if you still have the time, but I need you to do me a favor and keep any records off the precinct computers. You can verify with the Commander if need be but all correspondence needs to flow through me at my home unit or this line."

"It sounds like you're not playing well with others, Lieutenant."

"Have I ever?" laughed Ell.

"That answer may take some research. I'll let you know as soon as I have something."

"Thanks again,"

Ell disconnected and called out to the others scattered throughout the home. "Scribbler is meeting with our vic at nine. I assume we will have a decent image by early afternoon. I want one of you to circulate it back to those we've already spoken to as soon as it comes in."

"On it," replied Jones. "Hot stuff and I did a second run through on Jensen Dover's files last night. There are some mentions of the plea deal but nothing that helps us. If we were looking to charge him for colluding to misrepresent his client's interests sure, but there's nothing to indicate who was pulling his strings. The only oddity we found was a handwritten notation, 'Maddison, Wisconsin – December 84'.

We figured we'd run the city and date through the system to see if anything flagged."

"Sounds good, it's a loose thread so pull on it and see where it takes you. Rique?" she asked as they all conglomerated around the case board.

"Jane Sandusky checks out. Born in Winterest, Iowa in May of 1985. Lived a fairly mundane life until her parents both died in a hit and run at age sixteen. She bounced in and out of foster care for a year and a half then headed out on her own. She has a sealed juvenile record which smells like a minor drug offence but nothing serious on file. Four and a half years ago she testified in a homicide case against her then lover Jonas 'Cigs' Petruk. He received fifteen to life and is currently serving year four at the Iowa State Penn. She disappeared five days after testifying. No missing persons report has been filed. I've checked with the local Marshal's office but it doesn't look like this is official witness protection. I'd say the locals set her up with a new identity and sent her out east."

"Ok, so Claire Fenn's story checks out, let's switch focus to Unit H.L.A. I want you and the Colonel coordinating and digging into who and what we are dealing with. If someone has buried something, then there is or was something to find. I'm working on the theory that Sergeant Jellic somehow came upon information in regards to who they are or what they do, threatened to or did release the information, and ended up on the wrong side of the military machine. It's likely he took a deal, despite the lack of evidence, to save his own ass or possibly at the behest of Jensen Dover due to the payoff. If that's the case, something went wrong between the time the deal was made and the day he ended up in Claire Fenn's apartment. Pinpoint what that was."

Rique nodded, she could see he was reluctant to involve Colonel Craig but knew that, despite his reservations, he would follow her lead.

"What do we know on the collar? It had to come from somewhere."

"I've been working the list," responded Rique, "but call backs are few and far between. I get the feeling these people don't have a lot of trust in the police."

"You told them you were a cop? Jesus, Rique," she replied shaking her head. "Baker, get on the line and start making calls and emailing copies of the photo. You're looking to re-place a collar your new kitten used to have and wanted to surprise her by having it remade by the original artist. Find out who made it and then bring Mr. Wizard here in to do his 'I'm a cop' routine. I want everything you can find on who bought it and when."

The team split to their own makeshift workstations, Colonel Craig heading to the kitchen with Rique. The door-bell chimed putting everyone on edge. Ell, not expecting any-one, set her service pistol on the table beside the door, slid the French doors to the living room closed and took a look through the peephole. The face on the other side did not look familiar, a young woman of maybe twenty-five with steel eyes and an uncommon smirk. Ell palmed her pistol and slid it behind her back, opening the door with her left hand.

"Can I help you?"

"Ellison Frost?" she asked, an entitled tone in her voice.

"Lieutenant Ellison Frost," Ell repeated back to her with a steely gaze and emphasis on the title.

The woman smirked and let out a slight snicker. "You've been served, Lieutenant," she emphasized the title as Ell had and handed her a thick yellow envelope before turning and heading back down the driveway to a waiting grey Prius.

Ell stared at the envelope unsure if she should open it. 'Served? For what?' she pondered. Resolved that the only way to know was to look, she tore open the top of the envelope and pulled out the stack of papers within. The header on the first page was unmistakable, Janz, Sullivan and Dover followed by the bold print title 'You Are Being Sued'.

"Are you fucking kidding me," she screamed drawing the attention of everyone in the house.

"What's up?" asked Jones heading into the foyer at a fast walk.

"More great news. I just received a nice parting gift from my good friends down at Janz, Sullivan and Dover," she replied tossing the wrongful death claim at the detective.

Chapter Nineteen

Ell contacted Commander Nuez, noting that he was also listed on the lawsuit, and was advised that he had been served and the case had been forwarded to a union representative for follow up and defense. They would be in touch with her in the next few days. A meeting she was neither looking forward to nor bound to enjoy.

The team dug into their individual assignments and Ell tried to let go of the burning rage that the lawsuit had brought forth and focus on the case. She had placed her team on the most pressing lines of inquiry and freed herself up to make a call she had been trying to put off. Unfortunately, her options were becoming limited and while Rique and the Colonel may be able to turn something up through official channels the time it took to do so was going to be a problem. She stepped outside to the back deck, pulled out her cell and reluctantly dialed.

"And I was just thinking it was nearly breakfast and I hadn't received my morning wakeup call from home," answered Rob.

"We try to keep ourselves busy while you're out of town."

He picked up on something in her voice, a relaxation that had not been there for some time. "Ellison, you're relaxed, have you been breaking the rules?"

She laughed, relaxed was far from a good description but he always had a six sense when it came to her sexual frustrations.

"Relaxed? No, but less frustrated. And before you go threatening punishment, which is a pretty piss poor threat since I enjoy it, I didn't break your rules. I had company. I was joined by a studdly man in uniform."

"Interesting? I assume you didn't wake me up to brag so I'll torture the details out of you once I'm home later tonight."

"Mmmmm now that I can get behind, or in front of depending on your mood."

He laughed, "Definitely less frustrated. So what's up?"

"It's this bloody case we're working. The one in which Nuez had you scrub and transfer all the files. The shit has hit the proverbial fan. The Department of Defense stepped in last night and tried to shut it down. They're making a jurisdictional argument but I'm pretty sure they're just covering their own asses because everything I have points to some mysterious military unit."

"Christ Ell, when you step in it, you really step in it. Does this tie back to that information you needed on CleanSlate?"

"Yes and unfortunately that's why I'm calling. What's your day like?"

He could sense the apprehension in her voice.

"A few discussions and panels I'd rather not miss but I could clear most of it if need be. My flight out is at three and I should be landing around nine."

"Since when is it a six hour flight from Seattle?"

"It's not, it's four hours in the air and a two hour time change, and before you go off on a rant, consider whether or not that is the best use of the time you're ranting about."

"But... I... god dammit fine. In the interest of keeping the peace and saving time we can discuss it later. For now, this is a big favor but I need to know how long it would take you to bypass a high end firewall and all the other security garbage in place in order to get me some information."

"That would depend on who's firewall and how sophisticated the other security garbage is."

"GenData."

"Jesus Ell."

"I told you it was a big favor."

"To answer the question, and assuming you want this done covertly, probably the better part of my day. That said, I have a good relationship with these people, unless you think they are directly involved in something I'm pretty sure I could get them to play ball."

"Not on this, you mentioned they do a thorough vetting of all their clients before selling a copy of CleanSlate. I need everything they collected on a military client referred to as Unit H.L.A. Asking is an option but the odds are against us and I can't risk anyone finding out that we asked. Once they know we're digging they're going to bury everything five times as deep."

"You know that if I do this without a warrant it won't hold up. Not with you requesting it."

"I know but right now I'm swinging at shadows. Who they are and what they do may be motive evidence at best. If I lose that, so be it but until I can pin them down and understand the organization, I don't have a hope of finding something to tie them to any of this. Trust me, if I had another option..."

"Yeah, this doesn't feel right, Ell. These guys have been good to me."

"Rob, I have two bodies in the morgue and two more in the hospital. I can't weigh feelings at this point. I'm sorry."

With a deep sigh he agreed. "Here's hoping I'm as good as I think I am."

"Whips and chains," said Ell.

"After this? You can bet your sweet little red ass on that."

The hours ticked away without a major break. It was fatiguing and being cooped up in the house wasn't helping. By eleven-thirty Ell was itching for a break. She was about to call Scribbler for an update but decided she needed to escape the monotony of the house.

"I'm heading to St. Pete's to check in on Scribbler and see if there is any update on officer Kohl. Is anyone up for a road trip?"

They all grunted in response, too involved in their own angles or too frightened of her driving. She wasn't sure which. Ell shrugged and thought, 'Solo it is.'

The trip to St. Pete's was quick but relaxing, She took the opportunity to take out some stress and anger on the barrage of other drivers on the road, swerving and cursing there incompetence at near light speed. It was one of the small joys she reveled in. Her first stop was the admitting desk, having assumed Jerry Kohl would have been moved out of the ER once he was out of surgery and stable. She flashed her badge at the young lady behind the desk and asked for information on Officer Kohl.

"Lieutenant Frost," the lady checked a list on her computer. "Yes, we have been asked not to release information on that patient but I see that Officer Danuski has authorized you for updates and entry. He is in unit 430, would you like me to call up and advise them you are on your way?"

"Please do," she responded and headed for the stairwell.

"There is an elevator just around the corner," called out the admitting clerk but Ell waved her off. She'd played that game once too often this week.

The unit clerk gave her a similar grilling before releasing any information. He advised her that Officer Danuski was in room 43009 if she wanted to speak with him. Jerry Kohl had still not regained consciousness, however the doctors were optimistic. His brain function appeared normal and blood flow was good.

Ell thanked them for their time and decided not to bother Danuski. She had the information she needed for now. Heading back to the stairs she climbed the remaining two floors on her way to Claire Fenn's room. Once again she found the door guarded by a young uniformed officer, though this one appeared much more relaxed than the last.

"Lieutenant, Scribbl... sorry, Ms. Cue is still in with the victim. Per your orders no one but the two friends, police and medical personnel have been allowed in."

"Relax, officer. Did Denise give you any indication on a timeline?"

"No, sir, though she has been in there for a while now without a break."

"What about you? Had a break recently, Officer?"

"No, sir but my shift just started at seven."

"I'll tell you what, go stretch your legs, grab a coffee and whatever else you need. I'll watch the door for fifteen since I'll be waiting for Denise either way."

The kid smiled and leaped out of his chair. "Thanks, I could use a coffee and a chance to purge the last few."

Ell took a seat noticing that even the hospital chairs made her office guest chair seem like a cement block. With little to do but wait, she pulled out her cell and began scrolling through the slew of unanswered emails. Ninety percent were offers for sexual enhancements and free porn which she quickly deleted. The only message worth noting was a one line cryptic message from M.E. Sanders.

"Ell, I've been reviewing the notes you gave me on my latest jam and think I've come up with a new angle for the piece. You really need to hear it."

Either Sanders had finally lost it or he'd been advised that someone was likely monitoring her communications. She assumed the latter and responded in kind.

"It appears I have some time on my hands now that the Jellic case is someone else's problem. I could swing by for a listen in about an hour."

The officer returned promptly, fifteen minutes after she relieved him. He again thanked her and she considered telling him to take another fifteen just so she didn't have to give up the chair. As the thought was reverberating through her mind the door to the room opened and Denise Cue strolled out. "Have you been demoted to guard duty, Lieutenant?"

"Some days I wish that were possible. I was here checking on Officer Kohl and thought I'd save time and come see how you managed."

"How is he?"

"He's doing as well as can be expected, still in a coma but stable."

"I worked a few cases for Jerry before he transferred. He's a solid officer. I honestly can't believe it, we always feel so secure at the precinct. You'd never imagine something like this is possible."

"You don't need to tell me. I've worked a lot of gory scenes but when it's in your own home it has a completely different effect. Kohl's down in unit 430 if you want to see him. Room 43009. His old partner, Danuski, is playing guard dog. I'm not sure if you know him but if not have him call me. I'll vouch for you."

"Officer Danuski and I are..." she paused, "familiar. I'm sure it won't be a problem."

Ell gave her a raised eyebrow, the pause giving away something Denise would rather not say.

"It was a few years back." Scribbler didn't go into detail so Ell didn't push.

"So, did we get anything worthwhile from the victim?"

"I think so. Let's find a quiet place to take a look and discuss it," she motioned towards the door to indicate she would rather not talk about it within earshot of the room.

They made their way down the hall, finding a small visitor's room with a couch and T.V. Ell ignored the "Please leave open" sign and pulled the door shut.

"What's up?" asked Ell.

Scribbler rolled out a photo like image of a male, mid thirties with short, brown hair, a firm jaw and deep blue eyes.

"Damn, that's a hell of a lot more than I expected."

"Me too, which is what I wanted to talk to you about. We extrapolated on the jaw and hair. The girl indicated that he was wearing a ball cap and bandana but I wanted to leave them out for the sketch, so we drilled into what she had seen and worked with probabilities. Standard procedure."

"I hear a 'but' in there."

"I've done my share of these, Ell, and over the years you start to get a feel for how easy or hard it should be based on how much someone saw. What parts of the face the victim will focus on and what parts you need to really work. You accept and expect some minor discrepancy. I don't say this often, but this time it was too damn easy. She had details I wouldn't expect. Clear and precise and not just things that are usually blurry in a quick glance but things she couldn't have seen like the jawline. Either she saw more than she knows or more than she's letting on."

"Could it be the trauma?"

"Hell, I'm no psychologist, but I've never seen trauma increase the perception. Normally, I'm digging and clawing past it for a valid picture."

Ell didn't know what to think, it was possible her victim was hiding something but given what the girl had been through it was more likely that she'd seen more than she remembered or was possibly blocking something out.

"Thanks, I'll run this past Grayson and see if she has any insight. In the meantime, scan the sketch to Rique and Jones as soon as you can."

Ell could see the apprehension in Denise's eyes. "Seriously? That's damn near picture perfect and you want time to play around with shading and shit, don't you?"

"Well..."

"Sorry, the clocks ticking on this one, we need to get that sketch on the street now. I promise, one day I'll let you be an artist but today it's time to put on the cop hat."

She reluctantly agreed to send it out as soon as she was back at the station and Ell thought about having a quick discussion with Ms. Fenn before leaving. Deciding that she would be better served sitting down with Dr. Grayson before that happened, she sent a quick email to her office asking for five minutes as soon as she could spare them. She noted that the meeting had to be off-site. Sliding the phone back into her pocket she headed, quickly, for the stairs. She had a 'jam' to listen to.

Sander's assistant Mindy was conspicuously absent when she arrived at the morgue. Instead a loud buzzer sounded as she entered and Davidson Sanders strolled out from a room in the back to meet her.

"Sorry, Mindy took the day off. She said something about an 'ultra mad concert with a sweet pair of legs'. Personally I'm just hoping for a detailed story when she gets back."

"You're a sick old man Sanders," laughed Ell. "So what the hell did you need me to hear?"

He quickly shook his head, pointing to the ceiling and then his ear. He motioned for her to follow him back to an empty room where he turned on a stereo which was playing what she believed was his band's latest demo. He turned up the volume and leaned in close to whisper.

"I'm not taking any chances."

Ell shook her head, "Do you seriously think they're bugging a morgue."

"It's the military, Ell. NSA, FBI, CIA and any other acronyms you can find, so yes, I assume they've bugged my damn morgue and my phones and they're probably reading my emails and texts."

"Fine, we'll assume we're in a bad spy movie. What did you find?"

"Before the Judge Advocate's office came in here and confiscated my bodies and files, I was taking a look at the medical photos and file on your hostage victim, Ms. Fenn. What I saw contradicts some conclusions we came to based on Dover and Kohl. Ms. Fenn's wounds indicate an odd assortment of angles, however when I run the probabilities, unless your perp inflicted the wounds while behind her and reaching around, which would be an odd torture technique, I'd wager that most of the lacerations, if not all, indicate a left handed attacker."

"So you're thinking two separate perps? He could be ambidextrous."

"It's possible but all the injuries on Jellic, Dover and Kohl indicate a right handed attack from the front and all Ms. Fenn's indicate a left handed attack from the front and top. Even the flogging came down from her right shoulder to left hip. I lean towards different attackers. Fenn's wounds were also much more superficial. With Jellic they pinpointed high pain centers and hit each with perfect accuracy. With Fenn they just sliced and beat, they didn't pinpoint any specific areas, at least none that would be considered high pain. It could be that your perp is switching things up to throw us off. We know that's in the profile, but it still feels like a pair to me. I figured I'd better give you a heads up."

"Thanks," she said then raised her voice over the music. "The new jam is sweet shit. Loving the bass line."

Sanders smiled, shook his head and mouthed, "Fuck off."

Chapter Twenty

$\mathcal{R}$ ob's call came in just as she was pulling back into the driveway of the brownstone. She waited until she had parked and answered with the handset.

"So, I've managed to break the trust of a good colleague and employer in order to retrieve the information you required."

Ell cringed. She didn't need the damn guilt trip but knew she deserved it.

"Thanks, and I'm sorry, and all the other things that I should be saying but can't think of right now. I appreciate it. I don't mean to sound like a bitch but that was quick, even for you."

"Yes, and honestly I considered giving Taillen a call about it. He's one of the primary shareholder's and should know that his research arm's security has a major hole. From the looks of it I wasn't the first one to use it and, given who GenData looks into and the type of information they gather, that scares the crap out of me."

"Wouldn't that call raise a metric shit ton of questions?"

"Probably, and it would likely cost me a lucrative contract and possibly a civil lawsuit so I'm not going to make it. I am however going to wait a couple weeks, go back in and leave a very obvious flashing red sign that they've been breached."

"With any luck they'll call you to come seal it," she laughed.

"I'll do it for free if they do. I need all the karma I can get to work off this guilty conscience."

"I'll do my best to make it worth it. Someone needs to pay for the bodies I have in the morgue. Can you send the file to my home unit? Discreetly."

"Already done. If there's nothing else my cops need, I'm going to catch one more panel on proper techniques when bowing to our robot overlords and then jump on a plane heading your way."

"All clear on this end. Your service is appreciated. Whips and chains."

"Whips and chains back atcha."

She headed back into the house, held up a hand to stop the questions and reports coming from her team and yelled, "Give me ten minutes then hit the living room."

She headed straight for her computer, pulling up the new file on Unit H.L.A that Rob had conveniently left on her desktop. She preferred not to think of how he managed to do so or the security risk it posed. GenData had a lot of research on the obscure military unit but most of it focused on the high level arm it fell within rather than the unit and its mission. She stared at the information, cursed silently and hit print.

By the time she had the file printed and in hand the rest of the team had gathered around the case board and updated it with new information they had discovered. She could see Rique and the Colonel had been tugging a line that lead to a high ranking officer they were certain had some connection to Unit H.L.A. She was impressed, given a few more hours they may have had most of the command structure. A redundant point given the file she was holding but it was solid police work and, if she let them pursue it, admissible. It put her in an awkward position. She now had to weigh the admissibility versus the time, a commodity she didn't believe they had much of. Based on what she had read, the organization had the means and opportunity for a full scale cover up and even that wasn't likely to stop the bodies from continuing to fall. D.A. Stranik was going to tear her a new one, assuming this case ever saw a courtroom, but she'd deal with it when the time came. For now she had to do what she could to push things forward as quickly as possible.

"Before we jump too far into the updates you should all review this." Ell handed out copies of the summary printout she'd worked up. "The full file is still printing. Rique, you and the Colonel can grab it once we're done here and see where it leads you. From what I've gathered, Unit H.L.A is a deeply covert, multi-branch military organization with no main base but operating, instead, through-out various military organizations within the country. Their operations all appear to be focused within the U.S. and their chain of command is as long and spread out as the organization itself. I'll let you defer to the file for the first three levels of that chain and start digging into the rest. The organization's purpose, full structure and authority are still unknown, so we need to focus our efforts on that. There is a note in the file that is not included on the breakdown because it's speculation at this point made by a source I neither know or trust. It, is however intriguing."

She held up a single page of the report, written in the margin were the words "H.L.A. – Homeland Assassins???"

"Jesus Christ," responded the Colonel. "Where did you get this?"

"It is a security dossier composed by the investigation arm of GenData. Information they gathered when vetting the organization."

"Which they just handed over to us? No doubt, breaking numerous client confidentiality agreements and possibly a couple federal statutes." asked Rique.

"They may not be aware that we borrowed it and yes I realize that puts us on shaky legal ground but I'm wagering good money that a military organization such as this isn't ordering hits on cops and attorneys. Whoever is doing this has a tie to Unit H.L.A. but I'm betting that whatever their mission may be, it's not authorized."

"It makes sense," commented Jones. "If this was an official operation they would never have brought in the Colonel or let us start investigating. They'd use an inside man to sweep it under the rug, clean up the mess, and ensure it went away without ever becoming a story."

"And," cut in Baker, "they'd have taken out Jellic long before his case became a press sensation, not the day after it was all over the airwaves."

"Amateur hour at the professional shop," commented Ell though the analogy didn't quite fit. "What else do we have?"

"The Colonel and I have about twenty percent of what you just handed us and we were feeling pretty good about it too," said Rique.

"Consider this a free jump forward."

"Scribbler's sketch came in just before you got back. I've

seen professional photos that are lower quality so I should be able to make some standard runs through the government databases without too much difficulty. Military is going to be a problem, without their cooperation. I'll get out on the road this afternoon and pound the pavement to see if anyone in the known areas may have seen him."

Baker responded, "I can tag along to lighten the load. I have calls and emails into all sixteen remaining jewelers. I've heard back from eight, all sorry to let me and my kitten down as the original was not one of theirs. I can field incoming calls while slogging through the neighborhoods."

"Perfect, and when you get a hit on either the photo or the collar call it in immediately. I'll be back on the road this afternoon for an update with Grayson," they chuckled quietly to which Ell gave them the evil eye and continued, "and I need to update the Commander with this new information though I'm unsure as to how or where yet."

"I hear Angel's new club on fifteenth is bouncing," smirked Baker.

"A regular laugh riot in here. I'm surrounded by clowns." muttered Ell as she headed back to her desk to make some plans.

Dr. Grayson was expecting her at two o'clock in a small coffee shop three blocks from the eleventh precinct. 'The easy meeting,' she thought as she pulled up to the curb. Her second meeting of the afternoon was likely to prove more troublesome. Finding a quiet, secure location for a rendezvous with the Commander, whom she assumed would be under surveillance, had been difficult. A call to her newest friend 'Ginny' Collins had secured a location which should provide the cover they required, though Ell was sure it was going to cost her in the long run. Virginia was the exotic sort and when she called in a favor you knew it was going to be interesting if nothing else.

Dr. Grayson was waiting at a small table inside, a foaming cup of something sitting in front of her. Ell could smell a sweet musty scent wafting off of it.

"Is that?"

"A low-fat Chai vanilla latte with a double pump of simple syrup. It's divine."

Ell had been hooked on them ever since Rob began delivering chai lattes to the office. It was a guilty pleasure, one her ass disliked but she really didn't care if it cost her an extra ten minutes in the gym. She flagged over a waitress pointed to Dr. Grayson's mug and said, "One more liquid orgasm, heavy on the fat in mine, please."

"So your message didn't say much, are we here to dish over 'liquid orgasms' or do you have something more official on your mind?"

"Unfortunately the dishing will have to wait. Something came up this morning in a conversation with Scribbler, shit sorry, Denise Cue, and I thought I better run it past you."

"Just don't let her hear you call her that and your secret's safe with me."

"Old habits... so, earlier today Denise was doing an interview and sketch with one of my victims, Claire Fenn."

"This was the hostage rescue, correct?"

"Yes, she was taken at the scene of the Jellic murder, held, ransomed and tortured. I've interviewed her and she only caught a glimpse of her attacker. He kept her blindfolded or hooded for most of her time captive. What she did remember was pretty clear but it was literally seconds. Denise started digging today, as she does, drawing out the information she needed and she said it was too easy. There was too much there. She thinks the victim is either hiding or repressing something and I wanted to get your thoughts."

"I could probably give you a better idea if I spoke to her but I take it you'd like to avoid that."

"If she is hiding something I don't want to tip her off before I confront her and honestly, she's most likely going to need some professional help but the police psychiatrist is probably not the best option. She'd be immediately skeptical and unlikely to open up."

The waitress set Ell's latte down in front of her. She smiled and immediately took a sip followed by an audible and highly erotic moan. The waitress smiled and whispered, "Now, that I can relate too."

Dr. Grayson did her best to stop from laughing but could not help the grin that formed.

"Why don't you tell me a little bit about her captivity and what you know of her past," she said, trying to remain professional.

Ell gave her the details on the hostage situation, the manner in which she was found and the 'ghost' history that surrounded her. Dr. Grayson looked pensive and remained quiet.

"There is a very real possibility the young lady has suppressed much of the trauma she experienced. For most people, it would be natural to block out the pain without blocking the events but for a woman with a troubled background, a woman who managed to escape and form a new life, this could be a very serious triggering event. Taking her back to a place and time where pain, addiction, and servitude were the norm. The mind would cling to its new paradigm and refuse to acknowledge anything that could bring forth a shift. A coping mechanism and one with serious consequences, eventually."

"Denise was able to coax the truth from behind the wall?"

"It's possible. Denise does have a certain touch with victims and witnesses. You understand that I can't be certain on this. It's a best guess based on the profile you provided."

"A best guess will have to do. I was leaning towards a similar assumption but thought that, perhaps, my sympathy for Ms. Fenn was clouding my judgment. This helps."

"Always here to help," replied Dr. Grayson. "And when you're ready for that dish session, perhaps over another latte or something a little harder, give me a call. I'll clear my schedule."

Chapter Twenty-One

*T*hanks to the events of the Bouton case along with Virginia Collins' continued infatuation with Rob, the main offices of Collins International had received a significant upgrade in electronic surveillance and security. No cost had been spared and Virginia had insisted that Rob take on the task as general contractor for both the system specification and install. It had been another lucrative side contract but Ell had a feeling her stud had to put up with a lot of ogling along the way. Ginny, as he referred to her, made no secret of her plan to whoo him into submission. Unfortunately for her, submission wasn't Rob's usual role.

At Ell's suggestion, Virginia had put in a series of calls through contacts at the mayor's office, requesting an immediate sit down with Commander Nuez to discuss a possible donation to the fine men and woman that had helped her and her organization months earlier. It was a ruse, leaving a trail to explain the Commander's visit, but Ell suspected there would be a donation forth coming anyway, under the guise of covering her tracks but, in reality, just providing Ms. Collins a viable excuse to use with her board of directors.

Ell pulled into the underground parkade, using the private code she had been provided, forty minutes in advance of their meeting. She was attempting to avoid any surveillance that may have been put in place. She knew that the building would protect against eavesdropping and, with Rob's security in place, it was unlikely they would be able to get eyes inside. It was as secure a place as she could provide and, given the discussion they were about to have, she was glad it was available.

She had no sooner parked and pulled open her door before she heard the voice.

"Ellllll," screamed Virginia Collins, her arms open as she approached. "You know you don't need to make these elaborate excuses to see me. Just pick up the phone, dear."

The list of people wanting to 'get together' for one reason or another kept growing. Ell considered sending them all out together and staying home in hopes that it would solve the issue. "But what would we possibly talk about if there wasn't murder and mayhem in the midst?" she responded.

"So true, perhaps next time you could just bring that sexy boytoy and we can let him do all the talking."

"Hell, if he's going to be there then I may as well stay home and out of your way."

"I'm not opposed to an audience, dear. When it comes to that boy, I'm not opposed to much."

The two of them laughed and Virginia suggested they go wait out the remaining half hour in her office, where they could sit down and be comfortable. She escorted Ell to the elevator and watched as her head swiveled back and forth between the death cell and the stairs.

"Ell, it's thirty-two floors. I don't think the stairs are an option."

"Fuck," she muttered as she stepped through the doors. "These things and I haven't been getting along recently."

"Well, no worries there, this is my baby and she runs smooth as silk. We'll be topside in no time."

True to her word, the elevator rose quick and smooth, settling on the top floor with a gentle stop and two consecutive dings as the doors opened into Virginia's penthouse office. It was just as Ell remembered it, large, lush, and full of gallery level artwork, but comfortable. The barren space on the picture wall, which Virginia had told Ell she was saving for a 'special' piece, was now filled with a painting of a naked man, tied to a bed, blindfolded and gagged. It was a beautiful work that Ell remembered being captivated by in the "Fantasy Exhibit" of the Collins' art auction earlier that year. The artist had a gritty edge, managing to find both the freedom and fearlessness in the man's eyes. She was still taken by it.

"I see you won the piece you were after," she commented, unable to take her eyes off it.

"Not yet," replied Virginia with a lust in her eye, "but the painting will do for now."

Ell smiled. Virginia Collins was after something, or rather someone, and you could bet she'd have him. The woman was relentless.

"Please, have a seat and let me get you something to drink."

"Just water," Ell replied, settling into one of the soft leather chairs in the sitting area of the expansive office.

Virginia handed her a stunning crystal glass which nearly brought Ell to laughter. 'Who drinks water out of these?' she thought but she knew the answer. Virginia Collins.

"So, dish girl. What's with the secret hush, hush rendez-vous and need for a room in my security palace?"

"I'm dealing with a crazy case and an even crazier bad guy. I can't really get into it, Virginia, and, trust me when I tell you, you wouldn't want the details if I could."

"There's plenty of scary out there, Ell. I deal with some of it in the board room and others at the negotiating table but compared to what you deal with, who you go after, well... Let's just say I can't even imagine it."

"We all play our roles. I lock up the worst of the worst and you.... buy up the world? Honestly, I don't have a clue what you actually do. I know you're in charge, running this giant ship, but aside from the billboards and galas I don't know what Collins International actually is."

Virginia smiled, it was a kind, confident grin, one Ell expected she saved for those people in her life that she considered friends. "I could give you the big speech on all the industries and research arms but what it boils down to is Collins International makes money. That's really it. We find a way to make money, we implement it and we pass on those dollars to the people we hire. Well, most of those dollars. I hold back enough to maintain my glorious lifestyle," she laughed.

"Yeah, but isn't that just all business. I mean what do you really do?"

"We are all businesses, Ell, all successful businesses."

Ell still didn't have a clue but she accepted that the company was massive, Virginia was the big dog in charge, and she would likely never understand what any of that meant. To her, everything about Virginia Collins was an enigma, yet for some reason, Ell adored her.

Ell could not help but laugh. "Honestly, I have no idea what that means other than you have pretty much all the money."

"Not quite all of it," she paused for dramatic impact, "yet."

"Well then, I will take your free water, probably distilled from Antarctic glaciers, in your fancy crystal glass and just be thankful I have friends in such high places."

"That, I will drink to," replied Virginia, raising a glass of brown liquid that Ell assumed was very expensive scotch.

They discussed trivial nonsense and the thirty minutes disappeared as if it was five, yet Ell felt as though she had been relaxing for days. Virginia Collins had a gift for slowing life down and taking her away from the stress of her work. As she rose to head down to the conference room set aside for her and the Commander, she stopped, turned and, for some unknown reason, embraced Virginia in a deep hug.

"Thanks again, not just for the meeting but for this as well. I needed a couple minutes downtime."

"Downtime is one of my specialties, dear, and you are always welcome to join."

The Commander sat in awe, his eyes wide, taking in the luxury of Collins International Tower.

"This is what you get when you have all the money," commented Ell as she strolled into the room.

"Is that all it takes?"

"That and something about being all businesses. It's beyond me."

"Well, either way please pass on my appreciation to Ms.

Collins if the opportunity arises. While this made our meeting much easier, I don't know if I should be pleased that these steps were required. I assume this," he waved his hands at the expansive room," means you have concerning news."

"We've started to break through on Unit H.L.A. I still don't have a full picture on their mission, though I do have some suspicions. We've begun nailing down the unit structure and have identified a number of high level officers in the chain of command."

She laid out all the pertinent details as she had for her team earlier that day.

"You think this organization, one ran by high level military officers, is responsible for all of this, including an attack on a uniformed police officer in my precinct?"

"Culpable perhaps but I don't buy responsible. Not yet and not with what we have. We know this unit is involved in the Jellic case and we are fairly certain it was their tech used to bypass the precinct security, but I can't wrap my head around any reason an organization like this would risk the exposure those acts have caused. It's too sloppy. Right now I'm leaning towards a rogue member or someone tied with the group peripherally. It would explain the D.O.D's involvement from the beginning. They were unsure if it tied back to them but needed someone on the inside in case it did."

"It would also explain why my precinct was invaded, stripped clean and placed under heavy surveillance by the Judge Advocate's office without any argument from the Mayor or Chief."

"If I'm right, then the full force of this unit will be currently focused on eliminating this problem, however, justice will be far from their primary concern. They won't be looking to bring someone down for the deaths and attacks so much as sweep them under the rug. My victims mean nothing to them. It's cover your ass time and they'll want this buried fast and deep. I've been playing with an angle that may prevent that."

"I'm not going to like it, am I?"

He was right, he wasn't going to like it but Ell was convinced it was the best way to proceed.

"These organizations hide in the shadows, they thrive on secrecy, so fame and notoriety are just about the worst thing that can happen to them. I think it's time we leveraged that fear for our benefit."

"You want to threaten to expose them?"

"No, I want to do it. I want to shine some light onto their deep dark shadow and see what scurries out. A threat gives them time to plan, to hide, to bury and shred. It puts all of us on the block as possible threats to their security. I'm not fond of how these people deal with threats. Let's get this out there, flood the airwaves with what we know and let the public fill in the blanks with a fear of the all powerful big brother. They'll come up with theories far more frightening than the reality could ever be and it will give us the support and justification we need to dig into this properly. Right now this group is covering their asses and no one is going to talk because they have protection, elected officials helping in the cover up, but if the public turns, those elected officials are in a pretty tight spot. I think that protection falls by the wayside and our investigation gets the support it needs."

"Or it backfires and you, me and everyone else involved in this case end up sitting at home tweaking our resumes."

"In which case I have an in with the woman who has all the money and all the businesses."

Nuez cracked a smile but only for a brief moment. Ell knew the downside of what she was suggesting. This would drain any political capital they had. As much as she hated it, she knew that the trust of the Chief, the Mayor and all the other political wings was something they had to balance every day. The Commander took that weight on his shoulders and she was asking him to burn everything he'd established through years of schmoozing.

"You know you are a major pain in my ass, Frost. Your a damn fine cop and a huge asset to the department, but a major pain in my ass." He went quiet, almost too quiet as Ell could see he was contemplating the option.

"If we were to do this, who would you use?"

"Cindy Shepard, she's trustworthy, has been fair to us in the past and I kind of owe her an exclusive for helping me spread the word on that phony hostage rescue distraction."

"So two birds with one stone?"

"Why a stone?"

"What?" asked the Commander as if he hadn't heard her reply.

"Never mind, it's a different discussion. Cindy would be my girl. She is also one hell of a researcher so by the time this breaks I have no doubt that she will have more information than we have now."

"Would she work her release schedule with us so that we can control the timeline?"

"If I make it part of the deal she'll honor it."

"How do you plan to ensure her "source" is protected so that this doesn't blow back on you?"

"I don't, sir. I plan to announce it. I plan to look them in the eyes moments before all hell breaks loose and make damn sure they know who did this to them and why. I'm sick of getting run over by a bunch of bastards who think they are above the law, by people who are too busy covering their own asses to stop a murderer. Had they co-operated to begin with, I have no doubt that I'd have one less body in the morgue and officer Kohl would be home with his family."

"And you're prepared for the fallout that comes with that decision?"

"Yes, but, honestly I'm not sure there will be any. The politicians will get up in arms rallying against corruption because next year kicks off campaign season. They can't be seen colluding, so they'll jump up screaming about the will of the people and all that crap."

"In public," said the Commander. "In private, however, you'd be naive to think there won't be backlash against the cop that made them have to get up and dance. They won't be able to come after you right away but these people have long memories, Ell. You may be guaranteeing you'll never sit in my seat and, honestly, right now, that is a solid opportunity for you."

Ell stared at him as if he was crazy. She didn't know how to react. "With all due respect, sir, why the hell would I want your seat? I'm flattered you think I have the ability to lead at that level, but I have no interest in playing politics and trying to manage the nightmares associated with having cops like me beneath you. I'm an investigator. On most days I'm a damn good investigator. I'm where I should be. The big chair? That's for someone else."

She could tell she had surprised him. She was driven and most people confused that with ambitious. She had no interest in climbing the chain of command because she was doing exactly what she felt she was meant to do. She had enough leadership and autonomy for her liking and while the drive to do her job well pushed her forward every day, it didn't push her towards command.

"Honestly, I don't know what to say. I just assumed that the day I moved on you'd be stepping in to fill that spot. I'm..." his pause dragged on.

"Speechless?" she suggested.

He nodded, "Yeah."

"Not the best thing to be right now, I need some direction here, sir."

"Sorry, I'm not going to lie, from every angle but one it's a piss poor plan and the fallout may be more than we can handle. Unfortunately that one angle is the truth and if that's not our top priority then I don't know what is. I can't believe I'm going to say this but go home, clean up your resume and give Shepard a call."

Chapter Twenty-Two

$\mathcal{S}$he didn't wait to get home and she damn sure wasn't about to update a resume. Instead, after working out the timing details with the Commander, waiting for him to leave and rushing down thirty flights of stairs despite Virginia's insistence that her building elevators ran as smooth as clockwork, she jumped in the S550 and called up Cindy Shepard's number.

By the time her wheels hit the street the call was ringing through the hands free system.

"Well if it isn't the media's worst enemy, not that they'll hear it from me."

"Some people just shouldn't report without verifying the facts."

"Touché. So to what do I owe the pleasure of today's call?"

"I owe you an exclusive, don't I?"

"Seriously? You caught the scum bag?"

"No, but what I'm going to give you is just as juicy and far more controversial."

"Ell, we had a deal here. I've been pushing my editor off with promises of an exclusive on the Jellic murder."

"Trust me, Cindy, you want this. It ties in with the Jellic case and if I know you, it'll be twice as juicy by the time you're done with it."

"Ok, you can stop with the hard sell. Give me the basics and I'll let you know if it evens the scales."

"By the time this one's over you'll owe me three or four, Cindy, but no basics over the phone. We need to meet and there are going to be some ground rules before you go to print on this."

"Nothing is ever simple with you, is it? Most of my sources call me up begging me to print their story, Ell."

"Most of your sources don't give you pullawhatsit prize level material."

"Pulitzer?" she laughed.

"Whatever, you knew what I meant. Give me the when and where, and it needs to be today. You're going to print with this in tomorrow's noon edition."

"Pardon? Ell, you can't be serious. This isn't Channel Six. Research, writing, editing, this shit takes time."

"Sorry kid, that's the option available. If you can't break the story by noon then I need to find someone that can."

She knew that would push Cindy to the edge and she knew the girl could get this out in time if she took it on.

"Shit... Shit, fuck, damn. I hate you Frost. I hate you with sugar and a fucking cherry on top. Meet me at the Chronicle in twenty and be ready to spill fast because you just put me on an impossible deadline."

Ell had anticipated the location and was already en route.

"I can be there in ten. Get a private room ready."

She hung up and accelerated through three lanes of traffic, cursing the other drivers as she roared past.

She pulled into the Chronicle parking lot in seven minutes flat and took the opportunity to call Rique and check in on the team. Baker and Jones were still out circulating their new sketch. He and Colonel Craig had been digging into the command structure on Unit H.L.A and had a good run down on potential areas of operation. They believed they had identified two agents on the lower end of the structure, possibly lead field agents based on what they thought they were dealing with.

"It looks like they're setup with a lead agent as a communication go between and only a single active operative in any given area. We can't find anything on their actual mission parameters, but there are some kinky reports that seem to tie in to the locations we have flagged. I'm talking national security level stuff, L.T. Terrorist cells that have been under surveillance for months or years and suddenly there's nothing. No surveillance and no terrorists. Just reading this shit has me looking over my shoulders."

"Better get some eyes in the back of your head because I'm about to bring the whole thing into the light. I have a meeting with Cindy Shepard in two minutes and she's running the story in tomorrow's noon edition. The Commander is on board and he's setting up a meeting for tomorrow morning. I get to look into some D.O.D. assholes' eyes and explain what's about to happen."

"Jesus, I let you go off on your own for one damn day and you go bat shit crazy?"

"Tell the Colonel to strap in, this ride's about to get bumpy."

She disconnected and headed for the door, ready to give Cindy everything she had.

She had to admit, Cindy Shepard didn't scare easily. The story Ell just fed her should have sent her running for the hills but instead she sat there, enthralled and ready to blow the lid off the entire thing. Ell had left it with her and knew she'd have all of it and more ready for print first thing in the morning.

The sun was dipping behind the horizon as she exited the building in search of her car. She wasn't sure where the day went but her clock read six forty-two so she figured she had better head home, do one last update with the team and send them off for some rest. All hell was going to break loose in a little over sixteen hours so they may as well sleep while they could.

She could smell fresh grilled meat the moment she opened her door and realized that she hadn't eaten since breakfast.

"If you're messing up my kitchen I'll have your head on a spike and there better be some of whatever that is left," she called from the front door.

She found all four of her team spread amongst the kitchen table and counters, fresh steak, potatoes and some type of treeish green thing spread out on plates before them. Baker reached out and handed her a plate minus the green things and she said a silent prayer.

"It's sooooo good, L.T. Tony hooked us up."

"Tony?" she asked flashing Baker a slight glance.

"Don't look at me. He said the Colonel this, Colonel that didn't seem right given the circumstances. It wasn't personal enough."

"Trust me Tony, the last thing you need is the red head getting too personal."

Baker took a swing, trying to stab her in the shoulder with her fork and Ell sidestepped it.

"Better get back in the gym, you're getting slow." Ell knew the comment would cost her next time Baker got her alone and she was really looking forward to it.

The steak was delicious, Ell let out a slight moan as she took her first bite. "Jesus, keep making this stuff and I'll call you whatever you want."

"I figured, given the plan you've put into motion, you should at least have a decent last meal. Seriously, I hope you know what you're doing, Lieutenant, because this is going to blow up fast and hard."

"I'm counting on it. A little pressure may make them think twice about stonewalling us and letting a killer roam free. The more I see the more I am convinced they know who this is and have been putting a lot of time, energy and money into covering it up because somehow this ties back to the dirty little secret I am about to expose."

Ell took another bite and melted in her chair. "Is this unicorn? I'm pretty sure only unicorn steak could taste this good."

"It's just good old fashioned cow. With a few secret herbs tossed on to help,"

Between the steak and latte, Ell was glad she'd been running stairs all week. Minutes later she slid an empty plate across the counter while the others were still slowly savoring the meal. "Finish up and we can hit the board. I want a full review before we shut down for the evening." She pulled open the fridge in search of a drink, took a quick look at the clock, shrugged and grabbed a beer. Suddenly all eyes in the room were staring at her like lost puppies. "Christ, have a damn beer and stop looking at me like that."

Rique began passing out bottles as she headed for the living room. Ell took a couple minutes to review the board. Rique had updated the command structure and location chart for Unit H.L.A. and she could see the pattern they were referring to. In each flagged location there were very distinct security threats that just disappeared. Most of their data had been collected from public records such as search warrants and court records, so it was likely there were plenty of other scenarios they were not picking up on. She noted that there was nothing flagged close to home but she was willing to bet her job on the fact that Unit H.L.A. was active nearby.

"My guess is that they have individual couplings in most major centers," said Colonel Craig from behind her. "We've made the assumption that each area would have only a single operative. We haven't been able to back that up because we haven't been able to identify any of the low level players but it's a solid assumption based on what I've seen in the past. With a wide spread structure such as this, you need to keep each pod small. A two person team would be ideal. Your lead agent sits as a buffer between the street operative and command, providing security to those that call the shots and allowing for direct control over the operatives. It's quick, clean and quiet."

"Is there any indication that Jellic was digging into this?"

"Not that we've come across. In fact, we haven't been able to find any direct connection between H.L.A. and this case aside from what brought us to this point. This sort of thing, civilian wetwork, doesn't fit with what Rique and I are finding. Of course, we haven't been able to tie back any of what we found either. So far it's just speculation. Educated guesswork."

"In my experience educated guesswork is often the best first step. Unfortunately it's not enough to do anything with. We need some facts to connect the dots and without names of the people on the ground those are going to be difficult to come by."

"You're leaving a lot riding on the D.O.D. playing ball. I'm not sure outing them is the best option."

Ell thought about it, thought about the work that they assumed Unit H.L.A. was doing.

"It's the only option. Even if this is some rogue agent or someone only peripherally connected, whatever this unit's mission is, it shouldn't be done in the shadows. It shouldn't be done without the oversight of the public. I understand the need for secrecy when preparing an operation but when it's all said and done, the people need to know what was done in their name. They need to be able to determine if it was what this nation stands for. Without that you are allowing covert to become a cover word for corruption."

"There are some things that the public simply can't handle. Things that need to be done yet most would never understand."

"Tony, I know we come from different worlds. I deal with local crimes, murderers, rapists and your standard neighborhood scum bags. You deal with those same personalities but on a much larger scale. The thing is, what applies to my small scale, the oversight and rule of law, has to apply to yours because that is how we as a nation ensure that our morals and our honor, are being properly represented by those sticking their necks out to protect us. It's not about safety and security because those things don't matter at all if we lose who we are. If we lose what makes us human."

They could hear the troops in the kitchen begin to toss dishes in the sink.

"A conversation that we definitely need to continue," said the General. "For now, let's table it and see if we can't nail this murdering bastard."

"That we can agree on," said Ell as the others made their way into the room. "Updates," she announced.

"If your sketch is accurate, and since it's one of Scribbler's you can guarantee it is, our perp is damn careful," said Jones. "No one saw him or anyone resembling our guy near the Fenn/Plante apartment. I got the same response within a six block radius of the Sandbox. I even reached out, discretely, to a dozen officers at the precinct the day of the breach, twelve cops trained to observe and remember and not one of them saw this guy."

"I assume we also drew a blank on standard databases."

"Good assumption, I couldn't run it through military lines but if they are burying this the way we think they are, it wouldn't have done any good."

"Do we have any good news?"

"I got a hit on the collar," said Baker nonchalantly.

"Jesus, let's lead with that next time."

"It was originally purchased via custom order from Dru Mitchell, a high-end artist in Carlisle Pennsylvania. The call came in about fifteen minutes before you walked in the door. Rique put the fear of god into him and we are expecting a call back this evening with the name of the purchaser and any other information he may have."

"Keep on him, I'm not sure how or if it will play into things but we need to drill it down. Is anyone else burying the lead?"

"Just what you see on the board, L.T." responded Rique. "We've been working every angle we can but we just can't drill down the organization more than a couple high end command levels. There are a few possible we are still digging into but its slow going."

"Well, there's not much more we're going to accomplish at this hour so please feel free to get the hell out of my house and go have some lives."

"The ladies have offered to take Rique and I out for a drink and show us a good time, care to join us?" asked the Colonel.

Ell could sense a nervous energy which she assumed was residual awkwardness from the night before. She considered going with them but could already hear her bed calling and was looking forward to a peaceful night alone.

"Another time, I need to be ready for this meeting tomorrow." She leaned in beside him and whispered. "Enjoy the red head but be careful. She'll eat you alive."

Chapter Twenty-Three

The call came in at 9:14 p.m. Ell had just finished preparing her notes and settled into a hot bath. She considered ignoring it but knew that whoever was calling at this hour probably had something important to say. She snaked an arm out of the bubbles, reached across to a small ledge on the wall and grabbed her cell. The number was familiar but she couldn't place who it was.

"Hello?"

"Frost," it was Commander Nuez, "I'm calling from Keith's cell because it was the safest line I could find. There's no quiet way to bring you in on this but that can't be helped. I just received word that two officers are down at St. Pete's. I need you to take the lead on this because there is no doubt in my mind that it's going to cross over with your current investigation. Officers Kohl and Danuski were pronounced dead on scene."

"Fuck!" Ell's breathing became deep and loud, the anger and frustration growing with each breath.

"I'm on my way there but I need you on scene as soon as possible. This one is yours.

"Give me fifteen minutes and if you get there before me clear the scene. I don't need some damn nurse traipsing through it and contaminating the evidence."

'Assuming there is any,' she thought.

"And I need Lund and his tech monkey's there stat. I'll contact Rique on the way."

"The hospital based M.E. is on-site but I assume you want to pull Sanders in as well."

"Yeah, it's going to ruffle some feathers but if these cases overlap and you know they do, he has the history."

"I'll coordinate and deal with the egos. See you in fifteen."

She jumped out of the tub, pulling the plug on the way, grabbed some jeans and a t-shirt and barely had them on by the time she was out the door.

In true form, she made the trip in less than eleven minutes and was in Unit 430 in under fourteen. The hospital staff and security had the wing cordoned off. She flashed her badge and pushed her way through. Commander Nuez was already securing the scene and moving all non-essential personnel out of the area. When she rounded the corner to room to 43009 it was like replaying a bad nightmare. Aside from the fact that both men were dead and one was laid out on a hospital bed, the scene was nearly a spot on match to the one at the precinct. The attack that landed Officer Kohl here in the first place. For a brief moment, Ell froze. She didn't need to examine the bodies to know the cause of death or the angle of the blade. In fact the slice across Officer Kohl's throat appeared to have just reopened his recently stitched wound.

"Cameras," she screamed.

Looking back at the nurses and doctors conglomerating

at the edge of the hall she repeated, "Who has access to the damn cameras?"

"I can get you access," replied and older, grey haired security guard. "Give me a couple minutes and I'll get the last hour queued up on my station. It's just past the unit desk."

"Perfect, I'll be there in ten, give me footage of this hallway and any that tie into it."

"Yes, ma'am," he replied as he headed down the hall.

Ell took a deep breath and reminded herself that he was trying to be respectful, though she wanted to tell him exactly where he could put his "ma'am".

"Where the hell is Lund?"

"En route," replied the Commander. "He was clear across the city when I tagged him. Sanders should beat him here but..."

An older, portly nurse cut him off. "Excuse me, are you Commander Nuez?"

"Yes."

"I have a gentleman at the nurse's station that is asking to speak with you. He says he is from the Judge Advocate's office. General Costan, I believe."

Ell turned as if she was heading out and the Commander stopped her. "My fight, Frost. I need you in here doing what you do. I sit in the big chair so I get to deal with the political douchebags."

"When you kick his ass, be sure to get a good shot in for me and if the fucker tries to weasel in on my scene remind him that I have two dead cops and no current evidence that indicates any relation to whatever the fuck he's busy covering up."

"I may reword that a bit."

"Add all the expletives you need," she called out as he followed the nurse down the hall.

Rique rounded the corner just as she lost sight of the Commander. "How the fuck did this happen? I thought his location was being restricted?"

"A lot of good that did," said Ell. "I should have seen this coming. Unfinished business."

"Come on, L.T., he wasn't the target. He was collateral damage why would they come back for him."

"Because he saw their face..." she paused. "Oh, shit."

Without explanation she bolted down the hall around the corner and up two flights of stairs. Officer Smitts was now back on duty outside Claire Fenn's room and snapped to attention when he saw her flying down the hall towards him.

"Report," she said coming to a halt in front of him.

"No one in or out since five. My shift began at noon and two separate nurses have been through since. One at two and another at five."

"And the patient?"

"Fine last I heard, expected to be released tomorrow morning."

Ell took a deep breath, prepared for the worst and opened the door. Claire Fenn was sitting in her bed, the back raised to a seated position, reading a book.

"Lieutenant?"

"Claire, I was here on another matter and just wanted to check in and see how you are holding up."

"Good, my body is healing and the doctors said I could be out in the morning. The sketch, did it help? Your artist is very good and I think we came close."

"We are working with it now. You did well and Ms. Cue was impressed. It will help."

"I'm glad. I'm glad I could help."

Ell still couldn't get a read on the girl and really hoped she would seek assistance to get past the trauma that she had endured. She just seemed so detached.

"How are you holding up, mentally?" she asked.

"I've been better but I'm dealing with it. I had a nice long talk with Liz yesterday and that helped. Jon came with her which was nice considering how things ended. I guess he just wanted to make sure I was okay."

Ell thought better than to mention that it was more likely he was there to support Liz.

"I'm glad. Listen, I have to go deal with this other case but if you need anything please give me a call."

On her way out she updated Officer Smitts on the attack on the fourth floor and how it tied in with the Fenn case. If he was surprised, shocked or saddened by the news, it didn't show. He assured her he would remain vigilant and that he would pass along the information at shift change. Ell walked away even further convinced that the man was part android.

Both Lund and Sanders had arrived on scene by the time she got back to the fourth floor.

"Nail this fucker," said Lund as she approached, "and when you do I want five minutes alone with him."

"I can't guarantee the last part but the first is my priority. Is anything in there going to help me do that?"

"Don't know yet. I'm just waiting for Sanders to give the all clear on the bodies, but if the past few scenes are any indication the answer is no."

"Find me something. I have to go check on the security footage. Maybe we got lucky and the fucker forgot about the cameras."

"If so I'm spending this week's salary on lotto tickets."

"If we're that lucky you should only need one."

She found the old, grey haired security guard sitting in front of a flat screen monitor staring at it intently.

"I don't think you are going to like it, Detective."

"It's Lieutenant. Lieutenant Frost."

"Take a look, I can't explain it."

Ell scrolled through one hour of footage. The only person to enter or exit the room was Officer Danuski who stepped out forty-two minutes before the bodies were discovered and was back in the room within seven minutes of leaving. Two nurses and one doctor were seen on tape in the adjacent halls but none of them came anywhere near the door.

"Could the footage have been altered?"

"I suppose, I barely know how to pull it up. I'm really not the guy to be asking."

'No,' she thought, 'the guy to be asking is stepping off a plane from Seattle in about thirty-five minutes.'

She pulled out her cell and fired Rob a text.

"I know you won't get this until you land but I need someone to verify some security footage stat. Call me when you're down. – E"

She nearly ignored her phone when it buzzed a couple seconds later.

"Where is the footage from? Can you have it emailed to me? – R"

"Did you catch an early flight or did the robot overlords finally decide to synchronize time worldwide? – E"

"I'm still about a half hour out. You're experiencing the joys of modern technology and $7.00 in-air wifi. – R"

She could not wrap her head around the concept.

"I can't get signal in my basement but you're good to go at thirty thousand feet? I need to hire a better tech. – E"

"Perhaps you're just not paying the right currency. – R"

"Later, probably much later given the night I'm having. Two down at St. Pete's, both cops. I'll have the footage sent as soon as possible. I need to know if it's been tampered with. Whips and chains. – E"

"W&C back atcha. – R"

Ell gave the security guard Rob's email and directed him to email copies of the footage as soon as possible. He thought he could figure out how, but knew who to ask if he had any problems. She left him to it and headed back to the blood and gore portion of her evening.

Sanders grabbed her on her way back into the room.

"Do I need to give you the run down?"

"Probably not, any differences?"

"Officer Kohl was horizontal in bed and the slices are a little deeper. He probably figured more pressure would equal more dead and less chance of someone saving him this time. Aside from that, the angle of attack, likely height of attacker, right handed nature, are all the same. He used a different blade, thinner and shorter but just as sharp. It may have been a scalpel."

That was something different, but how did it fit in? A scalpel would have been a tool of opportunity, that tied with the items scrounged at the Jellic murder. They had used items found on scene but, once again, it didn't fit her theory of a planned attack. It didn't fit a professional.

"Time of death?" she asked though she knew that if the footage was authentic it was between eight-thirty and nine.

"I'll give you a small window for now and tighten it up once I have the bodies back at the house. Probably within fifteen to twenty minutes of discovery."

'Long enough,' she thought.

"Thanks, I'm going to go curse out Lund and see if it helps him find something."

"Enjoy it. It looks like it's going to be a late night for all involved."

Her phone buzzed just as she entered the room.

"Tape's authentic. – R"

"How could you possibly have received it and verified it that quickly. – E"

"The email hasn't shown up yet so I found a backdoor into the hospital server and reviewed the original. Nothing fishy, you're seeing whatever happened. – R"

'Which was nothing,' she thought.

"Thanks, I'll likely be working this till morning so come say hi when you get a chance. - E"

"Wouldn't miss it. – R"

She abstained from the traditional sign off and just sent him a picture of a heart.

"Lund, I need a secondary point of entry."

He actually laughed. "Unless teleportation is an option you have the door or the window and the window is a sheer brick face four stories up. Not an easy climb."

"Print it and check the frame, glass etc. It just became the only entry option."

"Well, that's something, let's hope it pays off."

She left the techs to their job, grabbed Rique and headed

out to find the Commander. He was still having a few heated words with General Costan when she approached.

"Sorry General, I need the Commander on an active double homicide. Feel free to take your bitching and complaining to a different higher authority, I need this one."

The General launched into a tirade but Ell just pulled the Commander away and down the hall.

"I'm betting you didn't use enough expletives and from the sounds of things he's now cornered that market. I'll let you go back and take some more abuse in a second. I just need to know where I'm working this, because it's looking to be a late night."

"Keep everything where you are for now. That may change tomorrow after you drop the nuke on the D.O.D. but I'm having enough trouble shutting up the General here and don't need his crap flowing into your case."

She thanked him and sent him back into the line of fire as her and Rique headed for the parking lot.

"Tell the red head to quit dancing on the tables, the party's over," Ell hollered into her hands free system, trying to raise her voice over the background noise on the other end of the call.

"Christ, Frost. Neither of these two is in any shape to work," replied Jones as the music behind her faded out. "I'll be lucky if I can get them to the station upright."

"We're not going to the station. This one ties in so it's being run out of the house. It turns out I have a couple nice beds and much better coffee than the bullpen so toss your collective asses into a cab and get back there. The party animals can sleep it off for a couple hours and deal with the repercussions from there. I've got two dead officers, Jones. These are our people and we damn sure owe them a little sacrifice."

"We'll be there in fifteen but I'm warning you, Baker is plowed. She won't like this and she's going to be a supreme bitch when you tell her to go sleep it off."

"Me?" laughed Ell.

"Yeah, you. It's the bonus you get with the fancy title."

"Yippee, and here I thought it only came with stress and responsibility."

Ell pulled in ten minutes before the cab with Rique still right on her tail.

"Damn, you actually kept up?" she said as they exited their individual vehicles.

"It's pretty easy to go mach twelve at this time of night. Still ludicrous, but easy."

"I'm surprised that piece of shit department issue could even do it?"

"She may look like crap, L.T. but she runs... well... like crap too. Whatever, I'm here."

"The rest of the team is right behind us, though I doubt the Colonel and the bombshell are going to be much help for a couple hours. Jones said they really let loose once I sprung them."

"Yeah, they were dancing on speakers when I got the call. By now we'll be lucky if they're walking."

"We'll toss them in a bed, actually make that separate beds," she corrected not wanting to even think of the trouble a single could bring, "and give them a couple hours to sober up. After that they can deal with the fucking hangover and work it off."

True to her word, Jones was nearly carrying the other two as she came through the door.

"Damn it Froosty, we haben't getted to the good part yet. Colonel Cutie's still got his padants on," slurred Baker as they came through the door.

"Blame it on the bastard who left me two corpses as a present. You," she pointed at the Colonel, "master bed and you," she shook her head at the giggling Baker, "spare room. Go get a couple hours and sober the fuck up. I need your eyes on this and your minds a hell of a lot sharper than they are right now."

"Murder and maynahem harshing ooll my fun," pouted the redhead as she stumbled off to the guest room.

"And how are you?" Ell asked Detective Jones.

"I'm fine, had a couple but nothing crazy. Once those two got going and Rique was called out, I figured someone should be sober enough to babysit."

"A good call, given the circumstances. If this was anything else I'd have left the three of you out of it until morning but…"

"I get it, L.T. Dead cops change everything. Give me a run down on the scene and let's see if there's something we can do before the city wakes up."

Chapter Twenty-Four

$\mathcal{J}$ ones nearly jumped out of her seat and let out a small yelp when the front door swung open at just after midnight.

"You said to stop by in the morning when I was free. It's morning, I'm free and I assumed you could use some help," said Rob as he sauntered into the foyer.

Ell's heart stopped, just the sight of him caused her temperature to rise and her skin to tingle. She hadn't realized, until that moment, how much she had missed him. His smile, his laughter, his mere presence, brought a sense of both calm and excitement.

"Did it occur to you that we could be sleeping? It is after midnight," smirked Ell, knowing that he knew her too well for that.

"Two dead cops? I don't think sleep is an option for anyone on your team. Though I don't see that rambunctious red head at the moment."

"Spare room, it turns out sleep is an option when you're too inebriated to walk. I had given them all the go ahead for some downtime since the case had hit a plateau. It sort of backfired on me. This entire case has been one mess after another so why not add some drunk cops and consultants into the mix."

Rob reached out to brush the hair from the side of her face in a comforting motion, forgetting about the company in the room. Her eyes went steel hard with fear as she took a step back and forced a smile. She was sure her team knew about her and Rob but having it right there, out in the open made something inside her scream in terror.

She took a deep breath and mouthed, "Sorry," seeing the confusion and hurt in his eyes.

He nodded and turned his attention to the case board.

"So why doesn't someone fill me in and we'll see if a fresh set of eyes can help shake something free."

The four of them sat down around the board and Ell began going through the case and what they had found, starting with the Jellic murder and moving forward. When she mentioned the breach and murder at the precinct Rob stopped her.

"Whoa, hold on, at the precinct, as in at our precinct, the eleventh?"

"Yeah, I called you on this and told you about the security breach using CleanSlate."

"You told me about 'a' security breach using CleanSlate and that a witness was killed and an officer wounded. You didn't mention that it was at the precinct."

She assumed his ego was taking a bit of a beating right now, finding out that it was his security system that had been breached.

"Shit, sorry, I hadn't realized," she said.

"No, Ell, you don't get it. They just made their first major mistake. When I landed the contract with GenData and discovered what they were working on I knew that, eventually, someone else would be looking for a system that could fight against their new software. That's how the security industry works. You build a better lock, they build a better key. You build a different lock, and so on. I figured it could be a lucrative side business once word of CleanSlate got out."

"Isn't that a bit of a conflict?" asked Jones.

"Maybe, but I didn't have a hand in the actual CleanSlate code, just the software security and because my contract licensed my code and I retained ownership there was no need for a non-compete agreement. I'd have given GenData a heads up before I went public with something and they'd have started on a new way to break what I built. It's business. Anyway, the point is I began developing something and needed a system to use as my guinea pig."

"You're kidding," said Ell, eyes wide.

"Not in the least. The eleventh precinct has a redundant security feed that is most likely unaffected by CleanSlate."

"Most likely?"

"I don't have access to a copy of the software so testing hasn't been easy. At this point it's theoretical but I suppose we are about to find out if it works."

"I should have known," said Ell shaking her head. "God forbid someone be able to beat one of your systems."

"It's happened, but I guarantee it doesn't last long."

"Get me the damn footage and let's see if you're as brilliant as you think you are."

"It's going to take a bit, I can't access it remotely so I need to be at the precinct and the system is completely offline. Assuming it was successful, I'll need to burn the footage out to a secondary hardrive and get it uploaded for you. Can you send me the details on the date and time? Give me an hour," he said grabbing his leather coat from the edge of the couch. Ell stood as he did, perhaps out of instinct and, without thinking, he leaned in and kissed her cheek before rushing out the door.

Her face began to flush as Jones and Rique stared at her. She could feel her heart racing and struggled to focus her mind. Looking at the two officers, each now smirking, she smirked back and said, "Yeah, that's a thing. Now can we please get back to fucking work?"

Ell prepared her notes on the hospital crime scene, trying not to focus on how responsible she felt. Jones and Rique combed through hospital records and visitor logs looking for anything that might pop. It was a long shot but until the crime scene techs managed to pull something together, long shots were all they had. The time ticked away and when one hour rolled into two she was starting to get nervous. When she finally couldn't take it any longer she pulled out her phone and composed a message.

"Your hour is up. – E"

"There's a bit... just call me. – R"

She hit dial and tried to keep her voice low as to not disturb the sleeping partygoers.

"Sorry," he said, "but I can't really text and work this algorithm."

"Can I assume your redundant system didn't pass the beta test?"

He was impressed she knew the phrase but wasn't sure she actually knew what a beta test was.

"This wasn't even close to the beta testing stage. Without the CleanSlate software to test against I was running on instinct and assumption. I have the video but it's still scrambled, I didn't anticipate a secondary encryption on their bypass. The good news is it's not wiped just fucked and I'm fairly certain I can un-fuck it. The bad news is, it's going to take time."

"What are we talking, days, weeks, months?"

"I'm aiming for hours but this is virgin territory."

"Something you're not used to."

His head was so deep in the code that he didn't catch the joke.

"What?"

"Virgin territory, something you're not used to. Jesus, never mind, it loses the humor if I need to explain it. Let me know if and when you've got something."

"You'll be my first call."

Ell was about to hang up when she paused. "Is Lund at the precinct?"

"He was when I came in. He and two lab techs had their heads into something serious. Fuck, yeah that's it baby now I've got you."

"You sweet talking little devil. I'll let you go play king of the microchips."

She was happy to hear that Lund was still in. It increased the odds that he'd found something. She was tempted to call but weighed the interruption versus the effect of her pushing him and decided that with two fellow officers in the morgue he was sufficiently motivated.

Her mind was racing and her body wanted to follow suit but she found herself staring at the case board, drawing a blank on the next step. She was stuck waiting for more data. She needed a new lead but she was stuck spinning, a situation she despised. In an effort to feel useful, she began detailing the major discrepancies she had encountered thus far.

1) Jellic scene, precinct and hospital had precision slicing and professional clean-up.
2) Jellic scene used items found in the apartment showing lack of planning.
3) Sandbox scene showed random slicing and indicated a left handed attack.
4) Sandbox scene also showed same level of professional clean-up
5) All other scenes indicated a right handed attacker.
6) Hospital wounds were possibly made by a scalpel. Again, an item available on-site showing lack of prior planning,

There was something else missing and she was struggling to pinpoint what it was. It had been gnawing at her and she was continually drawing a blank.

"Don't forget the perps wound," said a whoozy, sleepy eyed Baker from the doorway to the room. "There was a lot of his blood at scene one but nowhere else so somewhere in between he had to take care of whatever wound was leaking."

It was a good point, not the one she was digging for but a solid observation that Ell had passed over.

"Even when you look like death you've got a solid detective's mind."

Baker wasn't sure if it was a compliment to her mind or an insult to her appearance but both applied.

"Do you have any Advil in this house? If I'm upright and semi-sober I may as well be helping."

"Advil is in the second drawer in the hall bathroom. Hot, non-tar, coffee is in the pot in the kitchen waiting for you."

"You're my new hero, Ell. A bloody godsend. Do you want me to wake up sleeping cutie?"

"No, let him crash. We're pretty much spinning wheels and waiting for more information on the hospital scene. Rob may have a line on footage from the precinct but it'll be hours before we know for sure."

"Rob's home?" she seemed surprised and happy.

"Yeah, he blew in just after midnight and blew out just as fast once he found out the breach was at the precinct. He thinks he has a line on the video because of some redundant test system he's been playing around with."

"Gotcha, blah blah tech, blah blah Rob's awesome blah blah may have the video we need."

Ell smiled as Baker tried to wave the mess of mangled red hair out of her face. "Yeah that pretty much sums it up."

"Ok, pills then coffee. Back in five."

Jones and Rique had worked their way through the hospital staff and visitors, nothing popped as out of the ordinary. She hadn't expected to find anything but you had to put in the leg work and eliminate the obvious.

"Why don't you two find somewhere to crash and try to get a couple hours in before dawn. I think Baker's up for the night. She and I will keep running through the data looking for inconsistencies. There's not much else we can do before the tech team gets us some data."

Ell stared at the board, still searching for that missing piece when suddenly a steaming hot mug of coffee slid over her shoulder.

"I figured you could use one too. It's been a long day and I'm pretty sure you didn't sleep much last night." Baker was smiling and running her tongue across her front teeth.

"I slept great."

"Yeah, I'll bet you did. Just not for long. How was he?"

Ell shook her head and let out a sigh as a smile began to grow across her lips.

"He was... different. Not better, not worse but different. He was a little tentative at first but aggressive enough in the end."

"So? Plain?"

"Yes, but a nice change. Not an everyday meal but a decent snack once in awhile."

"If it wasn't for you and your damn double homicide we could be comparing notes right now. I had him just where I wanted him."

"You had him drunk and not happy, friendly drunk. Damn near passed out and barely walking drunk. You'd be lucky if he could have gotten it up and even then one or both of you would have been unconscious before it was over."

"Okay, maybe my plan had some holes but we'll never know now, will we?"

"I'll make you a deal, when we solve this case I'll make sure you get another shot at Colonel Cutie.

"Yeah, I hear a condition coming."

"Don't hurt the poor guy too much, he really has no idea what he's walking into."

Chapter Twenty-Five

$\mathcal{E}$ ll finally crashed just after 4:00 a.m. having relented to the fact that she was going in circles and knowing that she needed to be on the top of her game for the meeting with the D.O.D. later that morning.

She awoke, sprawled out on the couch, to the sound of her team gathered in the kitchen reviewing the list of discrepancies and possible explanations.

"It has to be a two man crew," said Rique. "It's the only way most of this makes sense."

"But our victim only identified a single perp and she was at two different crime scenes," replied Jones.

"She was hooded and blindfolded, maybe she only ever saw one of the two."

Baker chimed in, "If that's the case it doesn't explain the difference in right and left handed strikes. She saw the guy at the Jellic scene and he was the one that took her and tortured her. But the lacerations on Jellic don't match up with hers."

"Thank you all for loudly elaborating the conversation that has been circling around my mind for two days," said

Ell stumbling into the kitchen and grabbing a fresh coffee. She caught a quick look at the clock. Eight-forty. "Christ, why didn't one of you wake me?"

"You looked peaceful," replied the Colonel, "and given that you're meeting with the D.O.D. to throw your career under a bus, we thought you could use some rest."

She checked her phone, unsure if the Commander had given her a time and noticed an email calendar invite. The D.O.D. meeting was in Commander Nuez' office at 10:00 a.m. She was surprised and delighted that he had managed to have them come to the precinct. Home field wasn't much of an advantage but it did lend a bit of comfort.

An hour and twenty minutes didn't leave much time for anything else but she figured she could at least head in early and check with Lund and Rob beforehand. She slammed back her coffee and told the crew she was going to grab a shower and head back to the precinct. As she passed the edge of the room, Baker lifted her eyebrows and mouthed, "Want company?" Ell barely managed to make it out of the kitchen and down the hall without starting to laugh at the thought. If Rob's peck on the cheek had left Jones and Rique staring, she could only imagine what that image would do.

"Fuck you. I know you're going to break eventually so you may as well start now."

Ell recognized Rob cursing out an inanimate object as she approached the swank, spacious space he called an office. She paused in the doorway for just a moment, taking in the site of the I.T. demi-god in his natural habitat. He was glaring at the conglomeration of four sleek monitors that adorned his desk, a large bottle of, almost empty, grape soda to his right and a stack of books spread out, open to a series of strange glyphs, to his left. He didn't process the fact that he was being watched, too intent on the job at hand.

"Fuck!" he screamed throwing his mouse across the room at a speed Ell did not expect. She watched it explode into a slew of tiny pieces and nearly laughed. Only a stubborn computer could break through Rob's calm demeanor and even that was a rare occurrence. Part of her was glad to witness it.

"I guess I don't need to ask how it's going."

He took a couple deep breaths, determined not to take out the anger and frustration on her.

"I'm so fucking close but I can't break through the final barrier. I have a choppy, wavy, pixilated video at the moment but I just can't find that final piece to snap it back together.

"Can I see what you have?"

Rob waved her over, jumped between a couple windows on the screen, typed in some unrecognizable robot script and a video popped up on the far right monitor. He was right, it was choppy, wavy and had next to no detail but there were colors and shapes. She thought she could make out a hallway and a grey blob travelling through it.

"Is that my killer?"

"That or swamp thing. At this point I can't distinguish."

"You have something here. It's not much yet and an ID is going to need a hell of a lot more, but you have scale. Would that still be distorted?"

"A little but it's going to be close, I've managed to reimage back to an 83.7% zone."

"Close as in inches, feet, yards, what are we talking about here?"

"Blob man is probably within a couple inches either way of what we are seeing."

"Okay, I can work with that. We know the angle of that camera and the frame it covers, correct?"

"I assume it hasn't moved and I have footage from earlier in the day to verify. You want to know the coverage height," he said catching on to what she was doing. "Genius. The current angle gives us eight feet three inches of wall, if we factor in the angle and distance from the camera that puts the blob between..." he did some quick math, "five foot five and five foot nine."

"Still a decent sized gap but it helps."

"He's small, for a guy nowadays even five nine is small."

"And his Napoleon Complex is running overtime," she leaned down and went to kiss his cheek. He turned his face in anticipation and devoured her lips with his. Ell could feel her heart pounding, the rush of ecstasy coursing through her as she pulled away slowly.

"Keep going, you're close," she said and he smiled, nodded slightly and relaxed.

She headed out to check in with Lund and called out over her shoulder.

"And get a new mouse. I think that one's done for."

She found Lund passed out in his office chair, thought about letting him catch a couple more minutes but shrugged and walked in.

"Is this what you tech monkeys do while the rest of us are out there serving and protecting?"

"Fuck you Frost," he said without moving or opening his

eyes. "We've been straight through since we left the hospital. Can you say the same?"

He had her there, "Nope can't say I was and don't think for a second it's not appreciated. Those officers Sanders has on a slab, they're getting the best team in the city and they know it. So what did your long night turn up?"

"A couple foot prints in the blood around the bodies. It's pretty standard considering it was close quarters work. We see it at most of these scenes, with that much blood it's impossible to get out with stepping in it. I've had the monkeys trying to extrapolate shoe size and such. No discernible tread but their thinking a men's seven, maybe seven and a half.

"Small feet, that fits in with what I saw on the video Rob's trying to recreate from the precinct attack. He's putting the perp between five-five and five-nine."

"Well the tiny bastard knows his way around a blade and can climb like a fucking cat. We found three small blood drops on the window frame. Two inside and one out. It looks like you were right, our guy scaled the wall somehow. That window is our point of entry. Once we knew that we dusted every inch of the sill, window, frame and surrounding brick but came up blank. Odds are he was gloved. Not unlike the other scenes, he did a decent job of cleaning up and ensuring we didn't have much to go on.".

"Ok, if that's the case what's been keeping you up all night," she asked, knowing he was holding back on her.

Lund finally opened his eyes and smiled. "Follow me."

He led her out of the office to the lab space across the hall and gestured to a tiny microscope. "Look what I found in the sheets of Officer Kohl's bed."

Ell leaned down, placing her eye to the scope. "Is that?"

"That, my dear Lieutenant, is a contact lens. One left during, not before or after, the attacks. We know this because it was resting between two layers of blood."

"It looks pretty clean to me."

"Yes, because I've spent six hours trying to find a way to clean the damn thing without disturbing the finger print beneath the blood."

"Shit, you've got a print?"

"People tend not to wear gloves when putting these things in, it makes it difficult. DNA is a bust, the blood and cleaning process would have made a match impossible, but I was able to maintain a partial print. In fact, I just finished with it about twenty minutes ago. It's running through all civilian systems now just waiting for a match."

"Hoping for a match," she corrected. Whoever this is has been covering their tracks well. There's a good chance their prints aren't in the system."

"Stop killing my victory buzz. I'll let you know 'when' I get a hit. Now, if you don't mind, I'm going back to resting my eyes."

"Fine, you've earned a nap but the second you hit on something, call me."

"Yes, mistress," he mocked as he made his way across the hall.

Chapter Twenty-Six

"*W*hat the hell is she doing here?" demanded General Costan as he strolled into Commander Nuez' office and notice Ell standing beside the desk.

"Seeing as this is my meeting and it is supposed to be with a ranking official from the D.O.D. and not the misogynistic bastard in charge of the local Judge Advocate's office, I believe that was my question, General."

His eyes flared and Ell could see the vein in the side of his neck pulsing. He was about to explode. The gentleman behind him, also in full dress military uniform, placed a hand on Costan's shoulder and gave him a stern look.

"General Tanner Marcus with the Department of Defense. I assume you must be Lieutenant Frost."

Ell flashed him a knowing grin. His name was one of the few they had discovered in the Unit H.L.A. chain of command. "Well at least they sent the right man."

"Pardon?"

"Why don't we all take a seat before we get into it," suggested the Commander. The men sat, however Ell continued to stand. With all the testosterone, alpha personalities and egos in the room she was at a disadvantage. The elevated position would help lend her an air of power. It wouldn't do much against the personalities present but it would help her to steady her nerves and focus.

After some polite greetings General Marcus began, "I assume we are here to negotiate the release of your missing case files and evidence? I must say, Commander, I am less than impressed with the professional courtesy we have received on this matter."

Commander Nuez looked up at Ell. "Lieutenant, this is your meeting. Would you care to address the General's concerns?"

"Honestly, I don't have the time or energy for the General's concerns, sir. General, I have no intention of handing over my files and allowing this case to be buried in order to cover up the D.O.D.'s dark secrets. I intend on solving the murders that your organization doesn't seem to care about and bringing this killer to justice. If that doesn't align with what you consider professional courtesy, I really don't care because it does align with basic human decency, with moral behavior, and with a word your organization throws around so often yet fails to understand, honor."

General Costan ground his teeth and stared at his cohort. "I told you she was an uppity little bitch."

"Costan, shut up," responded the General.

"I'm not sure what you think you are investigating, Lieutenant but I can assure you this is a military matter concerning highly classified information."

"Such as Unit H.L.A.?" Ell asked as if everyone should know about it. The General's eyes grew and shock registered across his face for a moment before he regained his composure. It was a reaction that made Ell wish this were a game of poker.

"Yes, matters such as that. Matters which are above your pay grade."

"Have you seen my paycheck, General. Pretty much everything is above my paygrade but here I am, taking down the scum infecting this city and digging into the organizations that cover it up. I'm not here to explain my investigation or myself to you, General. I called this meeting as a simple courtesy to allow you time to prepare."

"Prepare? Lieutenant you have neither the authority or ability to investigate, myself, the unit or the core. You're overstepping if you believe otherwise."

"Oh, I'm not investigating your organization, I have homicides to solve. The civilian media will be handling the investigation into your unit and your core. As of noon today everything I have on Unit H.L.A. as well as plenty more that the media has been able to dig up, will become very public."

"Your bitch cop is blackmailing us?" said General Costan, staring at Commander Nuez. Having shown her no respect and ignoring Ell completely he didn't see the fist coming before it connected with his left eye and sent his chair toppling over backwards.

"I gave you the first one for free but the name is Lieutenant Ellison Frost and I'm no one's bitch." It wasn't true, there were nights she'd had actually begged Rob to 'make her his bitch' but it sounded damn good.

"Let me make this clear, General, we are not blackmailing you. Whether you assist in our investigation or not the information goes to print in less than two hours. Not because I have a vendetta against your organization and not because you're fucking me over on four homicides, but because it is the right thing to do. The US military should not have the unrestricted ability to run covert operations inside our borders without civilian oversight. You represent and protect us, our way of life, and we have the right to ensure that representation is done in a way that demonstrates that our values and our honor matter. If your organization works and it protects the public, then I applaud it and I encourage it to continue but you'll do so in the light of day with the people seeing the outcome and understanding the costs involved. In the meantime, this man," she pulled out a copy of Scribbler's sketch. "I'll find him, find out how he ties in with your unit and I will take him down."

The General took a close look at the sketch, studying it for a second and said, "I can assure you, he's not one of mine. I've never seen him. Now, if you will excuse us," he pulled General Costan off the floor by the arm, "I have some people to inform before the story breaks."

They were heading for the door when he stopped and turned. "Lieutenant, we're not the bad guys. Some of what we do may not be perfect, but our justification is solid and what we do does make a difference."

"If that's the case then it will still make a difference, even if the public is watching."

He nodded and continued to drag General Costan through the door.

Ell sent Cindy Shepard a quick text. "It's a go," and turned to face the Commander.

"About the punch, sir."

He waved her off, "We'll deal with it if Costan raises a complaint. I'm guessing he'd rather wear the shiner and move on than admit publicly that you knocked his ass into next Tuesday."

Ell stared at the sketch trying to think back to the General's reactions. He had shown himself to have a poor poker face when she first mentioned Unit H.L.A., however he didn't flinch when he saw the sketch. His eyes barely changed.

"You believe him, don't you?" said the Commander.

"He wasn't able to hide his reaction to anything else. When he looked at it, I could see him thinking but there was no recognition. Either he's a far better actor than I believe or we're not dealing with a rogue agent. That leaves me with about fifty new questions. I need to regroup with my team."

"Go... and don't forget to put some ice on that hand."

Ell had just settled back into the leather driver's seat of her S550 when Rob called.

"You can thank me later," the jubilation in his voice was unmistakable."

"Seriously? You cracked it?"

"I'd say the video is at about ninety-six percent. Better than VHS quality not quite DVD."

"I'll take it and I'll even promise not to leave a poor review. What do we have?"

"I've got rear footage of her entering the Interrogation Room and a pretty decent face shot as she exits."

"Send me the still. Wait, did you say her?" Ell was expecting confirmation on the sketch.

"Yes, a female in her late twenties or early thirties and from the look in her eyes, a stone cold, emotionless one at that. The still shot is on its way to your phone. I'll toss the footage onto your home unit and then I'm heading out. I'm in desperate need of a shower and a few hours unconscious. Ell... Ell, you there?"

Ell was still on the line but had gone dead silent. She was staring down at the cold eyes in the photo she had just received. Eyes she knew, eyes that reflected the truly evil soul of Claire Fenn.

Chapter Twenty-Seven

"She played us like a fucking fiddle," said Ell, her team now gathered around the case board staring at the security footage. "The innocent paralegal taken hostage and tortured, she played on our sympathies and sent us on a hunt for some mystery man to cover her ass."

"It fits," replied Baker, "it crosses off all our concerns. The items at the Jellic scene that were scrounged from the apartment and not planned. It was her apartment and she knew exactly what she was using."

"The amateur slicing on her person and switch to left handed assailant at her scene, that makes sense if the wounds were self inflicted," said Rique.

"Yeah, so does the piss poor install of the door bomb. She had to make sure it was positioned not to damage herself while she was still tied up in that back room."

"What about the second sample of male blood at the Jellic scene?" asked Jones. "An accomplice?"

"More likely a misdirection. It would fit the pattern. She froze Jellic to throw off time of death, faked a kidnapping to give herself an alibi and provided us a fake sketch to waste our resources on, why not toss in some extra blood and DNA to keep us on our toes?"

Ell grabbed the night vision shot of Claire Fenn bound over the pommel horse. There it was. The thing that had been eating at her, something she should have noticed from the start. Dark lines streaking over the right shoulder blade and down towards the chest. Marks that should only be there if the flogging was self inflicted.

"We should have seen it. Look how tidy this is, blood pooled around the body in small sections yet nothing disturbed, no footprints, no tools too far out of reach."

"It's easy to beat ourselves up after the fact, L.T.," said Jones, "but this doesn't explain everything. How'd she know we had Dover or where to find officer Kohl, we kept that information tight."

"I told her. Fuck, I actually told her."

The others stared at her, unsure why she would.

"Not directly. She must not have been unconscious when we found her at the Sandbox. Which makes sense, why knock yourself out when you can play dead. She would have heard me talking to your team on the radio and confirming that we had Dover in custody. As for Officer Kohl I told Denise Cue his room number so she could go see how he was doing. The two of us were standing right outside Fenn's room."

"So she found a scalpel and went Spiderman, scaling down from her window to his two stories below?" asked Baker.

"That's how I'd do it," said the Colonel. "We did extensive repel and scale training in special ops, it would have been difficult but not impossible."

Ell stared into the cold dead eyes in the photo. "And I'll bet my reputation that's exactly where she received the training to do it. This is our local H.L.A. operative and something set her off. Baker, any word on a location?"

"The hospital says she checked out at nine and the roommate hasn't seen or heard from her. I sent two uniforms passed the apartment but it's empty. They are staying on-site and will report anything suspicious."

Ell continued to stare at the photo, "Who are you? Where would you hide?" Pinning it back to the board she turned to face the team. "New focus, we need everything we can dig up on Ms. Fenn. Rique, dig back into the Jane Sandusky story, considering that she gave it up willingly I'm starting to doubt its authenticity. I need to update the Commander."

She headed to her desk, leaving the rest of the team to do what they did best. After a couple minutes contemplation she pulled out her phone and dialed the Commander's office.

"You've reached Commander Nuez' office, Keith speaking."

"Keith, it's Frost, I need to speak with him."

"For once, your timing is perfect, Lieutenant, the Commander has just freed up."

"Keith, before you put me through, give me a second." She took a deep breath knowing this was going to be difficult. "The other day," she continued, "I was a little harsh when you called. I just wanted to say I'm sorry."

"Oh," he paused as if thinking, "I hadn't noticed, Lieutenant but I will accept the apology. If you'll hold one moment I will connect you to the Commander."

The line began playing some light jazz for a moment before the Commander picked up.

"Lieutenant?"

"What do you feed that kid, microchips?"

"Who, Keith?"

"Nevermind, we've had a break. Rob worked some of his wizard touch on the precinct video and got me a face."

"Didn't Denise Cue already get you a face?"

"Yes, but not the right face because, unfortunately, we asked our perp to provide the details."

"Claire Fenn?"

"That's the name she's going by now, we're still digging into who she really is. Rob has a photo of her leaving the Interrogation Room moments before I arrived."

"This is the hostage we rescued, correct. The one that was tortured and shackled?"

"The one that wanted us to believe she had been, yes. She manufactured herself an alibi for Jellic's murder. I'm still working on the motive but our main focus right now is locating her. She was released from St. Pete's this morning and is in the wind."

She could tell he was flummoxed. "We'll review how the hell this got passed us later, for now find her and get her in a god damn cage before more bodies drop."

"On it," she said and quickly disconnected, looking up and seeing a frantic Baker, phone to her ear, waving like a madman from the end of the hall.

She headed out just as Baker hung up.

"The collar was purchased by one David Jellic a little over fifteen years ago. Mr. Mitchell had to go digging through archived records to find it. It was a custom job ordered by Jellic but picked up and signed for by a Mary Rutherford."

"Interesting. At some point Jellic had a taste for the lifestyle and someone he cared for enough to collar. It sheds a different angle on the murder and the state of the corpse. Aside from the staged crime scene at the Sandbox, Jellic was the only one tortured and the only one posed. That speaks to personal and that has been the issue all along. This screams both personal and professional because it was. There is history between Jellic and Fenn. We need to find it."

"Her life is a black hole. I'll start with his and see where she crosses in."

"Perfect, loop me in if you need anything." She could feel the pieces starting to fall into place but knew they were still missing a crucial one. There was a motive here aside from her assumed position in Unit H.L.A. They needed to find it but more importantly they needed to find her.

Ell advised the others that she was heading out on a hunch and to reach out if anything new came together. She settled back into the car and tore out of the driveway. Once comfortably on the way she connected her phone to the hands free system and dialed Angel.

"Two calls in as many days, I'm going to start thinking you're in to me."

"Big crush," replied Ell, "had it since college."

"Mmmmmm, fun days."

"Definitely, unfortunately I didn't call to reminisce. When I called yesterday you were worried about the Jellic case crossing into the lifestyle, why?"

"Because it was seven o'clock in the fucking morning and I hadn't yet remembered to keep my damn mouth shut."

"You knew him."

"Let's say we had a professional relationship from time to time."

"He used your service?"

"Occasionally, he kept things light and tight lipped. In his line of work they don't look kindly on anything outside of vanilla. Ell, is this going down a path I don't like?"

"I'm not sure, what about Claire Fenn. Does the name ring any bells?"

"No, I can check my records and see if she was a one off but the name's not familiar. Give me a second." The line went quiet and Ell could hear the clicking of keys while Angel began a search.

"There's no Fenn in the client logs, we get a few that still don't trust my security and use aliases."

"Try Sandusky, Jane Sandusky."

Again the line was quiet.

"Nothing there either."

"Ok, I'm going to text you a photo, run it past the staff but keep it quiet and let me know if any of them recognize her."

"Does it make me a bad person if I hope they don't?"

"Just a little but I'm sure you'll get over it. Thanks."

"On it and you owe me another drink.

"Oh, how cheap my girlhood crush is."

"Cheap and easy. Just ask your partner."

The line went dead before Ell could provide a witty comeback. With a shrug she checked her notes and pulled up the number for Corporal Jon Strand. The line rang three times and went to voicemail.

'Shit,' she thought then left a message.

"Corporal, this is Lieutenant Frost. I need to speak with you as soon as possible. Please call me back on my cell."

She disconnected and pulled into the parking lot of a large grey building. The sign above the plain glass entryway read Judge Advocate General.

Ell had no idea if she'd get through the door. She assumed she was persona non grata. Even if she did manage to talk her way in, she had no reason to suspect that General Marcus would be there. The Department of Defense did not have a permanent office in the city so she was going off the assumption that he would be utilizing one of the J.A.G offices while he was in town. The entire scenario was slim and likely to get her tossed out on her ass.

She walked confidently to the door, pulled it open and was immediately greeted by two large men in military uniform, one on each side of the doorway, each with a bolt action rifle held firmly to their chest. The view set her back and she instinctively began to reach for her weapon before thinking better. She glanced around the room. Aside from the two armed guards it appeared to be a standard issue reception area. She had been concerned that General Costan would be in the area but she saw no one she recognized and relaxed as she headed up to the central desk.

A young woman looked up and asked, "May I help you, ma'am?"

Ell had to mentally calm herself, reasoning that a lecture was not in her best interest. "I'd like to speak with General Marcus please."

"General Marcus?" the woman looked confused, Ell

wasn't sure if it was because she didn't recognize the name or that she had not expected anyone to ask for him.

"Yes, General Marcus with the Department of Defense."

"Is he expecting you, ma'am?"

"No, but if you could let him know that Lieutenant Ell Frost would like five minutes of his time."

"Are you the Lieutenant that floored General Costan this morning?" she grinned then quickly regained her composure. Ell smiled and gave the woman a wink.

"I'll get you right back ma'am. Just give me two minutes to organize it with the General."

Apparently Costan's demeanor wasn't any more liked and accepted here than it had been at her precinct. She stood off to the side, waiting impatiently but trying not to let it show. The young lady made a phone call, keeping her voice at a hushed tone so that Ell couldn't make out what was said. The impression she got wasn't a welcoming one. A few minutes later the receptionist hung up and looked over at her.

"Follow me please."

Ell followed her through the halls with a steady fear of being suddenly wisped away to an unknown military base to be tortured and maimed. She patted her service weapon just to double check that it was still there.

She was led back to a small, modest boardroom and asked to have a seat.

"The General will be out shortly."

The center of the table had a pitcher of water and four small glasses. Ell's mind raced through the possible poisons and tranquillizers that could be held within and passed on trying it.

"Lieutenant, you'll excuse me if I can't give you much time. You're friends at the Chronicle have ensured my day is sufficiently busy."

She had not yet had a chance to see the story but knew it hit the streets at noon. The General looked concerned but not nearly as concerned as she expected.

"Excuse me for saying so, General, but you seem to be taking this in stride."

He shrugged, "What else can I do? Two things I have learned over the years are that any covert action eventually comes to light and no matter how hard you try you can't fight the media. All you can do is work with them when the opportunity arises and hope they will keep the story impartial and avoid sensationalizing it. The last part is harder to come by nowadays but I've found Ms. Shepard to be a solid journalist and not out for a good headline and quick fame. I must admit it was a relief to see who was breaking the story. The fame whores will latch on but at least we can start out with a fairly unbiased account of the facts."

Ell was genuinely surprised. She sat there slack jawed, unsure what to say.

"Look, off the record, I don't disagree with your speech back at the precinct. I've voiced many of those same opinions in my time, occasionally my superiors listen, occasionally they don't, but one thing I do know is that whether or not we always agree on the methods our common goal is the same. I respect those I am accountable to for just that reason. Now, what can I help you with? We should probably get you in and out of here before you're forced to shine up Costan's other eye."

Ell pulled out her phone and showed him the surveillance

photo of Claire Fenn. She was going to ask if he recognized her but the instant fear in his eyes made it unnecessary.

"From your reaction I assume you know Ms. Fenn."

"I've read the reports. She was taken hostage at the Jellic scene."

"Yeah, but you knew her before that, didn't you General?"

"I'm not at liberty to discuss it."

"Let me paint you a picture. I have four dead all of which can be tied back to David Jellic and a series of cover-ups that relate to his death. Claire Fenn is my primary suspect in all four of those deaths as well as the wounding of two police officers injured while attempting to rescue her from a faked kidnapping. I'm going to find Ms. Fenn and I'm going to lock her in a cage for a very, very longtime. What's already done is on her. But," she paused for effect," if anyone else gets harmed because you and your organization refuse to help then that's on you and I'll make sure it sticks."

"You can't honestly think she did this. It's simply not possible."

"That photo, it was taken from the security feed running at my precinct the day Jensen Dover was killed. That's her walking out of the interrogation room where he died two minutes before I found the bodies. I don't think she did this, General, I know it, and thanks to this footage and some sloppy work at the hospital, I can prove it."

"A solid bluff, Lieutenant but I've read the reports. The precinct footage was bypassed and wiped with the CleanSlate software. There's no recovering it after that."

She gave him a cocky smirk, "That used to be true, but when you build a better lock eventually someone finds a better key."

He stared at her trying to discern if she was being honest. Her eyes spoke volumes. "You're telling me you have a bypass? And this photo, this is what you recovered. This can't be. It makes no sense. It..."

"She's yours isn't she? She's one of your covert agents."

"I cannot confirm or deny that," he placed a solid emphasis on the word confirm. "I need to run this up the chain of command. Right now I can't say anything."

"Run it fast General and if you change your mind, you have my number."

Chapter Twenty-Eight

Things began to move quickly after Ell left the J.A.G. building. Lund called to let her know that he had no luck with a fingerprint match on any known database but that if she found a suspect he'd be able to use it to confirm their identity. Bad luck there but at this point they didn't need an ID. What they really needed, apart from a location, was a motive. Dover, Kohl and Danuski... she knew why they died. Dover knew something about H.L.A. and as Jellic's attorney he may have known something that tied him with Fenn. Killing him was cover up. Kohl had seen her and Danuski was just in the wrong place at the wrong time. Jellic, however, was the tipping point. That was the connection they needed to make.

Before she even made it home she received a call back from General Marcus.

"You asked me to clear it quickly so I have done just that. Based on the information you have I've been cleared to tell you what I know, within limits."

"Better than nothing, can I assume you don't want to do this over the phone?"

"Not unless you have a secure line."

"It's an open cell at the moment. I'm about five minutes from home. Any chance you want to come take a look at all those missing files Costan couldn't locate?"

He actually laughed. She gave him her address and disconnected. It was a risk but at this stage, with the media digging, she didn't think it was likely that he would storm in and try to take over. She may as well get the whole team up to date at once.

"Gather what you have, I want a full update and review before the D.O.D. pays us a visit," she called out as she came through the door.

"Pardon?" replied the Colonel.

"We are expecting a visit from General Marcus. He has background on Claire Fenn and has been authorized to discuss it. We were dead on with the assumption that she was an operative for Unit H.L.A., hopefully whatever he has can help us nail down either a location or a motive."

"That would be nice," said Baker walking in with a half eaten jelly donut in her right hand, "since I've been able to find nothing at all tying Fenn and Jellic together."

"There better be a damn jelly left in that box."

Jamie slid her right hand behind her back, panic crossing her face.

"You didn't?" Ell's eyes glowed with rage. Baker took a step backwards.

"Want half?" she asked with fear in her voice.

"Shit duty, sweetheart. Graveyard shifts and drunks. That's what you just pulled for the next three weeks."

Baker tossed a pleading look at Rique, the obvious culprit behind supplying the donuts.

"Don't look at me," he said. "I told you to leave a jelly or she'd lose her shit."

"Ok, pastrygate and the punishment therein can wait," said Ell "Give me what you've found."

"It's a quick update all around, Lieutenant," replied Jones. "I can sum it up with one word. Nothing."

"Remind me again why we're paying you people."

"Winning personality?' asked Jones.

"Good looks," said Rique

"Hey that was mine," complained Baker.

Ell tossed a glance at the Colonel who had remained suspiciously quiet.

"What? You're not."

Ell shook her head trying to act frustrated but couldn't keep the smile from giving away her true reaction.

"Well, in that case, thank god for the all powerful military machine. Let's hope they can shed some light on what you four are missing."

Ell pulled the Colonel aside, "If you want to step out before the General arrives I'll understand. As it stands right now they don't know you've been helping us. If you leave now I can cover your involvement."

"I appreciate the offer but I think I'm done being on the wrong side of this. I'll see it through and let the chips fall where they must."

The initial greeting between General Marcus and Colonel Craig was awkward at best. For a moment, Ell thought she was going to end up having to tear the two apart, given the alpha male stare down that was occurring. It was Jamie that managed to break the tension by walking into the room, red hair flowing, seeing the two men staring each other down and saying, "Damn, no need to get aggressive boys, there's plenty of me to go around."

Rique and Jones nearly lost it, each struggling to hold in fits of laughter and the mood in the room quickly cooled off.

"Okay, General, this is the team, team this is General Marcus. Give us the run down and we can deal with formal introductions when we don't have a serial assassin on the loose."

The General nodded and began, "Your suspicions were correct, Claire Fenn is a ground level operative in Unit H.L.A. She was in place, trained and ready to deploy if needed but had yet to serve an active mission."

"And what, exactly would an active mission have been?"

"It could be any situation requiring specialized operational assistance from the military. High profile hostage situations, national threats, suspected terrorist cells. The unit has dealt with all of them. We plan, activate and operate on a covert level to ensure success."

"Homeland Assassinations," said Jones nodding at the acronym breakdown scrawled on the case board.

"Close, Homeland Assistance. Our operatives work, primarily in conjunction with a number of other governmental agencies. Assisting them where we can."

"So you're hired guns for the acronym squad," said Ell drawing a confused look. "NSA, FBI, CIA?"

"Yes and a few others. Our agents are trained to kill but not unlike your officers, only when absolutely required and authorized."

"So this Jellic mess wasn't an authorized operation?"

"Torture and murder? No, but Claire is the reason Jellic was on our radar to begin with and is partially responsible for his court martial. It was her that first brought us information on his intention to leak a dossier he had collected on Unit H.L.A. Her involvement, however, ended with that tip. My unit passed the information off to the Judge Advocate's office and they dealt with it from there."

"He hadn't actually done it, had he?" asked the Colonel.

"No, he had collected a dossier and threatened to release it but once J.A.G brought charges he shut down and whatever he had never saw the light of day. His attorney leveraged that information for a plea deal."

"And a hefty payoff," said Colonel Craig, fire in his eyes.

"A what?"

"You may as well come clean, General, the Lieutenant has Dover on tape admitting to receiving a payoff for talking his client into a plea deal."

"If that's so, it didn't come from our unit. As I said, we handed the matter over to J.A.G. and our involvement ended at that point."

"So how did your agent know that Jellic had this dossier."

"My report indicates that he threatened to expose her and us. He said he had information on her original identity as well as our recruitment and training."

"The identity change, that's part of the recruitment process?" asked Ell.

"Yes, our agents require anonymity and that means dropping the baggage, relationships and family that they currently carry. We work up a full new identity and implant them into the area they will be serving."

"And somehow," Ell pondered, "Jellic found out that Claire Fenn was actually Jane Sandusky."

The General laughed, "No, Jane Sandusky went missing, presumed murdered after testifying against her boyfriend. It's a solid cover story that we worked up for our female agents, should anyone realize that their identity has flaws."

"So who the hell is Claire Fenn?"

"I don't know... yet. Agent's original identities are above my clearance level. I've put in a request for the file but I haven't received it."

"Shit, L.T. this leaves us nothing. No history, no motive, no potential location, just confirmation of what we already knew or assumed," Rique's frustration was evident.

Ell sat quiet for a moment rolling through what they knew, looking at the board, studying the case notes, waiting for something to hit her.

"Who was her contact?" she whispered to herself.

"Sorry?" asked the General.

"Our research indicates a two man team, each operative with a specific team lead or direct contact."

The General gave her a smile, impressed with the depth of their research. "Yes, that would be correct."

"So who is Fenn's contact? Even if she's gone rogue, her direct contact would be our best bet on nailing her location. Who's the other half of her team?"

"You're going to love this. We try to keep the teams coordinated with the lead being a direct reporting officer to avoid a situation where the agent receives conflicting orders. Since Fenn is a paralegal with the Judge Advocate's office..."

"Don't, don't tell me it's him."

The General just grinned and watched the disgust, anger and regret roll over her.

Chapter Twenty-Nine

*A*sking General Costan for assistance wasn't an option at this point so Ell was going to have to rely on General Marcus' influence and the military chain of command. Given the situation, she was embracing the option with open arms. General Marcus wasn't overjoyed with the idea of her joining in the questioning but Ell had made it fairly clear that she wasn't about to stand aside.

In the interest of time, Ell insisted on driving. A decision General Marcus saw no reason to argue... at first. By the time they arrived at the J.A.G. offices twelve minutes later he was beginning to fear for his life. Ell saw him reach for the 'holy shit' handle above the door and shook her head.

"Pansies."

"Lieutenant I've had three tours in active war zones and, right now, I will gladly take that title if it means this ride will stop."

Ell laughed, hung a quick left into an open parking spot and slammed the S550 into park.

"Okay, how are we going to run this?"

"Run this?"

"The interrogation, what's our play."

"As Costan's superior officer I plan to sit him down, ask him what I need to know and leave."

Ell stared at him like he had lost his mind.

"Lieutenant, you simply do not understand the world I operate in. At this point I see no reason to suspect that Costan is involved in these murders. He's an ass but he has proven his loyalty to the core. That loyalty outweighs any he may have to Claire Fenn. It also guarantees that when I give him a direct order to answer our questions, he'll do just that. In your world that level of honesty comes from respect for you as an individual, in mine it comes from respect for the core in general and the requirement for the control that a properly established chain of command provides."

Ell stared at him. She had heard the words but a lifetime of interrogating both suspects and witnesses had taught her that just asking rarely garnered results.

"Trust me," he said as he turned and headed into the office.

'Trust him? How the hell did I get here?' she thought as she hurried to catch up.

"Where is General Costan?" he demanded to the young lady at the reception desk. The authoritarian voice almost made Ell sorry for the woman.

"In his office, sir. Would you like me to notify him that..."

"I'll deal with it, thank you."

The two of them pushed past the desk and down the hall. General Costan's office door was closed but Marcus threw it open without knocking.

"James, you have a problem."

He rose to his feet, seeing Ell, and rage crossed his eyes.

"Sit your ass back down," said General Marcus and watched as the man fought off his internal instinct to lash out and instead followed the order. "The Lieutenant is here to observe, record and if necessary ask you anything she must. You will answer as if her questions are mine, do I make myself clear?"

Ell could see the vile hatred in his eyes as he spat out a very reluctant, "Yes, sir."

"Good, now tell me you didn't know that your agent, the one you have been tasked with keeping an eye on, was the person responsible for the string of homicides beginning with David Jelllic."

"I did not, sir and the mere thought is ludicrous. Cla.. she," he corrected, "could not have been involved."

"You can drop the pronoun game, General," cut in Ell. "Everyone in this room is aware that Claire Fenn is a field agent for Unit H.L.A. and currently under your command."

"Then you are also aware that Ms. Fenn was held hostage and tortured by those responsible for killing David Jellic."

"We know that Ms. Fenn wanted us to believe that and faked her own kidnapping, cut and flogged herself and set up the ransom demand to facilitate a rescue. We know that in the process of doing so she put two members of my SWAT team in the hospital, just to make it look authentic. And we know that she is responsible for the deaths of two civilians and two police officers. What I don't know is why you didn't fucking notice."

"Listen you little b..."

"James!" hollered General Marcus. "Shut up or I'll allow the Lieutenant to shut you up... again."

Ell watched him fight back the urge to react and was

amazed. She paralleled the control aspect to that in a dom/sub relationship however here it was not about respect, care or love. Nor was it fear. It was something else. A devotion to something outside of one's self. A devotion similar to what she had with her job yet, so much more.

"What do you know of Private Fenn's relationship with David Jellic?"

General Costan ignored Ell completely, focusing on General Marcus as he asked the question.

"A little over a year ago she approached me and informed me that there may have been a security breach. Sergeant Jellic had gathered a dossier on both her and the Unit. He had evidence of her true identity along with her recruitment and training. Evidence that could be harmful not only to her but to the Unit as a whole. As you know I passed this information up the chain of command."

"How did Jellic compile this dossier?"

"I never found out sir, only that he had."

"And how did Ms. Fenn come to learn about it?" asked Ell from the side. General Costan maintained his focus on Marcus.

"He approached Private Fenn, threatened to expose her and promised silence for the right amount of money."

Ell knew there was something wrong with that story.

"When we failed to find his dossier or any evidence that he had leaked the information, that is exactly what we did. We paid him in exchange for a plea deal and his silence. Two hundred thousand dollars was wired to his attorney one week before the plea was entered."

"And how did your agent take it when she learned of the plea?"

"She was a little upset that we had given in, more so that the dossier was never retrieved, but she accepted it as soldiers do."

'Something about her past, something in that dossier,' thought Ell.

General Marcus resumed the questioning, "Where is she now?"

"I don't know, I haven't seen nor heard from her since this mess began. We had no contact while she was hospitalized and I understand she was released this morning."

"Where would she go if she was laying low?"

"Home, here, otherwise she'd stay on the move, not settle in anywhere but rather float through the city until it is safe to move on. That's how she was trained. It's the best defense when hiding. Hide in plain sight, float until you can move forward with the mission."

Ell began running over it in her head, tuning out the General for a moment. She wasn't home, wasn't settling, she was on the move, why? Because her mission wasn't over. Because she needed to hide until it was. So what was the mission?

"If she contacts you, you tell her nothing and I am your first call once she hangs up. If possible you get a location. Understood?"

"Yes, sir but I still think you're wrong about this. I know her, I know what she is capable of and going this far off on her own, that's not her. She lives and breathes for the Unit, sir. She would give her life to protect it."

"Perhaps, but I've seen the evidence, General and I have no doubt that private Fenn is responsible for a string of unauthorized kills."

Costan looked beaten down as they left the room. Nothing Ell could have done would have hurt him as much as General Marcus' parting words.

They were half way home when Ell's phone began ringing. General Marcus nearly had a fit when she transferred it to hands free while whipping through traffic at twice the speed limit. Thankfully, the distraction of the call slowed her pace to just above what most would consider safe.

"Angel, tell me you have something."

"If this leads to a break in your case do I get my boytoy back for some playtime."

"If this breaks my case I'll send over your boytoy a fire-plug red head and possibly a hot stud in full dress uniform."

General Marcus raised his eyebrows and Ell mouthed. "Don't worry, not you."

"Damn, you know how to buy a girl's loyalty. I passed the photo you gave me onto a slew of contacts and one of my friends from afar is pretty sure he recognized the girl. He said she dropped out of the game or packed up and disappeared about fifteen years ago so the picture's not quite perfect. Roll the age back a decade and a half and he's damn near certain it was this young gal he knew back in Carlisle. She was new to the scene, tied in pretty heavy to one young Dom. Name was Mary Rutherford."

Ell slid the car across to the right hand shoulder and slammed on the brakes.

"What?"

"Mary Rutherford. He said she was really tight with one

young Dom in the area. Really hot and heavy, there were talks of a collaring and then one day she just vanished."

"Angel, I may have to toss in a dead sexy I.T. tech."

"Shit with all that flesh flying I'll probably be left out in the cold. Just nail whoever you need to in order to close this one down and send that Latin Lover back my way. We'll call that even."

"Done, and thanks."

Ell disconnected and sent Rique a text.

"Gather the troops, home in five with a major thread ready for some pulling. – E"

Chapter Thirty

"**M**ary Fucking Rutherford," screamed Ell as she flew through the front door. "I need everything we have on her and I need it yesterday because, as of right now, she's using the alias Claire Fenn."

"Technically, we didn't know she existed yesterday," replied Rique earning a distinct glare from Ell as she cornered into the living room. "What? I said technically."

"Please tell me that we have something now."

"It wasn't a top priority, L.T. but I did a rudimentary run after talking to Mr. Mitchell." responded Baker pulling out her notes. "Born in, Jesus this fits, Maddison, Wisconson, thirty-two years back so the age works, moved to Carlisle, Pennsylvania at age nine. Her father was an air force mechanic. They hopped around for a while before they settled but no single stop was more than two years. He finally landed a permanent position in Carlisle and remained there for the next seventeen years. Rutherford and Jellic were close and had a lot in common, both with military parents etc. etc. I don't have anything on them as a couple but based on Mitchell's record she picked up the collar. It wouldn't be much of a stretch to assume it was meant for her. I'll need to make some calls to verify that. Both her parents are still alive. They filed a missing persons report six weeks after her seventeenth birthday. That would be about three weeks after she picked up the collar. The police have a standard investigation file, but found no evidence of foul play and ruled it a runaway. At age seventeen they didn't put any extra man power into finding her."

"She must have lied about her age," cut in Colonel Craig. "If we are assuming she was recruited by Unit H.L.A as opposed to disappearing, she would have to be eighteen."

"Not necessarily," suggested the General.

"Are you going to tell me you're recruiting minors?" asked Ell.

"With a parental signature, yes, but she wouldn't have begun training until her eighteenth birthday. If we found a recruit with promise we locked them in, recruited them as soon as possible and provided a solid education and life while we waited for them to hit the approved age. Once they did we would sign them on for a standard term and begin their training."

Ell could see the rage in her team's eyes.

"Let's not get into this now, we can discuss morality once Claire/Mary is in a cage. You said she'd need a parental signature. That doesn't fit with the parents filing a missing persons report."

"L.T., really?" asked Jones. "Have you ever known a teen girl that couldn't and wouldn't sign her mom's name?"

Ell shrugged, "Valid. So we have a teen girl, hot and heavy with a young stud, the two of them getting into some pretty heavy kink, dabbling in an alternative lifestyle and talking about a collaring, then suddenly she signs on with some secret military spy unit and poof she's gone? How does any of it play?"

"We wouldn't have targeted her for recruitment without a reason. The unit requires agents to leave behind everything and that means we look for those people with nothing to lose. Those stuck in situations they want to escape."

"She was just a teen, right?" asked Baker. "So she was still experimenting. She and her man were playing around with the kink, edging into the dom/sub life and suddenly he was hooked. He was full bore buying into it, so what does she do?"

The Colonel cut in, "A young impressionable girl with serious eyes for the man, she plays along, rides it out for a bit and gives him what he likes."

"Until she can't," said Ell. "Until suddenly he's talking about a collar and the fun game starts to look like a lifetime thing. If she's not buying into the life, not as invested as he is, that could be the trigger to bolt, to disappear and not look back."

"Fast forward fifteen years," said General Marcus, "and your girl is a highly trained operative in an elite military unit. Suddenly the man is back and threatening to expose her, to take down not only her but the very thing that saved her years ago. That could be your trigger, your motive for murder."

Rique nodded, "It also explains the crime scene. Tie him up torture him and let him feel what he wanted to put you through."

"And the missing dossier he'd gathered, she'd want to ensure it never saw the light of day. It's a reason to prolong the torture, to inflict maximum pain until he talked," said Ell, "but she's not finished. If she were finished she'd be out of hiding and holed up somewhere safe. Costan was right, she's still floating, still in motion and that tells me she's not done."

"Jellic's dead, the lawyer and witnesses are taken care of, what else is left?" asked Baker.

Ell stared at the board, rolled through the scenario in her mind and focused back on something General Costan had mentioned, "She lives and breathes for the Unit. She would give her life to protect it." That was precisely what she was doing, protecting not only herself but the Unit. If Jellic had gone public it may have hurt her reputation but it would also have done exactly what Ell had done earlier that day, it would have exposed Unit H.L.A.

"It's revenge," she said. "She's protecting her Unit, taking revenge on those that are aiming to take it down. Fuck!"

Ell reached down, pulled out her cell and dialed the number for Cindy Shepard. The line rang three times and went to voicemail, sending a sudden chill through Ell's spine.

"Dammit, I need eyes on Cindy Shepard," said Ell as she began frantically dialing Rob's line. Her team knew not to question but immediately started reaching out to any contacts they had who may be able to locate the reporter.

"Lieutenant, it's been three hours and how I've missed you," said Rob through the fog of sleep.

"I need a trace on a cell phone and I need it quickly, what can you do for me?"

"Do we know if the phone is on?" he asked recognizing the tone in her voice and dropping the banter.

"No clue, it rang three times and went to voicemail."

"That's a good sign. An offline cell will trigger the voicemail immediately. Give me the number and a couple minutes to figure out who the cell carrier is. I may be able to get what you need. You do know the carriers can do this with less... security hassles, right?"

"I don't have time to deal with some corporate asshole screaming for a warrant and protecting his own ass. The clock is ticking and I have a solid hunch that the owner of this line may be in imminent danger."

Rob went silent and she knew better than to interrupt whatever he was doing on the other end of the line.

"Wait... is this... Ell, this is Cindy Shepard's line. What's going on?"

"Just get me the damn trace."

Once again he went silent but she could hear an increased sense of urgency in what he was doing. Things became difficult when you were dealing with people you knew.

"I've triangulated the signal and can get you within a one block radius. The phone is out in Jalsedin Bay, somewhere between Pier 10 and 17.

'Son of a bitch,' thought Ell.

"That's as close as I can get without a GPS signal."

"Close enough. Thanks."

Ell disconnected. "Baker, Jones. I need SWAT notified and out the door in three minutes. We'll need to coordinate this one en route so make damn sure they're ready to roll when the trucks stop. We're heading back to the Sandbox."

"What can I do?" asked General Marcus.

"Observe and report," replied Ell. "We don't have time to call in your men, we'll be lucky if SWAT makes it on time. If you're up to it I could use you and the Colonel as part of my breach team. You'll have a better understanding of how she works, what she'll do and how well she'll be fortified."

Both men nodded without hesitation and the team headed for the door.

Chapter Thirty-One

*W*ithin twenty minutes Ell had her team, including six members of SWAT, in position outside the Sandbox. Heat signatures confirmed her fears and showed two people on-site, both located in the center of the abandoned club. SWAT advised that one heat signature appeared to be suspended in mid air and was growing faint. That information was enough for Ell to trigger an immediate breach.

Given what they had encountered during their previous operation and knowing that the first scene had been setup for show, they were going in low and slow this time. Colonel Craig had insisted on taking lead as he was intimately aware of the types of equipment Claire Fenn had at her disposal and how she may use them to fortify her position.

Breaching blind was a risk but their hand had been pushed. An innocent civilian was in mortal danger and they couldn't stand by and let something happen to her.

The two entry teams split off as they approached the building, one heading for the front access and one heading to the rear. Given their last encounter at the location the teams were diligent in watching for pressure sensors, trip lines and any other detonation devices. Ell, Colonel Craig and Rique moved in with three SWAT agents at the rear of the building. Baker, Jones and Colonel Marcus escorted an additional four SWAT members through the front access.

Ell watched as Colonel Craig scanned and cleared the way, gently popping the lock on the rear door and stepping carefully and quietly through the entry. The others followed but were quickly held back, the Colonel signaling as he came to a halt. They could see the damage inflicted by the bomb set off during their fake hostage rescue, Ell's mind began drifting back to that night and she fought to snap back into the present and focus on the job at hand. The Colonel searched the area carefully, assuming there would be some form of trap. Ell's eyes scanned the walls and ceiling around them. Noticing a black plastic box mounted to the corner of the inner door frame she tapped on Colonel Craig's arm and gestured with two fingers. The device was similar to the previous bomb but the Colonel noticed that this one was angled to direct the force of the blast wave directly down at the doorway. This one was focused to kill. He could not locate a pressure plate so on a hunch he reached into his rear pocket and pulled out a small aerosol can. As he sprayed the entryway a thick mist filled the air. A distinct red laser could be seen breaching across the gap at waist height.

The Colonel motioned to the floor by gently moving his hand downwards, held out flat with the palm down. His body followed suit as he laid flat and slid under the laser line and through the doorway. Once inside they could hear the moans and grunts of someone barely conscious, fighting to hold on. The moans were followed by angry murmurs and occasional laughter cutting through the silence. Ell and her team followed the Colonel's lead and they were soon inside the building, slowly making their way through the back rooms and into the main area of the club. The rear door to the central room was open and they emerged behind a waist high bar providing both cover and concealment. Ell motioned for the team to stay down as she slowly slid her eyes around the far corner to try and assess the situation.

In the center of the room, suspended by a series of ropes which were wrapped around an open beam, was Cindy Shepard. She had been hung by her wrists, her arms bound tightly together with wide leather strapping. Her clothes had been torn from her body, her head hung limp to the left side and small gashes of blood could be seen across her chest, torso and back. The cuts were similar to those that had been found on David Jellic and Ell knew they had been pinpointed to cause maximum pain. The floor beneath the body was littered with blades, whips, piercing tools and a twelve volt battery with jumper cables attached. Claire Fenn, aka Mary Rutherford, was slowly circling her victim, a small metal sickle in her right hand.

"Where is it, slut? This is only going to get more painful as the night progresses so you may as well spill now and I'll make the ending quick and painless."

Cindy moaned but was unable to speak.

"I know he gave you the fucking file, it's the only way you could have run that bullshit story. We both know you don't have the balls to withstand much more of this so, TELL ME WHERE IT FUCKING IS."

Ell slid back behind the bar and mouthed, "Stay and cover." to her team. The Colonel gave her a concerned look and began shaking his head but she waived him off with a hard stare. She crept to the edge of the bar, knowing she would need to time her actions perfectly. Her opponent was armed, but it was a short range weapon which meant her priority was keeping the perpetrator out of reach of the civilian. Once that was accomplished she would probably take some damage so she needed to ensure it was as superficial as possible. The girl was small but Ell wasn't going to misinterpret that as weak.

Ell waited until Fenn had her back to the bar and had circled past a point where the attack would be visible. When the time was right she leapt from behind the bar and ran full tilt towards the center of the room.

Claire Fenn was no amateur and immediately heard the movement, spinning towards the noise as she closed the gap between them. Ell dropped her shoulder and used all of her momentum to drive the soldier backwards while reaching down to scoop both legs and throw her to the ground. She succeeded in driving Fenn away from Cindy Shepard but the soldier sprawled her legs backwards and wide to the sides, thwarting Ell's attempt to gain leverage. The two women hit the ground hard, neither able to gain a solid advantage. The sickle clipped Ell's shoulder sending a white hot, searing pain through her as she fought to regain her footing. Ell managed to get her right foot firmly planted and was starting to find some leverage when a loud explosion rumbled through the room. Shattered wood, glass and metal rained down on them, the momentary distraction provided the highly trained Fenn the opportunity she needed. Out of nowhere Ell felt her right arm twist behind her back and a knee crush down into her spine forcing her back to the floor. The cold steel of the sickle found purchase around her neck. Just as she began to wonder if this was it, if this was her end, the blade stopped and she was pulled back to her feet.

"Stay back," screamed Fenn holding Ell in front of her, the blade inches from her throat. As her vision cleared, Ell could see General Marcus backed by Colonel Craig and six SWAT officers standing in front of her, weapons drawn, ready to fire.

"Drop the weapons or I spill every ounce of her blood right here and now."

"Private," said General Marcus, "you will disengage, stow your weapon and stand firm. This ends now."

His voice held a tone of authority but Ell knew it wasn't going to work. Not with Fenn. She was military but she didn't have the level of respect for the position required to follow the order.

"Can't you see what they are doing? They are destroying everything we have worked for. Everything we have trained for. They are attempting to undermine our honor with lies and falsehoods about who we are and what we do."

Ell could feel Claire's arm beginning to flex, the blade tightening to her neck. She knew she was going to have to make a move, soon.

"This is more important than them, more important than any of us," continued Fenn.

"Private, I said drop the weapon."

"Nooo," growled Fenn and Ell felt the rage within her as Fenn's arm twitched and began to pull the blade in. She struggled but could not move. She felt the edge of the blade cut into her neck, felt the warm flow of blood start to cover her skin. She pulled back trying to put distance between her throat and the blade when suddenly the arm holding her relaxed. Ell felt the body halt and twitch even before she heard the gunshot that rang out.

The sickle fell to the side and Claire Fenn dropped as Ell looked up to see Detective Jamie Baker with her arm extended, her glock nine millimeter still recoiling and a cold, hard stare in her eyes.

Ell was ready to beat the paramedics with one of the many whips available by the time they had finished poking and prodding at her. They had insisted on taking her to the hospital but after a few veiled threats and finally one or two very blunt ones, they stitched her up on-site and left her to the care of her fellow officers.

Baker's shot had missed her temple by just over an inch, coursed through Claire Fenn's neck just below the jawline and severed the spinal column dropping the woman instantly. It was a text book short-range, sniper shot and Ell reminded herself to smack the redhead for even attempting to make it.

The explosion had been triggered on purpose without any casualties. General Marcus had been hoping the distraction would allow them to get the drop on Fenn. Ell cursed herself for the lack of focus that had led to her being used as a human shield.

Cindy Shepard had suffered a horrendous torture. Both shoulders had been pulled out of their sockets in addition to three broken ribs and a spiral fracture in her left fibula. Thankfully, the slices riddling her body had been situated for pain and were not life threatening. She had lost some blood and would require months of rehab to regain full use of her joints and leg, but she would live. She had been rushed to St. Pete's for treatment and Ell made sure there were two uniform officers stationed outside and within her room. Eventually Cindy would throw up a fuss about the protection and Ell would have to remove them but, for now, she wasn't taking any risks.

General Marcus warned her that the crime scene would not be hers for long. The military machine would swoop in and try to clean up their mess but with one of the city's top investigative reporters involved, Ell knew they wouldn't be able to cover it up. With her suspect dead and her case re-solved, Ell was more than willing to turn over the clean up to whoever the hell wanted it. She was pulling back, out of the fray of crime scene techs and cops, looking for a quiet place to sit back and watch it all unfold when she noticed Baker sitting in a corner, tears streaming down her face, her eyes emotionless and stunned. Ell leaned against the wall and slid down next to her.

"It was a clean shoot. No one is going to be questioning it. There may be an investigation but it will be routine and the team has your back."

"I just... I don't know what to do."

Ell understood the pain she was going through. Clean shoot or not, taking a life haunts you, even if that life is a murdering bitch who needs to be taken down.

"You move forward, you reach out to your team, your friends and if necessary, Dr. Grayson. You put it right in your mind however you can and you walk tall because you did, not what you wanted to, but what you were forced to."

She put a hand on Jamie's chin and turned to look into her eyes. "And no matter what, you hold on to that soft, innocent piece that makes you who you are. You fight with everything you have to ensure that never gets lost. You fight because you have to."

Epilogue

*S*he wasn't sure how the hell she had let Rob talk her into this. Granted it had been a while since she'd had a night out to relax and pretty much everyone she knew had been on her ass for a get together, but seriously, what the fuck was 'girls night'?

"Remind me again, why the hell am I doing this?" she asked as she climbed out of the shower.

"Because you need it," replied Rob. "It's been four weeks since you closed the Jellic case, the Bouton trial begins in five days and you're set for a deposition on that stupid wrongful death suit in six. This is your chance to relax and enjoy yourself and it turns out you have a bunch of women that want to help you do just that."

Ell sat down on the bed beside him, let the towel she had wrapped around her slip open and slowly ran a hand up his thigh, stroking him through his jeans. "Call them off, call and tell them I'm sick and I'll make it worth your while. Everything you could ever dream of," she whispered feeling him grow in her hand.

"I can dream of a lot," he responded and visions of him

taking every inch of her began to fill Ell's mind. The lust was pounding in her eyes, begging him to do just that.

He fought past the urge, stood up and walked to the door, taking a couple deep breaths. "You're going, and when you get back I'm going to paddle you until you scream for leaving me in this position."

"Hey, that's your choice, stud, but I'll schedule in the paddling and be looking forward to it."

"Finish getting ready. Jamie will be here any minute," he called out leaving her alone in the bedroom.

"She can join if you let me stay," Ell called back.

As much as she had griped about it, she knew she needed this and more importantly, so did Baker. A little normalcy, if you could call girl's night normal, would help them both. Ell slid on a tight black dress, forgoing underwear, ran a comb through her hair and gave it a quick toss. It fell nicely across the edge of her shoulders. She stared into her closet, eyeing up the ankle killing stilettos that she would have slid on in an instance if Rob had taken her up on her offer, and instead opted for a pair of mid calf black Fluvog boots. She gave a quick spin in the mirror and decided it would do.

She could hear Baker and Rob chatting as she made her way into the foyer, but both stopped as soon as she was in sight and, in unison, as if planned, said. "Damn!"

She gave them a smirk, smacked Rob on the ass and resigned that tonight was going to be fun. As she and Jamie began to leave, Rob called out to her, "Whips and chains."

Ell stopped, turned back and took his face in both her hands. Her lips met his in a soft gentle kiss and pulling away she whispered. "I love you too."

About The Author

R. C. Butler is a software developer, graphic artist, freelance writer, and poet. Born in Edmonton Alberta, the need to create has been a running theme throughout his life. As a teen, Butler found his outlet in poetry, short stories and architecture, which eventually led to an educational background in software development and graphic arts. The mix of right-brain creativity and left-brain logic are the drawing factor in his love of the software industry.

As an author, he has completed numerous freelance short stories and poems as well as developed and hosted an online writing community. Honor Bound is his third full length novel and second in the Ellison Frost 'Bound' series.

Ellison Frost will return in 'Eternally Bound'.